Another English Civil War

(Tales from The Red Lion part 2)

Mark Fryday

Enjoy the next round

M. Fryday

By the same Author

Collapse of the Wave (Tales from the Red
Lion Part 1)

Amazon Reviews for Collapse of the Wave

*"At times funny, with sharply drawn observations of
mundane happenings, 'Collapse of the Wave' is
actually a marvellous study of love in all its guises…I
find myself looking forward to another chance of a
pint and a catch up with Dan."* (5 stars)

*"…publicans should buy it by the gross to give away
as a marketing tool!"* (4 stars)

*"The novel is carried by its sharp dialogue and
convincing characters - snapshots of life today told
with an assured and familiar voice."* (4 stars)

3

Copyright © 2018 Mark Fryday

www.markfryday.com

Cover illustration by Grant Wickham
www.grantwickham.co.uk

Dedication

For the 'Jens' and 'Debbies' in my life. Thank you for the pints we have shared and the lessons learned.

And for all those good people of CAMRA, without whom this book would have been a work of speculative fiction, and to all the other communities out there trying to keep the pubs they love open.

Cheers.

Firste note inn the mattere of The Red Lion Witch

Matthew Hopkins, Witch finder-General

Confess.

Confess witch.

There will be no escape for the likes of you. I have met with the Devill, and cheated him of his Booke, wherein were written all the Witches names in England.

And I see you. I can see into your damned soul. I will find out the truth of you. The rope and the ponde await ye.

So confess.

~

I sit by the pond, silently pick up a pebble and put it in my pocket. I stare at the water for answers. But all I see is water. Hydrogen and Oxygen. And the odd old rusty can and empty packet of crisps, all faded by the sun. Where can the solution possibly be found in that?

I could always ask someone. But I'm saying nothing. I can't even say a word.

Chapter 1

Everyone's gone.

About time too. I've almost run out of beer.

The last person leaves (Cousin Alan, who I have not seen for 15 years at the very least) and the door closes. I don't know why he stayed so long. He just seemed to have nothing better to do. I take a deep breath. And then I am on my own, in my own front room. I turn and look at the remains of the buffet and the empty bottles. I should really tidy this lot up now. Ten minutes later, however, I'm sitting in The Red Lion, halfway down a pint of 'Starter's Orders', 4.4%.

Don't judge me. It's been a bad day.

I'm sitting on my own again, which is not necessarily a bad thing. Good pubs can make you feel like this is a perfectly acceptable state of affairs. I've not had time to round up any likely compatriots for a cheeky mid-afternoon session on a Tuesday. I'm not sure that even if I had the time I would have been successful, especially as I couldn't bring myself to invite them to the funeral earlier. It's an odd time for most people anyway, Tuesday afternoon, even for my lot. Amy still has not managed to get sacked yet, Jez is doing his thing and Ted is travelling on some work-trip-of-mystery, so that just leaves me. I would normally be at work myself but, like I said, it's been a bad day.

I sense a slight ripple of astonishment waft over from the bar. If astonishment can be slight. I couldn't tell you if it was a sound, or something in my peripheral vision. It wasn't a smell anyway, that's for certain. Whatever it was, it made me look over at just the right moment. Tom, the landlord, is actually working behind the bar today, and he is looking slightly flabbergasted. So am I. Bloody hell, that's a turn up. *Frank is having another half.* Look, you know, he's having…another…half! No? Hmm, this may take some explaining.

Frank is, like me, a regular here. I have not mentioned him before as he comes under his own special category of drinker that I prefer not to talk about. Frank, you see, drinks halves. Not only that, but he only ever, and I mean *ever*, comes in, has one half of whatever and then leaves again. I mean, that's almost rude. Or at least 'hardly worth it'. What can you possibly get out of popping in for a half? This has been going on for years and years too. He was already notorious for this practice (within these four walls anyway) before I was old enough to come in here (but still, in fact, *did* come in here) and he has never strayed from his habits since. And now he has just sauntered up to the bar, to poor old unsuspecting Tom, bold as brass, in broad daylight, and ordered a second half. The cheek of it!

Tom has now come down to this end of the bar for a little sit down. Well, if Frank's on a second half there must be something monumental going on there. I'm going to need to find out, aren't I? Time for a refill anyway.

"Alright, Tom?" is my opening position to the landlord, as I arrive at the bar.

"Did you just see that? Bloody hell, did *I* just see that?" Tom says, shaking his head continually.

"We both, did indeed, just see that." I say. Then, a slight pause.

"Jesus," says Tom, not a man who normally is taken to turning to God, literally or in his vocabulary. "No one is going to believe this. You're my witness, right?"

I dramatically place my hand on my heart. Actually, it's probably a lung, but it is near enough for our purposes. "I shall indeed bear truthful witness to this very miracle, Tom. You can rely on me."

"Jesus, Mary and Joseph…" he carries on.

"Yeah…"

"…and all the saints…"

I cough politely. If he gets down to the bishops I'm going to get annoyed. And thirsty. Tom has seemingly zoned out completely now so I attempt to break the spell.

"It's enough to turn you to, er, *drink*, such an event, right?" I say, waving my empty glass.

Finally that is enough for Tom's landlord instincts to kick in, and he's back in the room.

"Starter's Orders?" he asks, his hand automatically going to the correct pump.

"Shouldn't really, it's my second, but since it's on offer…"

Tom gets me my pint in a flash and I give him the exact change at comparable speed. We're a well-oiled machine we are.

"Take it easy, Tom. You've had a shock," I say with a

smile and head off, not back to my seat of course, but down the bar towards where Frank is standing.

I can't say I know Frank that well. He's not the most natural conversationalist and doesn't really hang around long enough for you to get a conversation going, for reasons already explained. Over the years though, I suppose the minutes we have spent talking together have added up to something reasonably substantial, so me coming over and saying hello is no great shock. We've had quite enough of those today after all.

"Alright, Frank?" is my opening position again. At least I'm consistent.

"Dan, right?"

"Yeah, Dan. How's tricks?" He's not a magician, warlock or wizard or anything. I'm just asking him how he is. "Bit early for you."

"Bit early for you too," he responds.

"Yeah, well, I had a family event to go to, you know," I explain.

"Right," he continues. Blimey, he's not making this easy for me. Fortunately, I am on my second pint, so am not easily deterred. I point to his pint – sorry, his *half*.

"That's a good ale, is it? Should I try that one next do you think?" I ask.

He looks at his glass, then at me, then his glass again, weighing up the situation, and whether I'm likely to leave him alone or not. He then gives up and sighs.

"Yes, it's not bad," he says. "'Devil's Advocate', 3.7%"

I nod sagely. "Thanks for the tip," I say, being kind. It wasn't much of a tip. Regardless, I shall be trying it

11

next anyway.

Then, still staring at his drink he also says, "I got a letter today."

He takes the envelope out of his pocket. I can't believe he just got it today. It looks distinctly second hand already, all folded over and worn at the edges. He must have been taking it out of his pocket and putting it back in again since it arrived this morning. He's looking for the words. To say, I mean, not on the page. I know I should give him time to find them, but after a certain amount of silence I am compelled to fill the gap. I'm sorry but I can't help it.

"I don't get many of those these days. It's all emails and messaging now, isn't it?" I say. Well done, Dan, that really improved the situation.

"I'm not the online – is that the term 'online?' – type myself," he says, looking up from the envelope. "Not really the letter type either, not anymore, like."

I know already that he's going to tell me what's in it, so I just help him along towards the inevitable. "So, what's in the letter, then? Not bad news I hope."

Frank takes the tiniest sip from his glass. It would have to be tiny. If it was any bigger he would drain his drink in one. "Not bad as such, no. Not at all. Just, er, more like…unexpected…" he starts.

"Right," I say, just to show I'm still with him. Then, just like that, he tells me all about it.

Frank was in the merchant navy way back when. When he was a younger man, and a prodigious drinker by his own account, believe it or not. 'Work hard play hard' was the only accepted way of life on his ship. And when they played, they would stop off at all sorts of various places, Dubai, Ghana, Singapore the Philippines, and on and on. That way he got to explore the world and all the different kinds of women and alcohol it had to offer. As he saw it, this was much better than staying around here. It was boring round here back then, he tells me ('Back then! What about now?' I'm silently thinking) and he was in trouble with a local gang anyway, so getting away seemed like a good idea. And it was a good idea. For years. Then he got to Macau.

"We had a long stop in Macau for some reason," he continues. "Didn't care to ask why. So off we went to explore the locality, you know?"

"Not sure I do, Frank, but I have an image in my head anyway. It may be based on a James Bond movie."

"Depends which one, but just run with that, it doesn't matter. Beautiful place it was and it had some, er, *very* interesting bars. Not all that glitzy nonsense they have now. We made ourselves known there for a while, along with all the others off the ship."

"I can imagine," I say. I can't, but this isn't about me, so I'll just leave it there.

"One night though, I just wanted a change of scene, so I wandered off from our normal part of town, to have a look around the nice part of town."

"Nice. Always good to have a change of scene," I concur. Really, who am I kidding? I'm always down here at The Red Lion.

"Yes, well, I had just won a bunch of money playing cards, I had a belly full of beer, and a head full of youthful exuberance and overconfidence. Also, I didn't want to hang around and be persuaded to lose all my money again."

"Very wise," I add, between sips. I'm halfway down pint number two already. He's already a third of the way down his half as well. Tom is still down the other end of the bar, wiping a few glasses, pretending that he's not trying to listen. He's out of range though. I know these things.

"No one else wanted to leave," Frank continues. "Everything they wanted was laid out on tap right where we were. 'See you later, Professor', they said."

"Professor?" I enquire. "I had no idea…"

Frank shakes his head and smiles, looking down. "I just read a book occasionally. That's all it took to get a nickname on the ship. There were worse names to have. Anyway, they were used to me wandering off from time to time, so there was no fuss made. I eventually ended up near the Consulate. The British one. You always need to know where that is, in case you get into trouble. And it's always in a nice part of town."

"Hmm, yeah, London's like that."

"So I hear. Well, I find this bar in one of the nicer hotels up there, forget the name."

"Swanky though?" I ask. "Like the Ritz or something?"

"Never been. But yeah, I suppose so. I got some funny looks when I walked in, but that night I looked fairly dapper, for one of us. When I bought a drink at the bar without flinching at the price, that seemed to be enough for a small degree of acceptance. Tolerance, maybe."

I nod, mid-sip (not easy) and say, "Sometimes, that's all you can ask for."

"And then I saw her," Frank continues.

14

I thought it might be one of these stories. You get to recognise the sort of look on a chap's face when it's one of these stories. But I was now at the end of my beer. Frank now had half a half left. A quarter. I give the thumbs up to Tom and he brings over another 'Starter's Orders'. I was unable to request a 'Devil's Advocate' using just my thumbs. I give him another bunch of exact change. It was that sort of afternoon. I don't dare offer to buy Frank a third half. That was just beyond imagination. I seamlessly do all this while still continuing to pay full attention to Frank. To do otherwise would be beyond the pale, wherever that is.

Frank carries on. "She was a world away from the usual fare down the local bars. Classy, beautifully-attired. Suave. Elegant. Naturally confident. Demure…"

"Nice," I say. It may sound pathetic, but I find that this is just what you need to shift a person off an endless list of adjectives.

"Indeed," admits Frank, taking another sip. He is human after all. "I was feeling extra confident after my winning streak earlier. Probably felt I was still on one when I approached her table and coughed."

"Coughed?" I exclaim. "Isn't that just going to announce that you have some sort of tropical disease!"

I shouldn't have said that, but 'Starter's Orders' can do that to a bloke. It *is* 4.4 % after all. Thankfully this made Frank chuckle a bit, no mean feat.

"No," he explained, "it was more of an 'ahem'. You know, politely announcing my presence. Tropical disease indeed..."

"Sorry, carry on."

"Well, she looks me up and down, immediately clocking me for what I was, then readies her standard rebuttal…"

"I know that look."

"…then she spotted my book, peeking out of my jacket pocket. That seemed to give her pause for thought, so she turns her face up to meet mine for the first time and instead asks me what I am reading."

"Hmm, I sure hope it wasn't something embarrassing. Or Lady Chatterley's Lover or something."

"Ha! Yes, it could well have been. I took what I could get on that ship. Would read anything I could get my hands on. Luckily it was 'God Bless you Mr Rosewater'…"

"Oh lovely. I've read that. Marvellous. Hope she was impressed."

He nods appreciatively towards me. "She must have been. She asked to have a look at it while I went back to the bar to get her a gin and tonic."

"Kurt Vonnegut owes you a drink, then," I observe wryly, taking a sip.

"That he does. I'll forgive him though, in the circumstances. Well, I came back, and we started talking about books. That one and others. Turned out she worked at the Consulate and had spent some of her childhood in Macau while her father worked at the Consulate too. She normally would only see the likes of me from the ship when we got ourselves arrested, and she had to get us out of trouble. I must have been a refreshing change or something, because she seemed to take a shine to me." He sighed and took another small sip. "And I took a shine to her."

16

There's another pause. I may have to fill this one too, but I don't know what to say. This is not really my area of expertise. Thankfully, Frank's sip is small and so the pause is but brief before he resumes.

"We saw each other as much as we could after that. I was only there for a few more days but over the next few years we came back to Macau regularly, and I would always sneak off to see her whenever I could. This only served to enhance my status as 'Professor', since I now avoided the usual pursuits of my crew mates. Never told them what I was doing though."

"That's nice. Long distance though. Must be tough."

"Long distance was all I was ever going to have in my job. We wrote to each other too. I still have the letters. You keep them, don't you? And you read them again and again. Not like those emails these days. Letters are created with care."

I nod. I have a number of that sort of letter in a box in my bedroom, mainly old ones from Jen. I don't read them much now though. What am I saying? I don't read them at all. I do think about them though, and I feel their presence sometimes when I'm in that room.

Frank carries on. "The letters changed after a while though, and the job took us to Africa instead for a time."

"Changed?" I ask.

"Hmm yeah. Hard to put your finger on it, but there was slightly less affection. More facts, less emotion, that sort of thing. Subtle changes, but a move away. Thought I was making it up for a while, but I kept reading them again and again and it was clear that the change was there."

"Sorry about that. Did you get back to Macau then?" I

didn't want to rush him, but I wanted to know just what her problem was.

"Yes, later that year. We arranged to meet. It was ok, but not the same. I dare say I acted a little needy and she a little cold. But she never said why. I was due some home leave soon, so I gave her my home address and asked her to write to me there. I still live there."

"Did she write?"

"No, she didn't. Well, not until today."

"Bloody hell, Frank. How long was that? Lucky you didn't move."

"Lucky. No, not lucky." He shakes his head at me thoughtfully. The penny drops. Jesus, he stayed there for her, didn't he? All those years.

"You must have wondered what happened to her, Frank."

"Quite an understatement, Dan. I didn't know if she was ill, dead or just went off me and couldn't find a way to find out."

"Hmm. Well, she definitely wasn't dead then." I'm master of the obvious, me.

"No, not dead at all. She's still alive and well and still in Macau. And all this time she never wrote. I stayed in that same bloody house all my life, just to get that letter. Stopped the drink and all sorts else just so I would keep healthy and live long enough to get it."

"Good job you did, Frank."

"Um. And now the letter has arrived. When I'd almost forgotten why I was still here or why I don't drink."

"Sort of don't drink," I add, by way of correction.

"Sort of," he agrees, and smiles.

18

"Must be a bit upsetting though, that she never got in touch until now."

"Yeah, well. She says sorry, but she got married, you sort of had to back then, and felt that she shouldn't contact me after that, while her husband was still alive. She never stopped thinking of me though, she says. In here." He points at his heart. That's a bit poetic for this pub, even from a 'Professor'. Then he takes the letter out of his breast pocket and waves it at me. Ah, right, 'in the letter' he means. Fair enough.

"So, what are you going to do?" I ask. "Are you angry? Are you going to see her?"

Frank laughs. "Put it this way, you won't be seeing me in here again for a while." We both chuckle for a moment and shake our heads knowingly. Don't ask me why. And then, with that, he downs the rest of his half in one, impressive by his terms, and shakes me by the hand.

"Good luck, Frank. I daresay you are doing the right thing." I say.

"Thanks, you too," he adds with a smile. Then he is gone. I'm not sure he meant 'you too' literally. I'm not really doing anything.

As the door closes, Tom calls over, "Fill me in on that one and I'll give you the next pint for free. Starter's Orders."

I resisted, out of respect to Frank, but gave Tom the Landlord the bare bones, just to keep him happy. I liked that story. It's the sort of one I would tend to enjoy telling my friends later on, once they deign to come down from their positions of employment and join me. I'd have felt better about this one, though, if I thought that anyone would actually believe me.

19

"I don't believe you," Jez says, a few days later.

"Why not. Have you never been in love?"

Jez ignores this. "I knew it was bullshit as soon as you said he had another half. What do you take me for Dan? Anyway, another pint for you?"

I say nothing. He returns with another pint anyway.

"I never said I wanted one," I tease, taking a significant gulp from my new glass.

"Yeah, well we've not reached the three-pint minimum stay yet. You know the rules. If you can't do three pints, it's not worth coming in the first place."

We chink glasses. I like a man with principles.

"Unless it's for love," I add.

Jez shrugs and eyes me suspiciously. "I still don't believe you," he says.

And so, for those who do believe me, that is why 'Frank had a second half'. And, like a comet, such a cataclysmic event could only ever be an augur of darker things to come.

Chapter 2

Debbie's not working at The Red Lion tonight. I know this because *tonight* she is going out with me! Yes, yes, you heard that right.

I have no idea what *she* may be doing to prepare for this event. She's probably back at home getting clean and getting changed etc. Myself, I am preparing in the time-honoured way by having some dutch courage. Literally. I am having a pint of 'Dutch Courage', 4.6%. A bit strong for me so I'm only having one of those, out of respect for my date. Dutch courage, by the way, the concept I mean, not this particular beer, is one of those bizarre bits of drinking phraseology that I always adore. This one apparently originates from an observation by some British soldiers, back in some century or other, who were fighting alongside the Dutch against one of those King Louis's with a high number. Pardon me for the lack of detail. If you need any more I'm sure you can find it out yourself. Anyway, the Brits noted that their Dutch compatriots acted much more bravely after having a snifter or two of Jenever, a dutch gin, before heading in to fight the French. Whether this actually made them better fighters or not does not seem to be of historical note. This sort of courage may well have been seen as a poor cousin of actual proper courage, which the British, of course, thought they themselves had in abundance, so the term may have been a little disparaging. I don't care. The Dutch type is the only kind of courage I have access to. And it is much,

much easier to procure than digging up some of my own, or more likely, going down the yellow brick road to get some from the wonderful wizard.

This evening, I am also getting some timely sound advice about dealing with women. Fortunately, this is from a woman. My old school buddy Amy to be precise. I'm not sure that this necessarily means that the advice will be good though. Actually, what I meant to say is that I'm *supposed* to be getting such advice this evening. That was the plan. At the moment, though, she's not even helping me to get into the mood, not in the slightest. In fact, I think I am currently being admonished.

"So how *was* the funeral then?" is how she is starting, straight in there, no beating about the bush. She's not even on the 'Dutch Courage'! Just a pint of OMG, a mere 3.9%. Not that she ever needs any help to say what's on her mind. As I'm considering my response, she just carries on. She's been stewing on this for two weeks now after all.

"I would have come you know, Dan. All you had to do was ask." She is looking at me *that* way. You know the way. The way that makes you feel like you have done something wrong.

"I know, I know. I just didn't want you to feel like you had to, you know?" I say.

"No, I don't know," Amy replies immediately. "I could have taken the afternoon off you know. No problem. None at all really."

"Yeah, well. There was all my weird family you would have had to put up with…"

"I doubt I would have found them any more weird

today than I did as a kid. Jesus, Dan, you don't half overthink things. I really liked your Dad. You should have just invited me, all of us, and let us decide."
I *think* she may have a point, but this is not the preparation for a 'hot date' that I was hoping for. I take a sip and wait for what's next. Amy sighs and sits back, normally a good sign.
"How did it go anyway?" she asks.
So I tell her. Sort of.

"It was the music that got me in the end," I say.
"Start at the bloody beginning, Daniel. I missed the lot remember."
"A fact that I imagine I shan't be allowed to forget anytime soon." I begin, but she gives me that look again. "Sorry, I'll get back to the music presently."
"Please do."
She may sound harsh, but it's ok when it's with me. Really. It's how we have always been since we were kids, and, for us, it just feels comfortable. If she was actually nice to me that would feel a bit strange. I don't mean that really, but you know what I mean. Some relationships just go beyond the need for any social etiquette and this was one of them. Still, there are lines even here, and I have crossed one recently I know.
"Wakey wakey douchebag. You were saying?" That was her again. I think I was drifting off, and she can spot the signs of that quicker than anyone.
"Well, yeah, a lot of the family came. Aunts and cousins and stuff. About twenty or so in all. A few of Mum and Dad's friends. Maybe ten or so of them. Rachel was there of course, and Don, and the boys."
"I'm glad to hear your sister and her husband got an

invite," Amy says, taking another sip of OMG. Must be a spiky brew that one, despite the low ABV.

"I didn't want much fuss, so everyone met at the Crematorium," I continue.

"Right, fair enough."

"Me and Rachel came in from the funeral directors. There, we just did what they told us. Bit of a blur all that really." Sip.

"Yeah, I would imagine. Sorry."

"Yeah." Sip. Another sip, then I'm good to carry on.

"So we saw everyone for the first time waiting for us, as the hearse and our car drove in. I didn't know what to do, so I just waved at them. Rachel told me to stop it. She said that it made me look like the Queen! She was tetchy all day, Rachel I mean. But I suppose she had a point."

"Ha, yes. I can imagine you doing the posh wave from a posh car. If I stretch my imagination to its very limits. Anyway, do carry on."

"Yeah, well we got out and shook a lot of hands, said a lot of things you are supposed to say. Hadn't seen a lot of them since Mum's funeral. Makes you wonder how close we are that it takes someone to die for us to catch up."

We both take a couple of sips to digest that one. Amy raises her eyebrows in due course, to encourage me to continue. So I do.

"Well, I'm forcing myself to hold it together. For everyone else you know? As was Rachel. If I looked at her for too long I would start to well up, so I avoided catching her eye. She was the same with me. Look, if you and Jez were there I'd have just lost it, you know? Just because I *could*, you know?"

"Hmm…"

"If I kept on my own I could force myself to be strong. If I had the chance to unburden it all onto my friends then I think that I would have, and I'd have just lost it completely. So it's all still in there, you know. The grief, I suppose you could call it."

"Hmm. Well, as long as you do let it out at some point…"

"Yeah, yeah," I say, wanting to change that subject. "Anyway, we kept it short. Dad's brother said a few things. Then I thanked everyone for coming etc."

"Don't want to be rude, but you're not really giving me a sense of the occasion here."

"Sorry." Sip.

We stare at each other for a while. She sits back and sighs again.

"Ok, tell me about the song then."

"Billy, don't be a Hero."

Another sip break.

"Really?"

"Yup, one of Dad's guilty pleasures. He asked for that to be played, before he died. It's not really my bag. Still, when that came on that's when I finally did lose it a bit. So did a few people. I kept my head down, but I could hear the sounds of people losing it too, spreading around like a wave. Bit my lip and thought about something else for a couple of minutes."

"Paper…paper something?" Amy asks.

"Paper Lace…"

"Paper Lace. I knew it! One for the karaoke maybe? Hmm, maybe not now..."

"Hmm. Anyway, the coffin disappeared behind the

curtain and we were done."

"Just like that?" Amy enquires, her eyebrows raising to new heights.

"Well, I suppose it wasn't just like that. But that's how I'm going to remember it. Like I said, it was a bit of a blur. Anyway, then it was back to mine with the urn for some beer and nibbles."

"Rachel not tempted to host then?"

"I offered. It's just me there and much nearer the cemetery so it seemed easier. She did most of the food anyway. Thank goodness. I did the drinks." I add.

"You don't say."

"What are you going to do with the urn?" Amy asks me.

I nod downwards. "He's still in my bag under the table. I've been carrying him around sometimes, for some reason. Still, it's nice to have a last drink together. He hasn't been able to get down to the Lion for a while."

"I'm sorry to intrude on the occasion," Amy quips. "Bit weird though maybe. Come on, let's get him back and find a place for him."

"It's ok, he's going to Mum's tree when I'm ready. When me and Rachel are ready." I say staring at my glass.

"Ok, so for now let's tidy *you* up for your big night, Daniel! I take it that George down there," she says, pointing at my bag, "is not joining you for that one."

"Hmm…" I say, still staring at my glass.

"Ok, we'll go after the next one," Amy adds. "Since it's my round."

Amy's great. She always knows what to do in difficult situations.

Back at the flat, Amy sticks some music on, something I often forget to do. The Queen is Dead, by the Smiths, something I often forget that I have. She surveys the living room and kitchen (not altogether in pristine condition after recent stresses) with a disapproving look. I admit I have let myself go a little of late.

"This is a bigger job than I thought," she informs me. "Let's go sort you out first. Not that *that* isn't a big job either mind…"

"Ahhhh shaddap," I respond in some kind of voice from an old Warner Brothers cartoon. Daffy Duck maybe, possibly Bugs. All our group are liable to dropping that one in of late, but I could not for the life of me tell you who started it.

"To the wardrobe!" she announces heading up to the bedroom.

I don't normally find it easy getting women to head in that particular direction, but my relationship with Amy breaks all the rules. I do actually have a wardrobe, you may be surprised to hear. I mainly use it for storage of what can be collectively referred to as 'crap I may need, but probably won't' but there is just a little space for clothes left aside, as an afterthought. The ironing board is still up when we enter the bedroom. Amy raises those eyebrows again at me.

"I haven't put it back yet. It was for the shirt," I explain, "for the funeral..."

She nods appreciatively then asks, "And for your date too, yes?"

No. I just gesture down to the t-shirt and jeans combo

that I earlier changed into, the usual outfit of choice from 'Dan's House of Fashion'.

Amy tuts. Out loud this time. She often tuts internally, and I can tell when she is doing this too, don't ask me how. Another skill of dubious usefulness to join my rank of talents.

"What's wrong with wearing this?" I ask, pointing to my current ensemble. "Debbie knows what I bloody look like, better than most. A shirt is not going to fool her into thinking that I'm better looking than I actually am!"

Amy shakes her head, but with a smile. "That's not the point," she informs me, "that's not the point at all. You're looking at it the wrong way round. You're not trying to fool her into thinking you're attractive…"

"Cheers. Thanks a lot," I moan.

From downstairs, 'Frankly Mr. Shankly' starts up at this moment on my hi-fi, somewhat appropriately. We both have a laugh at this. "Only joking matey," she says, "we both know you are a top catch. No, it is not about that, you doofus. It is about you showing how much you care about this date, this chunk of time that you have set aside to be with this person, and that you are treating that time with respect. It's the effort you make that reflects how you feel about the person."

"Does it? Does it really?"

"It *does*. Trust me." Amy nods her head decisively to ram the point home. I have no argument against this.

"Well, you live and learn. You are a very useful friend to have around, Amy."

"Don't I know it. What would you do without me?"

"Wear this t-shirt probably."

She picks my only other shirt out of the wardrobe and gives it a sniff. It must have passed the test, whatever *that* is, as she announces, "Iron this and put it on. I'll be downstairs clearing up."

By the time 'Cemetery Gates' comes on I am be-shirted and ready. The living room table is clear, and I have a particularly strong cup of tea waiting in the kitchen. Without looking up from the first batch of washing up Amy tells me "You owe me more than a pint for this, Daniel." Then she looks round at me and grins "But it would make a good start!"

***

"This is a little weird."

"Is it?"

"Nice weird. But it is a little strange not to have the bar between us." This is Debbie finding things a little weird, and this is me failing to find something useful to say. We are sitting at a table, across from each other, as you may expect two restaurant-goers might do. Debbie then sticks up the menus between us like a wall, or indeed a bar.

"That's better!" she exclaims and starts laughing.

"Pint of mild and some peanuts, love. Dry roasted" I reply.

She mimics pouring a pint and hands the fictional beverage to me over the top of the menus. Peanuts is off, sir."

"How can peanuts be off?"

"Peanuts is *off*. If you don't like it you can take your business elsewhere."

"No, no that's quite alright. How much for the mild?"

29

"That's £1.25 for you, sir."

£1.25! Ooh, I think I'm falling in love.

Debbie knows all my usual stories by now, and I must know a fair amount of hers, but somehow we manage to fill the air between us with words. Effortlessly, as it goes. When she's on duty at The Red Lion, and when it's not too busy, I now always sit at the bar and chat with her. It's initially an odd experience, as you get interrupted in mid-sentence on a regular basis, but once you get used to it you can pick up where you left off without a thought. I told my sister Rachel this the other day. She said I should try having kids. Anyway, me and Debbie were now very good at this kind of exchange, so we don't drop a beat when the waiter takes our order and then leaves.

"Shame there's no proper beer here, Dan. You must be distraught!"

"I shall overcome. Well, I couldn't take you out to a pub on your night off. Busman's holiday and all that. This wine is nice though. Good choice."

"Well, I *do* work in the industry. Yes, it's better than what we normally have back at work. Must remember the name. Hey, have you ever wondered if a busman ever really went on a busman's holiday?"

"What, you mean drove the bus? On his actual holidays?" I ask.

"Yeah," Debbie continues, "you know like when you are in a place like this, or a plane or something, and someone keels over on the brink of death and someone always shouts…"

"…Is there a doctor in the house!" I finish. A little rude maybe, but she doesn't mind.

"Indeed. 'Is there a doctor in the house?' And there

always is."

I know where this story is going now, but that's ok. I'm looking forward to hearing how she tells it.

"Yeah, so at some point there must have been this coach trip, right? To Skegness, or Salisbury Plain or something…"

"…beginning with 's'…" I add for no reason.

"Exactly. Shoebury, that's it."

"You made that up," I suggest.

"Ah shaddap. You don't know that," Deb effectively counters.

"Fair enough, Deb. Do carry on."

"Many thanks, Dan. So the coach driver takes a funny turn. Starts swooning at the wheel. Some minor ailment."

"How about the runs?"

"Perfect."

"Not for him," I say. "He's on a coach. Not good for the rest of the passengers either, now I think about it."

"So," Debbie carries on, unabashed, "they are stuck on the side of the A666, while the poor driver monopolises the facilities."

"666? You're making *that* up."

"You don't know that either, Dan."

"You are enjoying the fact that I don't have any reception or wi-fi in here, aren't you?"

"Yes, I am. You're less 'full-of-facts' that way. Anyway, so someone at the front of the coach pipes up 'Is there a bus driver in the house?'"

"House?"

"Coach. Don't resort to pedantry just because Google has up and left you. So, Albert…"

"Albert?"

31

"Keep up. Albert is the busman. On holiday. Sitting thirteen rows back trying to ignore the situation. Poor Albert. He's been driving hard all year through the streets of Cheltenham, dealing with the notorious rush hour traffic in the town."

I finish my sip of wine and raise the glass to her. "Oh yes, the absolutely *notorious* Cheltenham traffic. Bet he really needed that break. Poor Albert."

"Oh, yes. Yes, he did. Then someone shouts up again 'Is there a busman in the coach?' But Albert keeps quiet and stares out the window."

"Gets away with it then?"

"Well, obviously not, or it wouldn't be the 'Tale of the Busman's Holiday'. Have you never heard of coherent narrative?"

I let that pass. "So…"

Debbie takes a sip of wine then resumes. "Well, his wife is sitting next to him, isn't she? Giving him a nudge and nodding her head to the front of the coach. 'Go on Albert, she says, *you're* a bus driver.' But she whispers all of this."

"Is that one of those whispers that is actually louder than normal speech?" I ask.

"Even louder than that. Gracie has a booming whisper. Albert tries to shush her but it's too late. It's a loud shush. A murmur then ripples through the coach…"

"Can murmurs ripple?"

"If I say so, yes." Debbie replies firmly. "It ripples round, and some bright spark shouts up, pointing at poor Albert. 'Here's one. We've got one here!' Cheers start to emanate round the coach. Maybe they will all get back to Shoebury…"

"Doesn't exist…"

"…to *Shoebury*, in time for tea. Well, by now Albert is totally done for, and he knows it. He slowly stands up, and, to a polite round of applause, shambles up to the front of the coach. 'I've got this' he says and takes the wheel." Debbie takes an imaginary wheel as she herself says this.

"Poor Albert." I say. "So…is that it?"

Sip. "Give me a chance. I'm making this up as I go along…"

"I knew it!"

"Except the place names, Dan. Well, anyway, back in the coach's W.C., the actual driver hears this round of applause, but this is just at the time he has made a particularly unfortunate noise from down below, so he glumly thinks it is ironic, and directed at him."

That makes me laugh in mid sip. Fortunately, I am well trained to deal with such a situation and am able to avoid spraying Debbie and our fellow eaters by means of a judicious semi-swallow. I'm full of these niche skills, I am. In two seconds flat, I am even able to say. "Hmm. I would think that too, in similar circumstances."

Debbie keeps going. "And, twenty minutes later the driver emerges from the toilet, prepared to make his heartfelt apologies. But, much to his surprise, he's now in Shoebury bus station and the coach is completely empty. And to this day no one ever knew how the bus got to Shoebury…"

"Except all the passengers, Deb. And Albert. And any one at Shoebury bus station. And their family. And their friends. Their Facebook friends…"

She swiftly kicks me from under the table then adds

"…and to this day *almost* no one knew how the bus got to Shoebury. And that is the 'Tale of the Busman's Holiday'." Debbie raises her wine glass on the completion of her tale and I chink it with mine. "Ok, ok, I liked it. The story, not the kick. Needs a bit of work, but I liked it. Interfering wife though? Bit of an anti-feminist cliché, right? You need to flesh out your female characters, Deborah."

"Ha, maybe. I wasn't aiming for a feminist allegory or anything, was I? Next time it shall be his gay partner. Happy now?" she asks.

"Very."

And I am. I find that I really am. I shouldn't be, I know, but I can't spend all day every day thinking about Dad, can I? You've got to move on in little ways here and there, even now, don't you?

Debbie then proceeds to tell me about this volunteer group she works with to keep old people company, and also to provide some help with dementia patients. She started helping while her mother was still alive, and she tells me that it helped her too, in a way. I nod some non-specific approval, then she asks if I would be interested in helping out too. Since I had some experience now. I'm not sure what to say. What I do not say is what I am actually thinking, which is that the prospect scares the hell out of me. But on the other hand, hey, it might help with the guilt. She sees my hesitance straight away and waves the idea away, apologising, saying it is probably too soon etc. I feel the familiar guilt rise in me again. I try to bat it away but end up saying words instead. These ones. "No, no, that *is* a good idea, Deb. I'm ready. I'm ready to try anyway. Let me know when next is good for you and I'll come too."

She smiles and takes my hand. "Thanks, Dan. If you are sure."

I'm not sure, but there's no going back now I've said it. Which is the only way I ever get things done.

Some context. Me and Debbie have known each other, in a shallow but fun sort of way, from the pub for a long time, but became closer around the run up to Dad's death. It turned out that her Mum had Alzheimer's too, way back, so she had an idea what I was going through then, once I had finally opened up a little. I don't know if it's strictly true that she knew exactly what *I* was going through, as each circumstance must be wildly different, but for some reason I did let her in, emotionally speaking, when I had largely been doing a grand job of keeping most everyone else at a safe distance. I didn't tell her everything, good God no, but we did evolve an understanding quickly, and I have come to rely on this already. Partly because of this, this is why we are here now, I suppose. So, it's no surprise that as the line in the bottle of wine descends and the food comes and goes, I change the subject from the volunteer group and start to talk about Dad's funeral. Properly this time. Not about the car and the cousins and the carnations. I tell her about the grief, the numbness, the feelings of unfairness, and the relief. Then the guilt. I tell her all about the guilt. All except the why.

"It's not your fault," she tells me, as she lightly holds my hand from across the table. Oh my, that's so easy to say.

35

Chapter 3

Obituory. No.

Obituery. Hmm…no.

Obiterary. Bloody hell. Dictionary.com.

Dad, despite being an all-round great bloke, was not a celebrity, local or otherwise. So he won't get his…hang on…obituary (of course that's how it's spelled!) put in The Times or anything like that. I could always have paid to put one in the local paper, I suppose, but I never got around to it and anyway the funeral has been and gone now. No, this obituary is just for his kids, i.e. me and Rachel. We are going to read it out when we go to the cemetery this afternoon and bury his ashes under the tree, where Mum's ashes are. Which is why the two of us are sitting in The Red Lion, trying to think one up over a drink.

"Dan! You don't even know how to spell the first word? Give it here, let me write it."
I hand over the pen. There's a distinct pause as we both try and come out with further words. Another thought inevitably distracts me. I open my mouth to allow Rachel to be distracted by this thought too.

"You know what we are now?" I ask, rhetorically.
"No, what?"
"We're orphans," I tell her.
"That sounds a bit sad, Dan."
"It *is* a bit sad, Rach."

"Hmm," she ponders. "It is a bit less sad since we happen to be grown-ups. Well, I *say* grown-ups…" she adds as she looks me up and down, then looks away, satisfied that her point is made.

"Hey!" I exclaim. "I *am* grown up. I'm drinking this pint, right? Therefore, I must be at least eighteen."

"Deeply flawed logic, deeply flawed, but I get what you are attempting to say. However, how long since that t-shirt got a wash, eh?" she asks, wafting her hand in my general direction, taking a sip of her white wine spritzer, and not even looking at my shirt.

I know better than to start any kind of debate with Rachel. Especially in this t-shirt.

"It's going in the wash tonight. It always was going to go in the wash tonight. Grown up, see."

Rachel chuckles and begins to write:

Our Dad, who produced two fine examples of a grown-up. Who taught me how to lace my shoes.

That's a lovely place to start. He would have liked that. Once that was begun, it was suddenly easy to make up a decent list. It didn't have to rhyme. It just had to be true.

Obituary

Our Dad,
who produced two fine examples of a grown-up

Who taught me how to lace my shoes
Who glued the eye back on my favourite bear
Who let me win the race to the lamppost
Who stayed with me until I wasn't frightened anymore

Our Dad,

38

who produced two fine examples of a grown-up

Who held me when we lost our Mum
Who bought me my first beer
Who made me curious about the world we live in
But will forever be missed in this world now without
him

That sort of thing you never see in The Times, nor, thankfully, in any poetry books, but it suits us and our own purposes for today. We could have gone on longer, but it was starting to get a little upsetting and we were getting near the end of our respective drinks. The full list would always be way too long to ever write down anyway, for any of us, wouldn't it? The last few lines were mine by the way, and the teddy bear thing.

Job done. Off we go then, back to the tree.

The plaque has been updated now. By which I mean the plaque on Mum's tree in the cemetery. We buried her ashes under this tree. Dad liked the idea of her carbon atoms being recycled in such a way that we could witness ourselves, in the branches and the leaves, as the tree grew bigger. So, although he never said, it seemed obvious to us that he would like his carbon atoms to join those of his wife. We already had asked the cemetery to add an inscription to the current plaque. There had been a space left on the plaque for just this purpose when we had it made for Mum. Practical, no doubt, and forward-thinking, but I

39

always thought it a little morbid too, before Dad died. So the plaque now says:

For Diane

Beloved Wife and Mother

Always in our hearts

And George

Beloved Husband and Father

Bon Voyage

That last line was my idea. I thought it appropriate since Dad liked the concept of his and Mum's remains travelling up the tree to the sky and beyond. Rachel didn't mind.

So now this is Mum *and* Dad's tree. Time for Dad to join it. I read the obituary out loud, at which point I discover it somewhat lacks rhythm. Then Rachel takes the urn and a trowel that she has brought with her (I don't have one, unsurprisingly) and kneels down by the base of the trunk. She digs a hole next to the one we dug for Mum. You can't see where that hole is now, but she remembers where it was, and so do I. I can visualise the hole there as if it was yesterday. She calmly digs, then puts down the trowel, the first job completed. She turns and looks back up at me. I just nod and smile weakly. She smiles back in much the same way and carries on. She takes the top off the urn, at the second attempt, and carefully pours the ashes into the hole. She then places the urn to one side, calmly picks up the trowel and puts the soil back on top again. And, just like that, the job is done. But Rachel just stays there for a while, still kneeling. I don't think she is praying. I watch all this silently.

I stare at the back of Rachel's head as she remains motionless by the bottom of the tree, and I'm looking for signs of emotion. After a few moments her shoulders start to shake, and she gasps a little. There are tears no doubt, but she doesn't want to show them at this moment, so I don't go looking for them. I just put my hand on her shoulder. There will be hugs later, but not now.

Sorry Rachel. I'm so sorry. I'm sorry, I'm sorry, I'm sorry. All in my head, these words, all just in my head. We always talk of actions and consequences. But they come in all sorts of shapes and sizes, do they not? And one of those consequences is a little break of something deep inside me, here and now. I know not what it is. I can just feel it, that's all, if that makes any sense. I hope it's nothing important.

Before you know it, we are back in The Red Lion, same table as it goes. To the casual observer it would have looked as if nothing much had happened between our sitting here previously, a mere hour or so ago. Like we had just popped out for a bit of lunch, or to the shops, then came back to resume our drinking. The very casual observer may not even have noticed that we had ever even left. Looking around, it makes you wonder what everyone else in here is up to today,

41

besides drinking, and what might be going on in their lives. Doesn't bear thinking about. On the other hand, it probably does. But not today.

Rachel is ok for another drink or two, since she is staying at mine tonight. She was actually quite happy for the excuse to get away from her husband, Don, and her two teenage boys for the night. With the funeral being so recent, no one was likely to argue with her this time.

"Part of me feels like I'm taking advantage of the situation," she tells me, on this very subject, while eyeing me over the rim of her spritzer (spritzer, I know, but what can you do?).

I shake my head. "Don't think like that, Rach. It makes perfect sense. You need to kick back once in a while anyway right? And if they won't let you now, then when the hell would they?" 'Dutch Courage' is making me marginally belligerent. I'd never say this to my nephews, not to their face. I find them a little intimidating if I am being honest.

Rachel smiles at me, in a slightly condescending way. The way that I always seem to attract from all quarters. "I can tell you've never been in a relationship before…" she begins.

"That's a bit harsh, Rach. You know I have."

"Sorry, yes…I liked *her*. I meant a family…"

"*You* know I've been in a family!" I exclaim, a little too loudly, maybe.

She raises her eyes up to the skies this time. Well, the pub ceiling at least. "This is like us being kids again. What I mean is *having* kids and all that. Of your *own*. You know what I mean!" She punches me on the arm, but in a nice way. Of course I know what she means.

42

I'm still not sure I'm wrong though.

She changes the subject slightly, before I can add any further words of wisdom.

"So how is that famous love life of yours then?" she asks. "I've been waiting since junior school for you and Amy to get together."

This causes a slight loss of Dutch Courage, by which I mean down the front of my t-shirt. Just as well this one was not fresh on today. I should have been more prepared, of course. As it goes, I've been getting this particular wind-up from my sister for as long as I can remember. I can handle it better now (slightly) than when I was ten, but this one never gets old apparently.

I give my usual headshake. "No, no, no. That's just not going to happen. I keep telling you, but you never believe me."

"Why ever not?" she asks.

I have to take a couple of sips before I consider my careful response. "Dunno," is the genius retort I come up with, plus accompanying shrug.

"Yeah well, she *is* too good for you I suppose."

"Er, I never said that. Anyway, I *am* seeing someone…"

This time it was a little bit of spritzer that left its glass without permission. No loss there then. This brings the first smile back on Rachel's face since we got to the cemetery. "Get away! Seriously?"

"Yes, seriously. It's not too soon is it? After Dad, I mean. Maybe it's a little impolite?"

"Impolite? Who to, Dan who to?" She wafts her hands at me dismissively. The spritzer is kicking in, clearly. She continues. "If there's one thing that death teaches you, surely, it is to live your life, right? You have to grasp the moment. Then at least one of us would have a relationship worthy of the name!" That last bit was news to me, sort of. I wondered about her and Don, but she normally kept tight-lipped about such things. She is in sleepover mode tonight though, so is letting her hair down. She, and the wine, are right though, I have to admit. In vino veritas and all that. Nice phrase, but one that is not always true. As we both know, it is possible to be very drunk *and* tight-lipped in certain special circumstances, is it not.

"Yes, I suppose so, I suppose so." I reply, avoiding any references back to her marriage. "Anyway, why is it so surprising that I have a date?"

Rachel's eyes flash upwards with a glint.

"Don't answer that." I add, just in time.

"I *was* going to answer that…" she offers.

"Please don't, or I won't tell you anything else."

Rachel holds her hands up in surrender. "Ok, ok. Go on then, who is she?"

"It's Debbie." I tell her.

"Debbie? Debbie…do I know this Debbie?"

"Sort of. She works here…"

"Oh *that* Debbie. I might have known. You didn't look very far did you, Dan?"

"Hey, that's not…"

"No, no, I'm sorry, I'm sorry," she says, holding her hands up again, this time in slight apology. "Yes, I know who you mean. Yes…she seems very nice."

"Thank you."

"Too good for you anyway."

"You just can't help yourself can you, sis? May I please rescind my previously expressed gratitude. Is

there *anyone* I am good enough for, Rachel?"
She laughs and takes another hearty swig. I do the same.

"Only joking little bro, only joking. Well, I don't need to ask you how you met. But how did you get together? Did you ask her out? Did you?" She's now leaning in and grinning at me like a kid.

"Sort of. We talk a lot. We started talking a lot ages ago now. About Dad mainly. She lost her Mum in much the same way. Took a lot longer with her Mum, as it goes."

The grin drops from Rachel's face briefly. Then she takes another sip and she recovers. After all, it really is still too soon for casual references to Dad. But she did ask. I carry on.

"So we've been talking a lot, when she's here you know? Then we'd talk about other things. Then one of us suggested we could talk about other things somewhere else. Like over dinner."

"Was that someone else you?"

"Yes, it was. The drunk version."

"That makes sense. He's more of the asking-out type."

"He sure is, bless him. Anyway, she said yes. And it was nice to spend some time with her when, you know, she didn't *have* to be here. It was all nice really. I never had to think about what to say next…"

"Dangerous…" Rachel quips, amusing herself.

"…ha, sometimes, but not then. Seriously. The chat just kept flowing. Stupid stuff really, but it meant a lot. To me, anyway."

"Ooh, Daniel, I dare say you are a little smitten."
I point to my glass, now containing the mere three

mouthfuls. She nods. Some spritzer drinkers know the rules too. "Daniel's in love," she sings to herself tunelessly as she leaves the table and heads towards the bar.

"Seriously though," she continues, when she comes back, "it is not too soon. Go for it. Dad wouldn't mind, would he? Anyway, it would be good for you to have a woman about the place for once."
I don't know, for once I was beginning to think that it had been really quite some time since I have actually had any *male* company.

Despite this realisation, the next day after work I find myself back in the flat, alone. I can feel the fissure in me that broke open at the tree starting to grow, or failing to heal at any rate. I could go out if I wanted. I *think* I could anyway. But the only company I can deal with right now is my own. Actually, even that isn't true. I can't really stand my own company either at the moment. So as an alternative I'm reading a book in order to ignore myself. This one is a big old history book on the English Civil War. I'm off popular science for the moment, so I just wandered around the library until something jumped out at me. I don't mean Strange Nick. He will actually *really* jump out at you, on a bad day. But you know what I mean, I'm sure. I can't say why I picked this book up and I'm even less sure now, as I leaf through these dense pages randomly, looking for inspiration. Looking for anything to stop me thinking about what is going on in my brain. Well almost anything – this is dry stuff compared to what I'm normally used to reading.

So, inevitably, the part of my brain that isn't me wins out, and thoughts of the funeral drift into the part of my brain that is me. And here is what I see, instead of the words on the page. I can see my knees. The knees encased in the black trousers, not the ones in the jeans that I have on now. The knees that I was staring at resolutely as an alternative to looking anyone else in the eye, during the ceremony at the Crematorium. Everyone wanted to talk to me. I'm guessing to say sorry, or something else more inventive but adding up to pretty much the same anyway. I did not want to talk to anyone. Every tear in everyone else's eye was like a stab in the heart to me, another shovel-full onto the guilt pile. What they maybe saw as empathy felt to me like they were just digging another hole deeper into my own grave. God, I'm an ungrateful sod, I know. I know I shouldn't be feeling that way. Nonetheless, my plan was that if I stared at my knees long enough, I would see less tears, and thereby feel less grief. So instead I just felt a succession of hands on my shoulder, briefly, from whoever. These hands cut deep too, but were easier to take, if I had to choose.

I haven't told anyone about all this, not even Debbie. I'm just telling myself. I could, in theory, have told Amy I guess, last time I saw her, told her how I felt on the day rather than just the bare events. But this feels way too dark to say out loud, so these feelings are just going to have to stay in here, until they somehow aren't here anymore. That's the plan, such as it is. A plan which doesn't look like it's going to work anytime soon, I'm guessing, but it's the best one I have. Sigh.

Back to the book for another go, to push myself away. This time I head to the index. There are a few references to beer (there usually are in books), which are entertaining for a few moments, but don't keep me busy for long. Then, back to the index, where I happen upon references to witchcraft. Which surprises me. What has that got to do with the civil war? So I start reading about the witch trials in Essex and Suffolk and the exploits of Matthew Hopkins, the Witchfinder General. As far as I can tell, once he got the job, he would just rock into a village, find the most likely looking candidate and accuse her of being a witch and kill her. Then the villagers would pay him for his services. Out of fear or gratitude I cannot tell. It seemed not to matter to anyone, with the exception of the accused of course, whether that person was actually a witch or not. The Witchfinder had to justify his presence and generate his income, so that pretty much guaranteed a witch being found in every place he stopped at. I'm glad we don't do that anymore. Then I think of the phrase 'media witch hunt' and begin to wonder whether we have just changed our methods, and not our habits.

This guy was shocking though. He was responsible for so many deaths, gruesome ones at that, and although the people around him may have convinced themselves that what he did was fine, or at least justifiable, he himself would have surely known that what he was doing was complete bollocks. A grade-A accuser. What a git. Blimey, so here's one man who was even worse than me. Hello Matthew Hopkins.

Hello Daniel.

48

Great. The fissure has opened up and let someone in. I've got company after all. Why him, of all people? Screw it, I'd best just go to bed, to 'not sleep' for a while. I put down the book, but he follows me up the stairs nonetheless.

Chapter 4

Ted was late, or I was early, so I rifle around the bookshelf in the far corner of the pub. Not with a rifle. Strange language is this English. I had hoped that Debbie would be in today. She told me her shifts for the week, but I had forgotten. I tried really hard to remember and I did remember, I really did, for about a day or two. But then all the days and times got misfiled in my head. Shame, as I would really love to see her, but can't decide if she would feel the same. Anyway, I need something to distract me and I'm not feeling capable of dealing with my current choice of reading matter on my own just now, so I look for something a little lighter. There's a strange mixture on this shelf, a mixture of books that people must have left, or lost, in previous visits. Tom the Landlord would never actually invest in a book collection, and I don't blame him. I look around at a few things, passing up on all the inexplicably large number of kids' books, then finally plump for a book on 'The Universe'. What's not to like about that? I take it back to my table and start to look through it.

"What's that you are reading?" says Ted, by way of hello, once he deigns to amble in.

"It's called 'The Universe', Ted. It's about…er, the Universe," I reply, holding the book up with one hand.

"You'd have thought it would have been a bit bigger then," he observes. Good point, that. We both look at the cover, which was a picture of just one galaxy, perhaps ours, and therefore only an infinitesimally small representation of the subject matter in hand. We both raise an eyebrow and furrow our brows, thinking that same thing at that same time, and therefore finding no need to say it out loud.

"Pint?" he interjects momentarily. Another good point. He's on fire today.

"Sure thing."

I can't read about Quantum Physics anymore, in case you are wondering. That was a thing for me and Dad together and it holds a certain weight of sadness for me, now that I can't share it with him anymore. Apologies to all the quarks and leptons out there, and there sure are a *lot* of them, but I'm officially into History now. I inform Ted of my new passion as he heads to the bar.

"The English Civil War?" questions Ted, as he brings the pints back from the bar, carrying on the conversation seamlessly from the point where we left it, when he headed off three minutes earlier. We are drinking 'Down and Dirty' this time. 4.0% on the button. I hope it tastes nicer than it sounds. Only one way to find out. Sip.

"Yeah, why not? We never really studied The English Civil War at school. It was all Tudors and that, and we sort of stopped there."

Ted takes his first sip from the top of the glass (always the best one) and nods. "Yeah, we had a lot of that too. A *lot* of that. Six wives, dissolution of the monasteries etc, etc. It felt like we studied that same thing three years in a row. Or maybe it's my memory playing tricks on me."

I carry on. "I've also studied the American Civil War,

the French Revolution, The Spanish Civil War and the Russian Revolution…"

"You sure know how to have a good time…"

"…ah shaddap…but I've never really got to grips with our own civil war. So, it seemed appropriate to do that now. I'm going to read *this*." I get out my history book, the one I recently procured from the library, and plonk it heavily on the table, carefully checking for traces of spilled beer first. You have to look after books, and definitely ones from the library. "Blimey," Ted muses, scratching his chin, "that's a big boy."

"Don't panic my friend," I assure him, "there's a lot of pictures, and some maps…"

"Hmm, even so…" Teds adds, unsure, as he takes another sip and continues to stare at the book in a concerned manner.

"…and a whopping index," I conclude. I flick through the pages until I get to the index then show him how much of the thickness of the book the index takes up, which is almost half the book! Ted watches this carefully, takes another sip, then finally sits back, apparently satisfied.

"Ok, that seems acceptable. I shall look forward to receiving some summaries of your thoughts in due course."

"Yeah, well give me a bit of time. It's been a long while since I've really delved into one of these. It's a little heavier than my normal fare."

"Well, it *is* about war…" Ted says.

"Indeed. Actually, it may not be the very best tome for cheering me up, now that I think about it."

"Oh well, you have it now, so give it a go. Anyway, I

shall be kind. Saturday will be fine for your first report," he announces.

"Jeez, Ted, it's Thursday now. Ok, I'll see what I can do. I may have to flick a bit." I proceed to flick a bit.

"Just do what you feel you have to, Dan. Just do what you feel you have to."

He's not wrong. That's me alright.

"Ok, here's something I read before," I begin.

"There's a bit here on beer taxes…"

"Trust you to fall on your specialist subject straight away, out of all of those pages. You must be some sort of beer tax diviner or something."

"Ted, do you want to hear this or not?"

"You had me at 'beer', Dan. Please continue."

"Well," I begin, furiously skimming my eyes across the page. "it says here that, er, Parliament… hang on I'll summarise…la la la… set up a central committee for collecting taxes, and organising professional tax gatherers..."

"…some things have never changed," Ted chimes in, sipping his pint in approval.

"Previously, tax collection was dependent on local officials acting voluntarily…"

Ted interrupts his next sip to add "… and, yet, there you go, some things *have* changed…"

I carry on paraphrasing. I like that word, paraphrasing. "Excise men were soon widely loathed…"

Ted again, "…no change…"

Me again "…and denounced as a biblical plague…"

Ted once more "…that is a change, well sort of…"

Back to me. This is fine by the way. It's how a pub conversation tends to work, anywhere past the zero-pint mark. "…The tax was imposed on meat, salt and beer, all of them staple elements of the diet of the poor…"

"no change …"

"It did not make them very popular…"

"…also no change again. Oh dear, you've spoilt my rhythm there.

"Oh, I am *so* sorry. Well, at least I can see that you are paying attention!"

"Yes, well that was of passing interest, but you have a bit more work to do for your weekend report."

I take a well-earned brace of sips. What Ted was on about is just what I have always liked about history. You can see both the changes and the similarities throughout time when you see things from a distance. We change for sure, our societies in particular, but in some ways we're not so different at heart to our ancestors. And in a biological sense, we have changed not at all. Evolution has no chance keeping up with us and our hare-brained ideas.

I flick through the book some more, looking for something else to jump out of the page. A mild ahem from Ted breaks my concentration. He holds up an empty glass. My goodness, where did *that* come from? It being my round next, I should certainly have been monitoring the progress of Ted's consumption and been at the bar by the time he had, say, the traditional three mouthfuls left. I'm losing my touch. I feel genuinely embarrassed.

"Time for you to contribute a little more to Parliament's coffers," says Ted, wiggling the glass in my general direction.

This is all somewhat of a relief, by the way. It has been a few weeks since I have seen Ted, which these days is highly unusual. We had to give each other a bit of space when Dad died, at least until the police, the coroner and all those types were happy, and we could get the funeral out of the way. Ted, more than anyone, had really been there for me in the dark days before the day itself, but chose to disappear once Dad had gone for good that night. That was fine for me. It was all a bit of a blur anyway. He did turn up to the funeral he tells me now, but chose to watch from a distance, so I never saw him. Sounds like a scene you get in every other spy movie, I tell him. He just shrugs. I thanked him for being there anyway. He just shrugs again. Which is fine. What else is there to say?

Anyway, I'm glad Ted is back, and we are getting back to normal. As much as things can be normal for us now at least. My family only seems to be getting smaller, so I'm going to need my friends more than ever.

Both new friends and old. Which is why I've met up with Debbie again, so soon after our last date. And why not? I think the first one went rather well, and she must have too, because she said, 'Great idea, I'll get my bag!' as soon as I mentioned the notion of meeting up. Since being at the Lion is like being at work, arguably for the both of us, and because it is such a nice day, we are instead heading to the riverside to share a fizzy Vimto and a bag of Wham Bars. I know how to woo a lady. I let Debbie decide exactly where to sit, as I do not necessarily want to pick the same spot where I used to sit with Dad and talk about the universe. But we end up sitting pretty close by. It is an objectively good spot after all. No worries then. As long as I know it's not me who is forcing the nostalgia, I'm happy to be here. I don't know it for sure, but I don't think forcing nostalgia sounds like a very healthy thing for me to be doing at the moment.

So, sitting here in this familiar environment, but with a more unfamiliar person, I can't help wondering what we are ever going to talk about. I'm thinking this silently as Debbie twists open the bottle with a satisfying hiss and pulls open the bag with a gratifying crackle. I'm *still* thinking of exactly what I could be saying about photons when Debbie laughs to herself and informs me that she is now going to tell me about the last boyfriend she had. Just to get that story out of the way, she says. Not necessarily the top of my subject list, but at least it will get us going, I guess.

"I knew he was an odd one from the start," she begins, "but I am prepared to admit that this might well just be hindsight." This starter not only piques my curiosity, but also provides a sense of comfort that I'm not going to have to hear about some great hero/stud character who cruelly left her and to whom I could never hold a candle, or any other flammable object.
"Not that there's anything necessarily wrong with odd," she continues. "He was definitely a confident chap. Not from round here, from London when I met him. He had short hair, but still had this hippy aura about him, you know?"

I don't. "Is it a scent?" I venture.

"No," she replies, then stops herself. "Well…yes, now I think about it. But that wasn't the thing."

"That *can* be a thing."

"It *should* be a thing, yes. But he was very distracting otherwise. Especially in the bedroom."

"Er, I'm not entirely sure…"

"Don't worry, this is not going where you think it is," she assures me.

"Right, ok," I say in a way that totally fails to obscure any relief I may be feeling.

"He *was* ok in that department, since you mentioned it…"

"I think it was *you* who mentioned it…"

"…in fact, he was awfully keen to get me back to his flat."

"I can imagine…" I muse to the sky, attempting to thread some of myself, and some humour, into this tale.

This thankfully makes her chuckle and she moves a bit closer, as she playfully pushes me on the shoulder.

"I mean *really* keen," she carries on. "So we had the requisite number of dates, the absolute bare minimum before any of *that* stuff is on the cards, then he was most insistent that he should entertain me back at his flat."

"I see. The forward type."

"That's what I thought. Then, when he got me back to his place…er …how do I describe it?"

"I daren't ask…"

"It was clothes off right away!" she exclaims. "Strips off right by his front door!"

"Blimey. The very-forward-indeed type."

"Well, Dan, I didn't know what to do…"

"So, what did you do?" I can't help but ask.

"Well, cookery didn't seem on the cards, so we just went to bed and…you know..."

"I do know, you'll be glad to know. I do *know*."

Despite myself, I may be getting slightly tetchy here, I don't know why. She's here with me now, after all.

"Good to hear. Anyway, so this carried on for a few more dates. I went around to his, he was starkers when I arrived by then, and we went straight to bed. Odd, but hey I could live with that. Then…"

"Then?" I ask, getting impatient for the bit where it all went wrong.

"One time he told me that he was a bit upset and asked me why I always wanted to get straight to bed. Like why couldn't we just chat for a bit, or cook together or something, and that it shouldn't be all about sex. I was taken aback a bit, I must say."

"So am I," I admit. "What was *his* problem then?"

"Turns out he was a nudist. Tackle out on the beach and all that stuff. He wasn't being sexually forward at all. From his point of view, he was just being comfortable, not randy. He told me that he thought I was 'way too horny' as he put it, and that I did not understand that the beauty of the human body is not just about sex. Boy, did I feel chastised at that point."

"What did you do then?" I ask.

"I put my clothes back on."

"Oh, right. I was imagining that you already had your clothes on at this point. Now I'm imagining you with your clothes off now…"

"Naughty…" she smiles and moves a little bit closer. I glance over at her and think to myself 'Don't think I haven't noticed'. But all I do is blush madly and exclaim "I mean, in the context of the story!"

"Yeah, yeah. You're all the same," she jokes, turning towards me on the grassy bank and brushing her leg ever so slightly against mine.

"I resent that slur. Ok, ok, so, your clothes are on…" I nudge her back along into her story as I nudge a little closer to her.

"Oh yeah. So, I told him that I was sorry for being so presumptuous. I mean I *said* that, just because he was all upset and that, but really… what was I supposed to think! Anyway, we do sit down and have a chat. And we do go to the kitchen and cook some dinner. But…"

"But?"

"It was just a bit too odd really. Me with my clothes on and him stark-bollock naked chatting about the weather."

"Oh, I was imagining him having put his clothes back on too."

"No such luck. Use that image if it makes you more comfortable. But this all made everything just that bit too awkward, you know..."

"No, I don't know. I really don't."

"…and frying eggs was particularly dangerous I recall."

"Ah, now *that* I can imagine! Ooh stop!"

"Ha. So we dated a couple of more times, out of politeness I guess more than anything. But then I stopped going round. He knew, and I knew, that it wasn't going to work out by then. I thought I saw him a couple of more times when I was out and about, but I couldn't be sure by then that I recognised him. Not with his clothes on."

"I tell you what…" I say.

"What?"

"I feel sorry for his postman. Imagine ringing his bell for a signature and getting more than you bargained for." She pauses and looks up at me quizzically for a moment, her face now close to mine, all personal space now out the window. "Sorry, shouldn't have said 'bell'," I add as I catch her gaze. This causes another snort and a chuckle and breaks any remaining tension that may have arisen, the type you might get when talking about exes. We pause again for a moment, her arm now somehow wrapped around mine.

"So…is this here a date?" I enquire tentatively.

"Yes, this certainly counts as a date. I am a fan of the Vimto and the Wham Bar."

"So that makes two dates then..."

"Yeesss…"

"And there is a certain number of dates that count as the bear minimum…"

"Yeeeessss…whatever are you getting at?"

"Nothing, nothing. Just checking!" I laugh. Then she grabs me and kisses me lightly. I close my eyes to enjoy the moment.

And so the particular photons that left the sun eight minutes and twenty seconds ago don't hit my retina this time after all. This may be a shame after coming all this way and getting ever so close. Apologies to those particular photons. However, I do feel them warming my skin instead, as me and Debbie hold each other, which still makes it a special moment.

And I certainly won't be spoiling it by mentioning Jen, clothed or otherwise.

You might think that the subsequent moments were in fact spoiled, if I told you that we then start talking about her Mum's, and my Dad's, illness and subsequent passing. But that wasn't the case at all. These overlaps in our experience are what made us close in the first place, that as well as the sheer amount of time we both spend in The Red Lion together. It was good to get away from the nudist ex anyway, and we are mainly just finding comfort in rehashing things that we had said before in the pub. But here and now, this is a different time and we are now different people. Different to each other anyway, which is the important thing. Also, there is something about this place, the weather and the moment that make it different. Not just different, but better, though I can't say exactly why. And so we drift in and out of this and other conversations, happy to watch the river drift things past us and away again between our words.

"Er, what was the hospital like?" I ask after a while, for want of a more insightful question.

"Oh, I don't know," Debbie sighs. "Perhaps you could describe it as a bittersweet place to die…"

"Bittersweet? How so?"

"Nice views."

"Hence the sweet…" I say.

"But death nonetheless."

"Hmm, but it's good you were there for her anyway."

That of course was the bitter part, but there's no point confirming it out loud. I left that topic there. What needed to be said has already now been said. Look, I never said I was always the best conversationalist. I think I'm more of a listener really.

"Reminds me of the fifth commandment really," Debbie eventually muses to the clouds.

"Coveting mules?" I guess lazily. I'm pretty sure this isn't right, but in the absence of the correct answer I might as well wind Debbie up a little, to get a reaction. Sure enough, the reaction is her sitting up and looking at me as if I'm an idiot.

"Seriously?" she asks, just as she realises, by the look on my face, that I'm being far from serious.

"Arsehole," she adds by way of conclusion, then confirms "Honour your father and mother" just to be sure.

"Right", I say, "I knew that."

"It's always been so important to look after your parents, so much so it's been written down for thousands of years."

"Yeah," I reply, "But shouldn't this be blindingly obvious? What sort of society needs to be told to look after your parents anyway?

"This one?" Debbie suggests.

This causes me pause. "Good point," I concede, then take this thought for a walk around my brain a few times. "Good point indeed. Just not sure God is going to get that point across to most people these days."

"I guess not," she agrees, "but who else steps in to tell us how to behave?"

"No one, I guess. We are on our own, Debbie."

"Well, we had all best grow up then."

"That's exactly what worries me," I sigh and let the topic drift away. We let another minute's worth of photons warm our skin at this thought, then Debbie breaks the silence again.

"What do you think about kids?" she asks out of nowhere. At first I internally panic, then give myself a few moments to think about how to reply to this, thankfully finding my way out with this:

"I don't think you should be serving them down The Red Lion," I tell her. This earns me a prompt slap on the arm. But then a hug and a chuckle, like I have passed some unknown test. We then silently watch a family of ducks drift down the river, followed by a soggy newspaper, before we have to go. Neither hold any symbolic reference, by the way. Both were just doing what they have to do.

Later, I say goodbye to Debbie at the end of her street, so she could get ready for work that evening. She picks this moment to inform me that she has some bad news, but that she wouldn't tell me today as it would spoil the mood. What the heck? Really? I really wish people wouldn't do that. Leaving things hanging like that, for my paranoia to chew on. But I was too tired to argue. I'm always too tired to argue. We part ways with a quick kiss, and despite the shadow of this 'news' I still find that I am grinning from ear to ear, watching her bounce along to her flat, then turn around and wave back at me before she disappears through her front door.

It is only a few hours after this, once the sun has fully set and I am back at home, that I stop grinning and begin to chastise myself. How could I possibly feel so happy, so soon after Dad? How could I even *think* of taking Debbie to the place where me and Dad used to go? What sort of despicable human being must I be, thinking that I should deserve to be even a little bit happy? My inner voice morphs into that of Matthew Hopkins, how I imagine a Witchfinder would sound, as I repeat these questions in my head. I know these thoughts should, in theory, make no logical sense, but that knowledge diminishes the feeling not one little bit. I stare at the empty armchair and wait for the feeling to subside anyway, knowing that I shall be waiting a very long time. Knowing that brand new photons from the sun shall be hitting my retina again before I will find any rest tonight.

Chapter 5

This 'bad news' of Debbie's was bugging me, as you may imagine. Why didn't she just tell me what it was there and then? What if she wanted to dump me? Before we hardly got going? Think this through, Daniel. Hmm, if she wanted to do that then surely she wouldn't have waited. There would be no ongoing 'mood' to spoil. No, even paranoid me feels comfortable enough to argue my way out of that theory. Surely not that then. Could be something worse though. What if *she* is really ill? Hmm, she didn't *look* ill. Don't be stupid, Dan, not everyone who *is* ill looks ill. Could be that then. Oh dear, I hope it's not that. Maybe it's…maybe it's…oh God I don't know what it is. We have not arranged to meet until the weekend. But I'll never make it to the weekend like this, so I'll have to go into The Red Lion while she's working to find out.

Which puts me in a bit of a position as I am supposed to know when she is working this week (since she actually told me), and, as usual, I had forgotten. There's only one thing for it. I will have to keep popping in until she is on shift, then I pretend that I was expecting to see her. That seems like the best solution. After the second session without her appearing, it finally occurs to me to just ask Tom the Landlord, instead.
"Don't you know?" he replies to me with a knowing wink. She must have been talking to him about us then. It's a fair cop.

I shrug and make that embarrassed male look that is only shared between other males. The one with a kind of grimace. He knows that look, so smiles and nods, as he takes some glasses out of the washer.

"She's in tomorrow night," he says, then turns to put the glasses away. I stay and have a 'Devil's Advocate', 3.7%, anyway. It would be rude not too. Just the one though, I'm trying to cut down. I know, it breaks the three-pint rule, but I didn't come in here for a pint as such at all, so that's ok, right? Either way, don't tell Jez please, or I won't hear the end of it.

The following evening, I breeze in with a nonchalant wave to Debbie, which I had been practicing at home before I left in front of the mirror, and approach the bar. She looks at me like I'm some kind of fool. Probably because I have never once before waved nonchalantly when approaching the bar. Oh well. Anyway, I then have to act normal for ten minutes or so before I dare to broach the subject of the 'news' again. She nods and nervously looks over at Tom. "I'll have to tell you later," she says, "hang on." What now? Is she seeing Ted as well? No, can't be that, surely. I think life was easier when I wasn't going out with anyone. My imagination could fly off in less self-destructive directions back then. Anyway, there is a pub quiz on tonight and Debbie is pretty busy on and off, so I pass the time instead by pretending not to listen to the quiz questions and, latterly, having a chat to Stan. He's another regular here who, as it transpires, has recently split with his wife, and not, as it turns out, just to get down to the quiz.

"Sorry to hear that, mate," is my sympathetic, albeit bog-standard, beginning, once he had updated me on his life. I had heard all of this already as it goes, but not from him, so I have to treat this as news.

"Yeah, well it's been coming a long time I suppose. It's ok really." Judging by the rate he is consuming his lager (whatever-%, I really don't care) things do not quite look like they are ok. I don't know though. Maybe he's just thirsty. Or relieved. You know what, if I actually pay some attention and let him talk I might actually find out.

"What happened, then?" I ask, "if you don't mind me asking…"

He didn't mind. At all. Many people might pretend that they come in here to get away from their troubles. But more often than not they end up being more than happy to totally confront their troubles by the end of the evening, with the help of a fellow drinker. All you have to do is ask how they are. It's like magic!

"Nothing happened, if that's what you mean. It wasn't her and it wasn't me. It was the 'us' that just disappeared over time, that's all."

This is not a surprise. He never previously mentioned his wife much at all, and seldom in a complimentary fashion if he did. I suppose in some other establishment in town somewhere, some female equivalent of me is getting a similar run down of the mirror-image of these events from Stan's ex. I wonder who she might be? And would I like her? Shut up, Dan and stay focused, I tell myself. Outwardly though, I just take a sip and nod, providing just enough encouragement for him to carry on.

"So no affairs, no gossip for you…" he begins.

"Not at all," I say holding up my hands, "I'm not one for gossip as you know…"

"Hmm. Anyway, it just fizzled out, that's all. I could tell really, whenever I bothered to pay attention. Each time I did, pay attention you see, it felt like there was a little less relationship there than the last time. Then, eventually, it just felt like there was nothing left at all. Turns out she was feeling much the same, once we broached the subject. Sad, but a relief in many ways."

"Yeah, I know," I say. I really don't though. My personal tendency is to get dumped well before I'm ready to do any of the walking away myself. So I shall have to use some pretend empathy this time.

Stan finishes the last third of his pint in one go, and, while gesturing towards Debbie for the next one, casually remarks, "I suppose the dating website was a bit of a distraction…"

I lift my glass up to my face to hide whatever look has just fallen upon it. I would need a mirror to check, as I can't be quite sure what look that might be. There will be shock and confusion in the mix there at the very least. Thank goodness I wasn't in mid-gulp or Stan would have been wearing 'eau de Devil's Advocate' for the remainder of the evening.

"Dating website?" I ask in a whisper, once Debbie has taken Stan's order and retreated again to the pumps. "When was that?"

"Oh, quite a while ago," Stan replies. Without a glass he's not sure what to do with his hands now, and he begins to fidget. Another reason why we like to drink. Keeps our hands nice and busy! "Not to do anything naughty you understand. Just to have a look, you

68

know? See what I was missing. Thought it, er, might, er, make me appreciate *her* more maybe." The 'ers' and the increased fidgeting here clearly reveal something else, but I don't press the issue.

"I've never been on one of those sites before," I say, to relieve the beginnings of tension. "Always felt a bit too self-conscious."

The pints arrive. One for me too. Wordlessly, we are in a round now. You just *know* when that's the right thing to happen, that's all I can say. Stan pays as I wink at Debbie, and she returns me a smile. Stan doesn't notice. We take a small break in the conversation to savour the first few sips of our new refreshments, but despite this we both know that it's Stan's turn to speak, so when we are both ready he starts up again.

"Oh no," he says. "It's so easy really. Just fill in a few fields, find a decent picture…"

"Which would be my main problem…"

"You must have one picture that's ok, Dan. I could take one of you now. Sitting here with a pint at the bar. That would tell a prospective lady all she needs to know about you!" He laughs at this and brings out his phone to mime taking a picture. In response I choose to pretend to be offended.

"There's more to me than that, Stan!" I exclaim, then immediately wonder exactly what that 'more' would look like in a pie chart showing 'at the bar with a pint' in red and 'more than that' in blue. I imagine something around 70-30 but I choose not to inform Stan of this. That would just give him more ammunition for piss-taking. Plus, I want to know more about this dating site. Not for me, you

69

understand. I want to know what he was doing on there.

So I ask him, "Tell me about this site then."

He needed no further encouragement, like anyone talking about their pet subject. "Well, no sooner had I put my profile up, then all these messages started appearing. Some of them a bit weird…"

Sip. "Weird? How weird?"

"Well, like a bit over the top, some of them. Going on like they were looking for husband material. I still literally *was* husband material at the time…"

"Yeah, someone else's husband…"

"Hmm, yes. But not all were like that. There were a few that raised my eyebrows I must say…"

"But you didn't act on them…" I probe.

"No. Well…" he begins, then takes another hearty swig. Jesus, why doesn't anyone want to just tell me things straight tonight?

"Well...?"

"Well, I sent a few messages."

"Oh, that's ok. I think…"

"And had a couple of dates."

"Er…"

"But *that* was it. Anyway, soon after that me and the missus broke up anyway."

"Right."

"So I might have followed up on those dates."

"Er, right."

"After an appropriate time."

I don't ask what that time was, although I am curious I must admit. No point stirring that pot. Different pot for everyone, I suppose.

"Are you still on the site then?"

"Well, I *was*."

"Oh yeah?" Ooh, this sounds interesting. Sip.

"Until last week. Had to change to another site."

"Really? How so?"

"Well I got my recommendations for the week as usual. You know, of suitable matches."

"Right."

"And you'll never guess who was on there. Only my bloody wife!"

He didn't actually give me time to guess, but I think I would have actually made a decent stab at that one if given the chance. Never mind. I laugh in response anyway.

"Apparently we are a great match!" he says, and joins in the laughter. I'm still laughing when I start to wonder whether this situation is really that funny after all.

" Oh dear, no," is all I can manage in reply eventually. "She must have got something similar too I expect."

"Yeah, I guess so. I never thought of that. I never sent her a message to check, that's for sure."

"No. That would have been just insane, Stan."

"Yep. Gave me quite a shock I can tell you."

"Makes you think though." I say.

Stan stops in mid-sip and turns to look at me. He's starting to look, and sound, a little drunk, even to me.

"Whatever you think I should be thinking about this, I have already decided that I'm not going to think about it. I think," he firmly tells me.

"Hmm. Probably just as well." I concur. Well, there's no point disagreeing right now, is there?

"Hey, you never know, give it a year or two and we

both might find it funny!" Stan concludes, then raises his glass towards me. "Cheers!"

"Cheers!" I reply, and we chink glasses. A fitting ritual after a shared moment.

"So," Stan carries on, "do you want details of this site then? Have a go yourself?"

"Er…"

"Not for my missus though…" He wags his finger at me.

"No, of course not!" I assure him. I glance over at Debbie, who is busy down the bar. She's smiling at a customer, coming back from the till. She looks particularly lovely when she smiles. I love seeing that smile, even when it's not pointing at me. "No, I'm alright Stan. Good luck to you though. And to her."

"Yeah, I can drink to that, mate."

And so on.

Once the quiz is over the pub clears substantially, and Stan has gone off, presumably to check his laptop or phone for potential new liaisons. Debbie is clearing the bar a little and finally we have a chance to chat. Well, I say that, but Debbie is decidedly not taking up that opportunity. Whatever this news is, it is not preying on *her* mind in quite the same way as mine. So I have to dig for information again, but, of course, I do this with attempted nonchalance.

"So…"

"So? What's up Dan?"

"You had some *news*. You know? That you wanted to tell me?"

She stops for a second, then the penny drops. "Oh, yes!" she says, and looks over to Tom the Landlord again. "Are you sitting down?" she asks.

"You can see I'm sitting down. On this bar stool. Where I've been all night!" Even I lose my patience eventually, albeit just a little.

"Look, I'm not supposed to tell you this…"

Urrghh!!

"…but I can trust you."

I gesture for her to continue. Opening my mouth will just cause more delay.

"Tom brought us all in for a meeting," she begins. Then she stops.

This had better not be the full extent of the news. I gesture again.

"I don't know how to tell you this…"

I gesture again, even more so this time. I'm going to take off if I flap any more.

"He wants to sell up. Sell up the pub. And it's going to close. He wants to sell it to a property developer. For flats."

Oh. So *that's* the news. Ok then. She's not dumping me. Then it begins to hit me. Oh no. Oh God no. No! Well, now I *am* glad I was sitting down.

"Sorry Dan. Keep it to yourself though yeah?"

I nod, absent-mindedly at first, then with some vigour, as I notice her eyes staring into me with some force.

"You ok Dan? Dan? Um…do you want a drink?"

I nod vigorously again. In the circumstances, I think that I better had. I even order a Big Britain.

Before I know it, it is 3am. My busy bladder has decided it does not want to keep in the Big Britain until morning and has dispatched a weird dream to my brain, in order to wake me up and send me to the bathroom. In this dream, I am in a courtroom, specifically on the witness stand. I know what you might be thinking, but I'm not being cross-examined or accused of anything in particular at all. I join the scene asking the judge whether I can be excused to go to the bathroom. The judge politely informs me that I cannot leave, as there are no bathrooms, but I could have a quick tinkle in the witness stand itself if that would help. For some reason, in the context of this scene, that strikes me as being an entirely reasonable compromise, so I employ my zip for its intended purpose and make a start. Trouble is, once I do start I just can't seem to stop, and, as the stream continues to flow and flow and flow, disapproving harumphs increase in volume around the court, as the torrent spreads across the floor. I blush, laugh nervously, start apologising and then…. wake up.

Jesus, that was weird. Just plain weird, not unusual weird. My bladder and my brain are regular close collaborators in such productions, conspiring against me and a good night's sleep. But there's no point fighting it, so off I go to the bathroom. However, back in bed a few minutes later I am not rewarded with a quick return to sleep. Oh no, this is where my real punishment begins. Traditionally I am employed to punish myself, but now I have Matthew Hopkins to join in and help. He likes the night in the same way that I don't. I don't know where he is in the room, but I can hear him.

"Glad you could join me," he says with a sarcastic edge.

"My pleasure," I say, maintaining the tone in reply.

"I know you. I see the blackness in you."

Blimey, he doesn't hang about. I try to ignore him

and think about something else. Jasper the cat pops out of my memory. He was a good boy. He always made me happy. Then he died. Thanks brain, that was no help at all. My mother. Same problem. Dad. No, don't think of Dad, don't think of Dad, don't think of Dad!

"Yes, I know all about you and your father," Hopkins says. "But you must confess."

I bury my head in my pillow and scream silently until he has gone. The light is streaming through my curtains by the time that happens.

You didn't hear any of this. I never said anything of the sort. If I told you this when I was drunk it's not true, I was making it up. You understand? Please? And I won't be drinking Big Britain again. Well, not quite so much of it anyway. It's bloody strong.

Chapter 6

I'm being punished. That's it. I must be being punished. The universe is out to get me. Or find balance again, at least. I could happily wallow in this train of thought for much longer, but I push these feelings from my mind for now. It is early evening, or maybe late afternoon, on Saturday, one of my favourite times of the week, and Jez has just walked into the pub. He likes a slightly early start too, bless him, and I need him to turn up on time today, to help me get away from myself. I don't tell him that though.

Jez starts by saying that he feels a little under the weather and may have a little trouble drinking today. He tells me this as he takes his first sip of 'Spin Dry', 4.1%, which is a little bit hoppy, I must say. I give him a suitable look of condolence. As we catch up on the week's news, he continues struggling through his first pint, which is usually the most difficult one in these circumstances. If you do manage to get to the third then you are generally considered to be back to normal, for the time being at least. He does indeed look a little peaky, but soon enough it is my round, so I say, "Doctor Dan prescribes another pint of medicine!"

Jez looks a little unsure and feels his throat. "Hmm, not sure. I think I've lost my beer glands today."

Beer glands. What a thought. Imagine if we actually had beer glands! Mine would look a little weathered I expect, but not entirely shot to bits either.

"Beer glands?" I ask, unconsciously feeling at my neck too. That must be where they are, right?

"Yeah, I'm sure we all have beer glands," Jez confirms confidently. "They must define how good a drinker you are. Some people have wine glands instead. I think that's an X chromosome thing."

X chromosome. This is Jez's way of trying not to be sexist when he is, in fact, being casually sexist, although I'm sure he means no harm by it. However, he does have a point I suppose, looking at the evidence. It is, as always, predominantly male in here and, should you be looking, you can find twice the X chromosomes on average in Corkscrews down the road, if you don't count the men hanging around the intended demographic there for other reasons. This 'X chromosome' code never helps Jez in practice though. Amy always swipes him across the back of the head with one hand, while sipping her beer with the other, when her genes are called into question. Fortunately for Jez, Amy is not coming along until later. Lightweight. Do not tell her I said that though.

"Would some food help?" I suggest. This is normally against the grain, if not the rules, but the poor bloke has his beer glands up, so let's just be nice. Hmm, I say 'food' but in here that may mean something different to what you are expecting. Jez raises his eyebrows and has a think.

"Hmm, yes, that could work. What have they got on today?"

"The Specials?" I say, which is a joke.

Jez starts singing 'Too Much Too Young' which is the usual second part of the same joke. We find joy in repetition, me and Jez. This is a great trick if you can

77

pull it off. It helps not having to always come up with new material.

"Back on Earth though, what have they got? I am a bit peckish," he says once he has completed the first verse, which is all he knows. I have a better view of the snacks hung up behind the bar from here, so I crane my neck and reel them off.

"Crisps. Usual."

"Hmmm…" Jez says, still noncommittal.

"Crisps. Those hot chilli ones."

"Oh god no, not today. My glands, you know…"

"Nuts…"

"Bit harsh, mate. Beer glands are real."

"Ha ha. How about these? Pork scratchings. Scratchings? That can't be right, can it? Is it cracklings?" I should know this, but I'm starting to doubt myself. I am plagued with self-doubt, like most people, but fortunately these doubts tend to surface around inconsequential things like this as much as the big stuff.

Jez ponders this then says, "Scratchings. Yes, it is scratchings. I've not stopped to ask why until now though. Still, I do think that it is indeed the scratchings that will sort my itchy glands out."

All this talk of scratching and glands is putting me right off the idea of a snack. Happily, I'm not that hungry anyway. Later on, this does not stop us chatting about food during our third, and for Jez, *key* pint. Key because if he gets through this he'll be out for the night, and will be here to get his head slapped by Amy later on. He then leaves me with a profound thought to ponder on as he heads back to the bar.

"Crisp sandwich?" I ask him to confirm, upon his return.

"You should not simply ask the question 'crisp sandwich'" Jez advises me. If he wore glasses he would be looking over them at me with academic disapproval. "The answer is, of course, *always* 'yes'. No, the real question is 'which crisp sandwich?'"

"Ah, I see!" I say, feigning a Road to Damascus moment. I haven't got time to explain that reference just now. You can look it up. I continue, "Well, why didn't you say so? I've now wasted two minutes precious thinking time on the incorrect hypothesis." It's best to use words like hypothesis now, since I won't be able to use them properly later on. That fact doesn't usually stop me however, I am reliably informed.

"No matter," Jez opines (another nice word for pint three), "the answer is always Salt and Vinegar."

"Always?" I say, my gut reaction being to question established norms, for the sake of the development of scientific knowledge. We both pause, looking for alternatives from our bodies of research, and take a couple of sips while we cogitate. Don't worry, this verbosity won't last much longer. After a few moments, I have to tip my head and nod in agreement, succumbing to the superior academic position.

"Always," Jez confirms, opening his, mercifully small, bag of Pork Scratchings. "You weren't going to say Prawn Cocktail were you?"

I shake my head confidently. "Oh no, not in a sandwich. Great on their own…"

"Indeed, Doctor Dan. I am glad we can come to an

agreement on this matter."
We should publish this work somewhere. It could save people a lot of wasted time. Plus an awful lot of bread and crisps.

We move onto the merits of Baconated Brussels Sprouts, as the level on Jez's pint gradually descends, almost without him noticing. We are reaching the Rubicon. You know, the point of no return. Jez is going to reach it any sip now. I'm silently willing him over the line. Is that really so selfish? After all, we're both enjoying ourselves here. Plus, I really cannot be left on my own today, not for a moment. I can sense my bad inner self and his new friend just waiting to pounce as soon as they get me by myself. So yes, it is selfish, I know, but who isn't? Anyway, one more topic should do it. And I think I have the one.
"You know how you get beer sweats, right?" I offer as a starter.
"Oh yes," Jez confirms, taking another sip. "That glorious scent of stale ale permeating from the pores of one's skin, usually on the morning following an extensive research session on the quest for knowledge of…"
He's getting pint-five rambles already, despite being on pint three, so I should really cut him off before he ties himself in verbal knots. Which brings me to interject, "Exactly. But why is it just *beer* sweats?"
"Well there is Sambuca…"
"Oh god, don't go there. Not in your condition. I meant other things, like food. Like food made out of grain too…"
"Like cake?" Jez offers, unsure as to where this is going. Or even why.

"*Exactly* like cake!" I enthuse.

"So… what you mean is, Dan, is…um, why don't we get the cake sweats?" Yes, Jez is starting to get it.

"Yes, why *don't* we get the cake sweats?" I ask.

"Maybe we do. I just don't think I've eaten enough cake to generate them."

"Me neither, Jez. We will need to talk to someone who eats a lot of cake."

"That's not just something, Daniel, you can go up to a person and ask," he says, "without getting into a certain degree of personal trouble. Believe me, I know." He raises his eyes in brief reminiscence, then winces a bit. I'll make a mental note to get the story on that one later.

"Oh yes, I see, I see," I say instead, once I do see. Jez sure is wise, albeit in a strange way. "Hmm, maybe we had best park that one right there then. For now."

"We should. And do not ask Amy about cake. At least not around the time when she was eighteen."

"I shan't. Good advice, my friend. So…how's the glands?"

"What glands?" he says smiling, and chinks my glass. Which is great for me. But it's going to cost him in the morning.

You might think that all this is inconsequential, and you'd be right. But that is the point. And this is just what I need right now. You must yourself surely have needed a nonsensical piece of chit-chat like this at some point too in your life, right? To take you away from…you. That's why so many people in here actually talk to me, I think. Even with me and Jez though, this level of insignificance can't last, and Jez, by and by, wants to know a little bit more about the funeral, and all that. It is pint four, so he's staying and he knows it, and we now have time, and are drunk enough, for more meaty subjects. In an instant we change tack, like an ice skater's pirouette. Hmm, remind me to work a bit more on my metaphors.

"You ok now, mate?" he asks. I've seen him a little since Dad's funeral, but we have studiously avoided the subject up until now, and he doesn't seem too upset about not being invited. We know each other so well, I suppose that we just instinctively know when the time is right for such things. It's different for every relationship isn't it, and our time was just a little later than mine was with Amy. That may have more to do with Amy than Jez though, or indeed me. "Ah, you know, I really miss him," I say, swilling my pint around and around my glass. Jez does know all about this sort of subject himself, as it goes. "It's all still pretty fresh. Half the time I think I've got to go and see how he is, then I realise I don't. That's a mixed feeling, I have to admit."

"Hmm," is all Jez says. Fair enough. What he doesn't really know much about is caring for a dementia patient, so he wisely backs off from an opinion on that one.

I carry on. "I didn't realise how much he had become part of my life again, since I came back. It seems like if I wasn't in here, in this pub I mean, I was with *him* pretty much."

"You can't have been with him *that* much then," Jez quips. It may sound heartless from the outside, but from within an old friendship, such things are more like the little hugs we never give each other for real. They really are. We both chuckle a little, then sigh.

82

Then I continue.

"It makes me think about all those years when I was in London and I didn't see much of him at all. Why didn't I go back home more often?"

"You can't go thinking like that, mate," Jez replies, "you had to go out and live your life. Become who you are meant to be and all that. That's what your Mum and Dad would have wanted for you."

"I don't even know if I ever became who I was meant to be anyway," I say, head down.

"Yeah, you did, Dan. Yeah you did." He leans over and chinks my glass without me looking up. Another little 'hug'. God, we're getting well into the melancholy part of the evening already, the part I most often try and navigate around, whether I'm feeling blue or not. It's just too big to avoid tonight.

After a while Jez tells me stories of Tina's funeral. Tina is his sister (she *still* is his sister, if you ask him) and was killed by a car some years ago. He's not trying to change the subject on me, you understand. He's partly trying to give me a rest. But mainly he's trying to show some empathy, some understanding, to show me that he too has a window into how I am feeling. That's how life teaches us to be 'experienced'. You just pick up stories that you can use elsewhere later on. I know for sure that at some point I'm going to be sitting in here, or somewhere similar, patiently listening to the funeral story of someone else or other, waiting to reel out the story of my own Dad's funeral, by then honed by endless repetition, just to show some empathy of my own.

So, he's talking about her, but he's really just trying to help me.

"That was super traumatic, and when you're in it you think it will never pass. In some ways it doesn't, but in others it does pass, Dan. It changes into something…smaller. Something you can handle, or hide."

"I think your body just eventually physically runs out of the materials to make those chemicals that make your brain sad." I add.

"You would say that," he says in return, with a wry smile.

We could go on about why I would say that, but that's enough of that sort of thing for now, we seem to agree wordlessly. There is other business to attend to.

"Have you heard, Jez?"

"Heard?"

"The news."

"Not since breakfast. Stock market is down. Some politician said something inconsistent. Blah, blah."

"No, not that," I say leaning in. "The news *here*."

"Here? What? Cider prices down? We've run out of Pork Scratchings? Tom went back on his promise to stock Cashew Nuts? Blah blah?"

"No, not that, Jez. What? Did Tom do that…? Never mind. Anyway. Look, I'm not supposed to tell you this…"

This piques his interest. Nothing on this planet, after all, piques your interest more than something you are not supposed to know about. "Do tell…" he asks, leaning in.

"You can't say."

"I won't." It's ok, I know he won't. Jez's love of

gossip only works one way, like a fact-valve. Information going in, nothing going out. Ooh, that's a better metaphor! Or am I just getting drunker?

"It's the pub, Jez. Debbie told me. Tom's going to sell up."

Jez, a natural optimist, responds with just a shrug of his shoulders. I'm not sure I'm getting the point across as to just how serious this is, because he just says, "I'll miss him. I will. But, you know, he's not the only landlord on the planet. I'm sure we'll just carry on pretty much as before."

"No, Jez. He's going to sell up to developers. For flats or something."

"Oh." *Now* he gets it. "Shit, that's out of order. He can't *do* that can he?"

"It's his pub. The freehold and everything. I don't know, but I think he can do that. I mean, you don't protect buildings like this one, do you? It's hardly on the 'Listed', er, list."

Jez looks around, as if seeing the place for the first time. "No, I guess it isn't. He can't just *do* that though, surely? I mean, this is our *home*!"

"I know!"

"Well, second home," Jez corrects himself, then stands up and finishes his pint with a renewed enthusiasm. "Jeez, that's bad news. What are we going to do?"

"Yeah. Well look, Debbie says she is going to look into it all anyway, so watch this space. And keep it under your hat for now." I finish my pint with a determined flourish, for no reason I can justify.

"Good. I will." Jez mimes a hat with something under it. That done, he then points his glass at me. "Another one? While we can?"

We've been drinking far too quickly tonight, and should not be this far ahead of Amy before she even arrives. A brief dilemma ensues. However, I bet she'll be drinking a sneaky couple at home. Probably. Plus, we will be slowing down from here on in, we always do. I'm sure there's another reason or two to help us justify having another one now. Oh yes, we've had food. Well, Jez has, and I've talked about it. Yes, that counts. And Jez needs medicine. Yes, that should do it. "Sure thing," I tell him.

The bar is busy now, and although it's only been five minutes, when he gets back I have already been hijacked by my bad inner self.

"I think I'm being punished." I tell him, as he sits down.

Jez looks genuinely confused. "Punished? Whatever for? Tom's not selling up to spite *you,* I'm sure. Anyway mate, haven't you had enough punishment lately?"

I consider this seriously for a moment. Have I? Oh dear, I'm already talking too much. Time for a deep breath and to rein myself in. "Sorry mate. I don't know what I mean," I say. "What's this?" I point to my drink, which is a distinctly darker colour than the last few.

"It's just come on. Mellow Doubt, 3.4%. We need a session ale or my glands, and Amy, are going to take bad revenge upon me."

I take a sip. "It's lovely," I say.

"Yup. And where are we going to get a pint like this when this place closes?"

"I don't know, Jez. There's always the

86

Shakespeare…"

"The Shakespeare? We never dare go in there after the sun goes down! We'll have to become…er… what is the opposite of nocturnal?"

"Er…diurnal?" I offer, uncertain of myself for a moment.

"Really? I thought it would be something else. Some word I had actually heard of."

"I have no idea how I dug that out, but yes…yes that's the word. But you have a point, we can't be diurnal drinkers."

Jez nods in agreement. "Too right. I can't even say it."

The thought of what we *are* actually going to do still permeates through my brain for the duration of the evening. This is even after Amy bursts in, berates us for our drunkenness, gives us both an *actual* hug, then proceeds to catch us up via the medium of cider. All in that order. And for those moments, those brief few moments, the recent changes in our lives are banished and the concerns of the changes to come leave with them.

Second note inn the mattere of The Red Lion Witch
Matthew Hopkins, Witch finder-General

Men sometimes have strange motives for the things they do, as God is my witness. This will not save you witch. We knowe your own damnable crimes are contrarie to God and nature.

We will take you to the pond. Float and you will be guilty then you will be hung by the necke until your death. Sink and may God showe you to be innocent and I commend your soul to Him.

Your test is about to begin.

Confess.

~

"Shut up Hopkins. Shut up. Shut up. Shut up! I'm not listening!"

As if. I can hear him all too clearly now.

I look up and see that I have walked the long way home again. And again find that I have stopped at the benches, the ones next to the pond that sit by the gates of the cemetery. The gates that are now safely locked up for the night, to keep demons like me out. I stare at the water and stare at the gates in turn. If I was in a room, the room would be spinning. But now it's my head that just spins instead. I don't want it to stop. If it stops I might just be able to do as Hopkins commands me, and jump into the water. To jump in the pond and prove my guilt. The water ripples in time with my spinning brain.

Then. I blink.

The sky is a little lighter to the east when I find myself at the gates instead, grabbing at them hard, trying in vain to shake them open, staring out into the dark

89

inside for a familiar landmark. When Hopkins asks
me what I think I'm doing I tell him.

"I just want to say sorry. I'm sorry! I'm sorry Dad!"

He sneers at me and just points to the pond instead.
And the only thing that is stopping me is the fact that
my fingers are locked so tight that I can't let go of the
gate. I don't let go until the sun finally does come up.
Then I'm safe for one more day, and I can return
home for the few hours of unconsciousness that I get
as a substitute for sleep.

And carry on like nothing has happened.

Chapter 7

Blimey. I think, by this point of the night, I've literally been talking now for hours and hours. Funny, because when I came out of my flat earlier I literally had nothing to say. Indeed, as I turned the key in my front door on the way out, I was completely bereft of opinion, interests and knowledge. I had been sitting on my sofa in a blank state, TV on, desperately trying not to think about anything. Which is why, when Ted sent me a message suggesting 'a cheeky pint', I was out the door in less than five minutes. I was meeting Debbie later anyway so it made perfect sense.

"Pint of Dover sole?" Ted asks me when I walk in. He must have messaged me from the pub, as he's here even quicker than me, which is pretty darn quick, I'll have you know.
"I don't know, Ted. Sounds a bit weird. Even I have my limits."
"It's *Soul* – spelt S.O.U.L."
"Ah right. Hmm. Um, even so, I've still got that first image in my head now. Can you get me a 'Certain Fate' instead? 4.6%."
"Fair enough. I'm not drinking the 'Dover Soul' either to be honest," Ted admits to me, then heads to the bar. It is his round because I got the last one on the last time we met. We both know this instinctively, experts in this field as we are.
I watch him as he gets the drinks in and exchanges brief pleasantries with Tom the Landlord about something or other. There's something about him that

is not quite right tonight. My radar is up because he was here before me, which as you know is most unusual, but there's something else. His shoulders are hunched maybe, or something like that. Can't put my finger on it, but he's not quite right. Nevertheless, he is smiling at me as he heads back and plonks my pint down on the table. So, what next? Since something is upsetting Ted at the moment, and he is my friend, we'll just talk about it, right? Wrong. Will we heck!

"I've been reading about the Book of Sports," Ted begins instead, which almost certainly is *not* the thing that is actually bothering him. Then he looks at me as if he is expecting some kind of reaction. I give him one.

"I don't really like sports, Ted. You know that."

"Not 'a book on sport', dingus. *The Book of Sports*. Right?" Then, after my blank look continues, he adds, "No? Really? I thought this was your new area of expertise!" He laughs at the end of this though. No one is really going to get annoyed here, and certainly not about anything like this.

"Er…" is the sum total of my contribution, as I try and work out just what he is getting at.

Ted takes out a book from his jacket pocket, with a library sticker on it, and proceeds to quote from it. This book appears to be a nice, short, readable history of the English Civil War. For kids maybe. It appears to have colour pictures! A book that I would no doubt have got out of the library instead, if it had been there, when I ended up procuring my more weighty tome instead. Yes, I would have got that book out instead quicker than…than I can down a third! Of a pint, that is. Which is pretty quick, just to be clear.

92

"The Declaration of Sports," Ted reads, "also known as the Book of Sports, was a declaration of James I of England issued just for Lancashire in 1617, then nationally in 1618, then reissued by Charles I in 1633. It listed the sports and recreations that were permitted on Sundays and other holy days. It was intended to resolve a conflict, on the subject of Sunday recreations, between the Puritans and the gentry, many of whom were Roman Catholics."

"Ah, I see," I begin excusing myself. "Yes, well, I haven't got to that bit yet. My book is considerably bigger than yours, I can't help but notice. Still, I can imagine how those chaps might have trouble agreeing on what to do on a Sunday afternoon. Couldn't they just agree to disagree and meet up again on the Monday?"

"Apparently, that is not how things worked back then. Imagine there being a list of things that you had to check against to see what you could get up to on the weekend?"

"I can imagine. It wasn't that long ago when we weren't allowed to be in the pub between 2pm and 7pm on a Sunday, remember? Apart from the lock-ins…"

"Oh, God bless those lock-ins," Ted muses and chinks my glass. "Anyway, it says here that permission was given for dancing, archery, leaping and vaulting, and for having of May games, Whitsun ales and Morris dances…"

"Not much of a list. I'll bag the Whitsun ales!" I laugh.

Ted surveys the list for his remaining selection, then gives up with a sigh and a chuckle. "Not much of a choice left," he admits.

"Indeed. The King was hardly the life and soul of the party."

"To you, maybe not. But he most certainly was when compared to the Puritans. They burned the Book…"

"That again…"

"Yes, that again. They burned the Book of Sports in 1643 and banned all sorts of sports and games until 1660 when Charles II brought it back in."

"And Whitsun Ales?"

"Almost certainly."

"I've gone right off the Puritans."

"I can't believe you were ever really *on* them…"

"Hmm. Hey, can we swap library books?"

"No chance."

And so on, our words effectively blocking out the world outside, for the time that they last.

"This will have to be my last one, sorry mate," says Ted after a time, while the round was on an even number. "But I'm sure you'll be alright here on your own, right?" This is most unusual, as we are almost always in for the session, and Debbie is not due here for a good while yet. I want to know why, but I don't want to *ask* why, and since he offers up no explanation we just leave it at that. We chit chat on for the rest of the pint about not much, then he swigs his last mouthful and gets up.

"Thanks, mate, I needed that," he tells me for some reason, his hand on my shoulder, and off he goes, disappearing through the pub door to God-knows-where. I hope he's not all upset because of me, and all that stuff that happened.

Secrets. Popular culture tells us that they always come out in the end. But they don't, actually. They can stay locked away forever. We *all* know that, right?

So it's just us now. Why not come on over. Sit down why don't you. Nice to see you again. You know, I think it's time for you to let me tell you about how Jen and I split up. Yes, yes, I know, I know, I have had a few, but I'll try not to get too maudlin this time I promise. And it's about time. Deep breath...

Sip. And...

We were living together in our flat in London, Jen and me. It wasn't much to look at I suppose, looking back on it, but I didn't care. All that mattered was that *we* were in it. I think she felt the same, except maybe for the lack of cushions, which always seemed to be an issue. Four was plenty as far as I was concerned, but apparently I was wrong. Enough about cushions anyway. I could see that the coving was tatty, at least once it was pointed out to me, and once I was informed what coving actually *was*. And the kitchen was too small for a washing machine, but that didn't matter either. Fundamentally, I just loved going back there. I loved going back there because Jen would be there to greet me with a big smile and a hug, at the very least, when I came through the door, or I would be able to wait in the expectantly empty flat for her to come back and return the favour. This was not perfect, I know that, but it was enough. It was enough for a while anyway.

Sip.

I'm glad she didn't dump me in our flat. It would
have spoiled the memories of the place somewhat,
plus I wouldn't have known where to put myself
afterwards. The flat was supposed to be my safe place
after all. She really didn't have to dump me while we
were on a weekend away at her mother's house
though. I really didn't know where to put myself
when that happened. We then proceeded to spend a
day and a half pretending everything was ok, when I
imagine it clearly didn't look at all ok to everyone
present. I do hope I did a good job pretending though,
and didn't embarrass anyone, not least myself. No
one *looked* embarrassed anyway, which is the main
thing round here. I probably just permanently looked
like I had been slapped. In the face or on the arse.
Both. I expect I often had that look about me at her
mother's house anyway, so maybe I did get away
with it. Ah, who am I kidding? They probably all
knew what was going to happen before me anyway.
'Last to Know' by Del Amitri is echoing in my head.
That song wasn't playing that weekend. It's just my
brain making unnecessary connections. Spoilt that
song for me nonetheless. Won't be able to get it out
of my head now. Stupid brain.

Sip.

I may have oversold this story now I think about it. I
can't actually remember the moment, the very
moment, when it happened. I remember the evening
before. We found a nice pub on some terraced street
near the football stadium and all had a good laugh. I

remember the possibly-awkward dinner afterwards
with my slapped-face look. We had a pork casserole,
then some ice cream. Raspberry ripple. The bit in
between though, the bit in between…sip. It was in the
spare bedroom, the one we were staying in…she told
me something…something like…no, that's it, that's
all I have. I think I have suppressed the rest. It's
probably buried deep in my brain, waiting for a nice
bout of hypnotherapy to come along and bring it out.
But I'm not about to do that anytime soon. The look
on her face is gone. The words are gone. The colour
of the curtains. Gone. What I do remember though,
very clearly, is the way my stomach turned upside
down, at the moment those unremembered words
spilled out of her mouth and into my ears. I think it
turned upside down in a vain attempt to keep up with
the position of my world, which had just done the
same, but neglected to warn the rest of my internal
organs.

Sip.

Sip.

That's a daft idea I know, as it probably really has
something to do with the endocrine system and my
adrenal gland, not my stomach. Either way, it didn't
feel good and it stuck in the memory like the last
drunk at the bar ignoring the last orders bell. Funny
how these things work. But would I really feel any
better if I forgot my stomach and remembered her
face? I don't think so. This must be some kind of
survival mechanism that we have evolved. Not the
most useful debt to evolution the human race has ever

received, admittedly, but I suppose that I am grateful at least.

Either way, my adrenal gland, or whatever, then enjoyed conspiring against me for around the next three years or so, after which time my stomach decided to realign away from the breach position it had found a home in, and settle back where it was supposed to be. Can't say why. It was a body thing, not a mind thing. By then, if I chose to think about it, I could still feel sad whenever I wanted.

Sip. Sorry I'm almost getting maudlin now, aren't I? Change of tack required now. Don't go just yet, I don't want to be on my own. Anyway, Debbie's due in at any moment, and she's the punctual type. And she is not going to want to hear about any of this rubbish, that's for sure.

Hey, look at what I'm drinking now. I know, funny isn't it? I'm upholding an old tradition here, drinking this. I am being the veritable custodian of history here, as I neck this pint. Yes, I think it *has* gone to my head a little, now you mention it. What I'm drinking is a half-and-half. I should explain. It's simply two different ales in the same pint glass. Two halves making a whole as it were, a blend of beer. What you mix betrays where you are from, or often does. People don't really do this anymore, but I got the idea from my Dad and so my idea of a half-and-half is from the North-Eastern habit of mixing a Scotch Ale and an Indian Pale Ale. Stay with me here. Scotch is not from Scotland, nor should it be confused with Scotch whisky, especially when you order Scotch Ale by the pint! Indian Pale Ale is not from India either. It was brewed in England for the troops and other folk out in India during the British Empire. It was formulated so that it travelled well. Just like Imperial Stout, which was deliberately made 12% or more, so it wouldn't freeze when transported over the freezing Baltic Sea to Russia. I'll stick to the IPA though. One Imperial Stout and I'll start rambling worse than this. Then fall over. You'd probably love to see that though, wouldn't you?

Sip. This isn't strictly a Geordie half and half. You just can't get Scotch down here. But they do have a Mild on at the moment, which is kind if similar, so I'm taking the opportunity to pretend that I'm having one of Dad's half-and-halfs (halves?). I'm doing this in his memory. Cheers Dad, wherever you are. If you get the two halves right, it can be quite a pleasure. Sometimes though, you can get it wrong and the ingredients end up being less than the sum of the parts. Which is why most people can't be bothered anymore. People were 'mixers' from as far back as the 50's, apparently because the quality of the draught beer was hit and miss, so you hedged your bets and masked the flavour of the bad draught beer with the decent flavour of the bottled beer. I really don't know why you would still want half of your pint to be a bad beer, but I kind of admire the stubbornness and sheer pragmatism that gave birth to this practice.

"That doesn't look like any of the barrels we have on today. Are you having a half-and-half or something?" Debbie is standing over me, blocking out the few lucky rays of sunlight that manage to get through the

99

foggy windows of this establishment. I think I have just fallen a little bit more in love at this moment. In response I raise my glass and hold it to the side, so that the photons can pass through my drink before they hit my retina. Lucky photons. What an adventure for them! They take millions of years to escape from the core of the sun to then shoot out to the Earth in a mere 8 minutes, and then, just before they find oblivion in the back of my retina, they get to enjoy a trip across my beer and change their wavelength to a delicious amber. Oh god, I'm back on the science again, I'm not supposed to be! Something about Debbie keeps making me think of photons, for some reason.

"Yes, just look at this." I say. "What a lovely colour!" She eyes me suspiciously and asks, "Just how long have you been here?"

I choose to treat that as a rhetorical question. Debbie sits down with a drink already in her hand. She seems to have managed to enter the pub, get served and make it over to my table before I even notice her arrival. I even positioned myself facing the door earlier to specifically avoid this scenario. I make a mental note to be a more attentive boyfriend, if that is indeed what I am now. She's having a gin and tonic, which she casually describes as a loosener. What exactly it will be loosening I will have to wait and see. She takes a deep breath and places both hands on the table, like the chairman of the board. She slightly places her little finger in a small puddle of half-and-half that found its way out of my pint glass somehow sometime earlier. We both silently conspire to ignore this, so as not to spoil the moment.

100

"Right then," she begins, "what are we going to do about this pub closing?"

"We?" A fair question. But this is the first time I've heard that I myself am supposed to do something about it.

"If not us, then who?"

"I wasn't planning on doing anything about anything for a while, actually…"

"Do you know how that sounds Dan?"

"Well…" I shrug, not sure how to bring Dad's passing into this without looking like I'm using the situation. Debbie saves me the embarrassment.

"Sorry, Dan. I know it has not been long since your Dad died. But believe me, it does you good to keep busy rather than dwelling on things. I definitely know how that feels."

I don't think she quite knows how *this* feels, but she may be on to something here nonetheless. Even I have my maximum brooding limits and I think I may have reached them lately. Plus I really need to keep Matthew Hopkins at bay, and I doubt a Puritan such as himself would follow me into a campaign to keep The Red Lion open. And because of all this I hear myself saying:

"Ok, maybe you're right. We should do something. If there is something that we could do."

"Wow, inspirational. Don't go into speech writing, Daniel, whatever you do."

"Ha, yes, it's not quite Churchill is it? But what good could I do here to keep the pub open?"

Debbie looks at me and rolls her eyes and looks around the empty tables. "I think you already keep this place open just by being yourself…" she muses, then proceeds to chuckle.

"I'm not here *that* much," I insist, fairly sure of my position. "There are some in here who really *do* keep this place going though."

"Yes, but we won't be asking *them* for help. You though, you sit in the middle. You're a committed enthusiast but still have most of your brain cells intact. Also, I would really be worried about you without this place to come to."

"Thanks. I think. But what about you?"

She laughs. "I just work here! But I would like to keep working here if possible. I've learned a lot being here. I would like to run a place like this. One day."

"I didn't know you felt like that. Ok, I'll help. What do you want me to do?"

"ACVs."

"JCBs?"

"ACVs idiot. Assets of Community Value. I've been doing some research on them. If we apply for The Red Lion to become an asset of community value, then no one can change it into flats. At least not without applying for permission themselves. That's normally enough to put people off."

"Rightho, sounds promising. Shouldn't Tom the Landlord be doing this though?" I ask, before my brain actually considers what I'm saying.

"Dan, it's him who wants to change this place into flats. We need to stop him."

"Ah, got it. Don't want to go against Tom though..."

"Don't worry about Tom," Debbie assures me. "I'll deal with him. But look. I don't have a computer at home and I certainly don't have one in the workplace. I need you to sort out the application. Can you do

102

that?"

"I guess so…"

"Or do you want to start drinking at Corkscrews?"

"Ok, sure. I'm on it, I'm on it," I state with a tad more conviction. "Where did you find out about all this stuff anyway?"

"It's happening up and down the country. People keeping their own pubs open. CAMRA are helping people do that too. If people like us don't do something, then we are going to lose a whole load more of them. All we need to do is write an application as to how this pub is important to the community. Sports teams, quiz nights, music venue, that sort of thing, get the land registry details and get 21 signatures."

"You've done your research," I admit.

"Yes, I keep my ear out for industry trends. I'm into this stuff."

"Me too, me too."

"Really?"

"Maybe in a different way, Deb. I always felt I belong at *this* side of the bar."

"Maybe. But I think you'd be right at home on the other side too."

I tasted, then swallowed that thought along with my last mouthful of half-and-half, 'Mr. Mild', 3.4% and 'Massage to India',4.6%.

Debbie then says it's not just us joining this campaign. "I have brought in some reinforcements," she explains. And as if by magic, Amy and Jez stride through the door, a gust of wind from outside blowing dramatically through their hair.

103

Well, it was five minutes later in real life, but it sounds better if we edit out that delay. There was actually probably none of that hair drama either, now that I think about it.

Oh, then ten minutes after that, Jen walks in. Actually, physically walks through that door and into this room. Yes, *that* Jen. And that would become plenty drama all on its own, even without any wind in her hair, and made this particular evening especially different from the night in front of the TV that I might have had instead.

Chapter 8

Well, that was a bit awkward. Don't worry, it's now a different day and all has gone quiet for the time being. I'm back down here (guess where!) on the precise understanding that there will be no more pub-entry surprises from you-know-who. Plus I really do need a pint. I suppose you'll be wanting to know how it all went, won't you?

Amy and Jez both choked on their drinks. That was the first thing that happened. There sure is a lot of that around these days. Debbie, who has heard of the legendary Jen, but has never seen her nor has she seen a photo, took a little longer to cotton on that something unusual was up. I saw Jez mouth the word 'Jen' in Debbie's general direction, while subtlely pointing towards Jen. By 'subtle' I mean that you would only have failed to notice it if you were in the toilets with the cubicle door closed. Later on, I tried this mouthing of the word 'Jen' to myself in front of the mirror, to see what it looked like. I'm not sure how useful that would have been really. I could have been saying 'Dan' or 'phlegm' or most single syllable words. However, Debbie's a sharp one and she seemed to get a hold of the situation quicker than I would have.

I saw Jen before she saw me though, which fortunately gave me vital seconds to run through the following checklist:

1. Panic

2. Disbelief
3. Momentary happiness
4. Self-retribution re said momentary happiness
5. Acceptance
6. More panic
7. Check reaction of Debbie
8. Check reaction of Amy
9. Check reaction of Jez
10. Assume air of cool nonchalance

As for '10', it may have been a bit of a stretch to actually have achieved it, but it was what I was desperately aiming for at least. Jen was by the door, looking around the bar for something. I don't think I'm being too arrogant to guess that this something was me. There's not really many things you could wish to come in here and look around for. Eventually she clocked me at the table, then squinted a little, as if that took away the years of degradation in my face since she last saw me, until she was sure it was me who she recognised. Then she waved, a little too enthusiastically considering all the history, and came over smiling, without first stopping at the bar. Actually, it would have been a bit rude if she had stopped off at the bar first, now that I think about it. That would have been her taking her own air of cool nonchalance a step too far. Anyway, you know what she said to me? Go on, guess…

… "Fancy seeing you in here," she says, plonking her bag down on the floor by the table. I can tell by her face that she is merely putting on this confident air. It is all bravado. I can almost see the pause, the double hair flick, and the deep breath she took, just before she pushed open the door of the bar. She's doing well so far though. She is five words ahead of me already. "How are you doing, Dan?" she adds, adding another five words to her tally. This is going to be a one-sided word-massacre at this rate. "Sorry, this is probably a bit of a shock," she continues. "I can explain." Now I'm losing count of the deficit. I'm going to have to add some words of my own soon. From my peripheral vision, I can see the heads of Debbie, Amy and Jez swing from side to side as they catch each other's glances and try to catch mine. My head is staying dead straight though. And still my mouth won't move.

"Shall I get you a drink first though?" she continues. "I'm going to the bar."

This, unsurprisingly for those who know me, brings me out of my stupor.

"Jen, hi. Yes, good guess finding me here. I *am* that obvious! Good job I'm not a wanted man! I mean, by the police or spies or something, not the other way. Yeah, good guess, well done you. Um, yes, yes, I'll take another drink. That might prove useful! Ha ha. Um, yes, I'll try a 'Latest Flame', 4.6%. Don't worry, no, no, I'm not winding you up, I'm not! They'll know it at the bar."

That must have got me ahead on the words stakes, if only merely by quantity.

"Ok, will do Dan! Hello Amy, Jack." Amy just nods her head, looking neutral. Jez waves with a smile and says hi, not too bothered about her getting his name wrong. At least the first letter was spot on. I think he is enjoying all this anyway. "Hello," Jen adds, looking at Debbie for more than a moment. Did Jen just size her up a bit there? As a rival? Or am I just being paranoid? Or is that being arrogant, even? Anyway, Jen grabs her purse from her bag and offers the rest of them a drink. Jez is about to say yes, but reluctantly changes his mind after Amy and Debbie politely decline. Jen then heads to the bar.

"That's…" Debbie says.

"Yes," I confirm.

"Did you..?" she adds.

"No," I assure her. "Not at all."

"Should we..?"

"No, you stay right here. I've no idea what is going on here, believe me."

"Business as usual," Jez quips into his pint. He is enjoying this just a little too much I think.

"Are you sure?" Debbie asks.

"Sure I'm sure. This is embarrassing enough as it is without you lot running out of here. It's fine…Amy?" I add this because Amy has gone quiet and is looking sternly across towards the bar. She's going headlong into protective mode. Protective of me, that is. She got an awful lot of the break-up chat, an *awful* lot, and saw me through a lot of self-pity sessions, on the phone at first and in the pub, when I came back home. Eventually, and after countless pints, that all helped bit by bit, just about enough anyway. I expect she now wants to protect her extensive investment.

"Amy," I say again. She slowly turns and looks at me without changing expression. "It's ok," I continue, and lean over to place my hand on her arm. "It's ok. Just be nice."

She shrugs and takes a sip, which happens to be of 'Avenging Angel', a cider that comes in at a

108

challenging 8.2%. I take my hand away and sit back. That will have to do, as Jen is coming back already, a drink in each hand. My heart is still beating like the lights on a fruit machine. I wish I had asked for the cider instead.

Of course, there was an awful lot of trivial chit chat before we got to anything of substance. I can skip that if you like. Suffice to say, we talked about how the pub hadn't changed much since…since…well, we had to let the 'since what' just hang there unsaid. There are precious few safe subjects in scenarios like these. We talked about her train journey from (where from, was it still Wales? Was she still with *him*?) …from wherever, I didn't ask. It was fine. Debbie introduced herself. As 'Debbie' I mean, not 'my girlfriend'. Was she even my girlfriend yet anyway, I was thinking? Jen then asked Jez how he was. Or at least how Jack was, whoever that is. Jez just grinned and said Jack was doing marvellously well, thanks. Amy said nothing and Jen and her merely swapped perfunctory hellos, then proceeded to avoid each other. They both knew the score there. Wow, weren't we all having such a marvellous time! Anyway, this was all getting a bit much after one drink. So eventually Debbie got up and kissed me on the cheek and said she would see me on Tuesday, which might have been a suggestion but sounded rather like an instruction upon reflection.
"Tuesday," I said, buying what turned out to be not enough time. "Tuesday?"
"My next visit to the old people's home?"
"Oh yes! Yes, I knew that. *That* Tuesday."
"Are you still sure you want to?"

"Sure I'm sure. I'm sure. Yes, Tuesday is *on*. And don't worry about *this*. I'll find out what's going on." I gave two thumbs up, which I belatedly decided looked suspiciously over the top.
Nevertheless, she kissed me on the cheek again, made her excuses and left. Amy got up too, much to Jen's relief, and dragged Jez with her. Debbie left through the door, and I assumed that Amy and Jez did too. I later found out that they just went around the bar and sat at another table in the corner. Jen and I eyed each other up, knowing that the chit chat was over. I took a deep breath.

Then I downed my pint and went to the bar for my round. Jen wanted a vodka and coke, evidently regretting her initial choice of cider. I briefly considered the 'Avenging Angel' myself, then changed my mind. Then I changed it back again and got one. Tom gave me a double-take sort of look but commented no further. He's still a credit to his profession, despite his evil ambition to sell up and sell us all out. I looked back over to our table as I waited. Jen was furiously fiddling with her empty glass, her back to the bar. I watched her while Tom got the drinks. I then noticed that I had been turning a beermat round and round and round with my left hand. My right-brain must be up to something I thought, which is not a good sign. Another deep breath and I headed back to the table, having procured drinks, courage and change. And do you know what she said to me when I sat back down? Go on, guess…

… "I've left…*him*, by the way. In case that matters." she says, gratefully taking the glass from me, without our hands touching.

"Right," I say. I am master of the non-committal, I am. My brain refuses to work out what I think about that just yet, which is just fine by me. But right now my right-hand is manically fiddling with the beer mat on this table, which should instead be making my pint glass comfortable. This means that my left-brain is now up to something. Definitely not a good sign, when both halves start ganging up on you. That's a different kind of half-and-half altogether! Sorry, I digress. Must be a bit nervous.

"Right," I say again, in case she missed it the first time, or might enjoy hearing that once more.

"That's not why I'm here though," she says, finally looking me in the eye for the first time this pint.

"Right," I add. Maybe a third time is a bit too much, so I carry on by using other words. "So what does bring you to these parts then?"

"My parents are getting divorced. I've come back home to see them. I jumped on a train when I heard, from my Mum. But now I'm here I'm not actually sure what I'm supposed to do. It's not like it's an anniversary party or something. I've just been helping Dad with some boxes today."

"Blimey, sorry Jen. I had no idea."

"That's alright. Of course you wouldn't. They've been keeping it all nice and quiet of course. 'What would the neighbours think' and all that. Anyway, I hear that you have had more, er, pressing things to deal with yourself, right?"

"Er…" I can feel Hopkins on my shoulder. Jen can't know anything about *that*, you idiot, I tell myself, while she interjects.

111

"I'm soooo sorry about your Dad. My Dad told me yesterday all about it. They still saw each other once in a while, apparently."

"All about it?"

She starts turning her glass around again. Round and around. What must both of us look like? Like we are doing warm up exercises for a juggler's convention, or maybe something funnier.

"The, er, Alzheimer's and that," she says. "That must have been horrible."

"It *was*, Jen. It *was* horrible. Like you would never guess. I hope you never find out yourself. Really I do." I take a swig of the 'Avenging Angel'. God, that stuff is strong. I take another sip, just to check. "What happened with your folks then?" I say, changing the subject back, at least for the moment. This conversation is going to end up being like parent-tennis, if we are not careful.

"No big drama," she explains, "but I think Mum found someone else. Dad isn't saying much at all. At least I know that they didn't stay together just for me. I mean, look at us. We are so old now! Sorry, I mean *you* still look fine, Dan. But it has been a few years, right?"

"A few, yeah, a certain number. So…what brings you down The Red Lion, then?"

"Well, once I heard about your Dad," she says, batting the ball back into my side of the court, "I thought I should give you a ring. But then I remembered I only had your old home number and I thought that wouldn't work anymore probably, but Dad mentioned that you had moved back, so I then thought that if I came down to The Red Lion often enough I would be bound to bump into you at some point…"

"Sounds like a decent plan, although no one likes to be too predictable, do they? How many times have you been down then?" I ask her.

"This is the first. Lucky eh?"

"Um, yes. Lucky." Sip.

Another sip. If I remember correctly we both hated awkward silences. Even so, it's her move. She takes a sip. I take another sip. No problem, I could do this all day. Perhaps not on 'Avenging Angel' though.

"So you've moved back here for good, have you?" she asks, finally.

"Yes, once I came back that was it. But I'm glad I did it. I wouldn't have had any quality time with Dad before he went, otherwise. Not just coming up from London once in a while. It's those moments I keep a hold on to now. Not the ones when he got, you know, ill."

"Hmm," she says, the appropriate response in any language for those temporarily out of their depth. Unless you are literally out of your depth, then 'Help, I'm drowning' might be more appropriate. Sorry, digressing again. I'm not myself today, but I hope you understand.

"But it's been nice to see Rachel a bit more again too," I continue. "Amy and Jez are still around, and we meet in here from time to time. Like the old days."

"Time to time?" She raises that one eyebrow again, like she used to. I expect she always will.

"Hey, I don't *live* here you know! I don't live *far* from here granted…" I tail off. I don't think my life

113

story quite has the impressive edge of adventure, so I'm not entirely sure what to brag about. You are supposed to brag about things in this specific sort of conversation, I have gathered. The sort of conversation that spawns from bumping unexpectedly into your ex. Jen spares me the effort anyway.

"I'm going to go travelling, Dan," she suddenly blurts out. "Once I get my parents all happy with their split. Then I'm going to, er, get me all happy with, er, *mine*, and be off!"

"Ok, where are you going to go? Round Europe of something?"

"The world, Dan. I'm going to go around the world!"

"Blimey, that's inclusive. Don't want anyone left out or something?"

That makes her laugh, for some reason.

"That's right, the whole damn planet," she declares.

"What about your job and all that?" I enquire. "I thought you were happy in recruitment."

"Happy?" she scoffs. "That was never quite the word. It suited me well for a while, yeah, and the job has helped me save enough. The savings weren't for travelling at first…"

"Homebuilding?" I'm pushing it just a little here, but this is my pub and she did come here without a by or leave.

She looks at me to gauge my mood, but I try to remain impassive. This cider does not help. If I manage to carry off even 'slightly pained' I would be happy with that. She doesn't seem to get what she wants out of my face anyway, and looks down at her drink for a moment.

"Yes, I suppose so," she admits finally. "I guess that

was the initial reason. New kitchen, better mattress. Kids. Things like that. Things I don't need now."

"Hmm."

"Sorry, I didn't mean that about kids. That sounds a little harsh!"

"You don't have any though, right?"

"No!" she exclaims, then calms down a little. "I mean, no that never happened. Just as well really…"

If I was just her friend I would have asked what happened etc and she would have told me all about it etc. That's not going to happen here though. Which is somewhat frustrating, as I would love to know what went so badly wrong with that relationship. I would love to know *all* of those details. Sorry, you, like me, are just going to have to use your imagination.

"Anyway," she carries on quickly, also understanding the moment, "the home and career and all that somehow seem like a bit of a disappointment now. It's all been somewhat disillusioning I must say. Like I could not see the treadmill while I was on it, you know?"

"I'm not sure. I'm probably still on mine."

This perks her up, and she gets up and goes to the bar, holding a finger up. Not the rude one, the one that says 'hold that thought'. She brings me back another pint. She guesses wrong, but with good intentions I suppose, wanting to show she still understands me or something. But, thankfully, the last 'Avenging Angel' of the day is behind me.

Jen then started telling me all about the trip she has planned. New York, San Francisco, Hawaii, Fiji, New Zealand, Australia, Thailand, probably some others. I found the details a little overwhelming to tell you the

115

truth, and took a break eventually by getting my round in. Italy too. Almost forgot that one. Call me paranoid but I got the feeling that she was trying to sell me the idea, like a travel agent. Then do you know what she said? No, don't worry, that was rhetorical, it wasn't that obvious...

"Did you know, Fiji is not an island but actually a collection of islands? Guess how many?"
I'm a little calmer now and, in a weird way, glad to see her, but I'm still on edge and not sure if this light affability is entirely appropriate. However, for lack of a better response, I play along.
"Three hundred and thirty-three?" I try, scratching my chin.
"What? Oh, yes. That's right." She looks a little deflated. I briefly regret bursting her bubble, but not much. "How on *earth* did you know that?"
I raise both my eyebrows. I can't raise just the one, as dictated by my genes. Then I take a sip, holding her gaze. It's actually a nice beer. I must find out which one she picked.
She slams her hand down on the table, politely though, and says "Ahhh, pub quiz! You overheard it in in pub quiz! I'm right, right?"
I raise my glass in affirmation, and smile. I've been trying not to smile, but I'm guessing that this is not the first breach this evening, nor will be the last.
"You should have been a researcher or something, you know," she says. I don't remember her ever suggesting this when we were together, but no good will ever come of me saying this now, so I let that pass. Sip. Another awkward pause is looming.
"Are you working, then?" she enquires.

"Yeah," I say. "Nothing special. Spreadsheets." I spread my arms out wide, using the internationally recognised sign for spreadsheets, according to no one. "Really, Dan? Really? You always hated them."

I'm pretty sure that *this* had come up in conversation during our time together, so I was happy to reply, "I sure did. But I'm having one more go, just to be sure. That's a joke, by the way."

She eyes me up and down, formulating something or other inside her head. "Hmm, there was always that lack of ambition with you. And I always found that unattractive…"

"Jesus, Jen! Have you come all this way to bring up my career choices again?" This is the 'Avenging Angel' talking, I think, not me really, but I dare say that I agree with him, or her.

"If you let me finish…" she begins, raising her hands in surrender. "I said I always found that unattractive, but…"

"Oh, there's a 'but'…"

"…*but*, now after all these years of hard work and homebuilding, and all that getting me precisely nowhere, I'm coming around to the idea that you might have had a point."

Surprise catches me unawares for a moment, but I recover momentarily and manage to raise my glass in victory. "Cheers. Finally, you got there."

"So I'm done with the future, I'm going to live for the present!" she declares.

How ironic, I think. This was the first time in my life I was actually thinking about the future for once. And not just next Tuesday. Which made the next thing she said all the more disconcerting.

"Why don't you come away with me, Dan. Come on, let's see the world!"

It is only then that I spot Amy, walking from the Ladies, back to an unseen table. As she does so, we swap knowing glances, without me actually knowing quite what they were supposed to mean, but it was a comfort nonetheless. I give a weak thumbs-up from under the table as she passes. That seems to be enough. For now. The Gents is over the other side of the bar, which must be killing Jez, or 'Jack' as I may start calling him, because this means that he has no excuse to wander over here. Looking back over at Jen, with an expectant look in her eye, I dearly wish both of my friends were sitting here with me here right now, merrily changing the subject.

But since they weren't I had to say something. So what was it that I said to Jen? How did I reply to this life-changing revelation? I said this:
"What you having, Jen?"
"It's my round, Dan."
"I know. I was just interested in what you were having."
Like I said, master of the non-committal.
I really wasn't myself, though. It wasn't even her round.

Chapter 9

I'm looking over the table towards this bloke called Harry. We are separated by two cups of tea and a packet of garibaldis. If we were separated by two pints of beer and a packet of dry roasted peanuts I'd be chatting away happily by now, but I'm currently struggling to decide on the next topic of conversation. I look across the common room to Debbie, who is engaged in effortless banter with two old ladies, possibly on the subject of knitting, although it could just have easily been the Palestine question. If I can't think of something soon I'm going to have to find those dominoes. Again. I am ashamed to say that it is Harry himself who breaks the silence.

"Were you in the war?" he asks.
The war. This is an easy one to answer as such, since I have not been near any wars. I've hardly been near Star Wars. I think he means the Second World War though. He'd be about the right age for that one, I'm guessing. Shame, as I'm reading about the English Civil War at the moment, and I think he's a little over-young to have been in that one. Don't worry by the way, I've not aged terribly due to recent events! It's just that Harry gets confused, and keeps forgetting who I am, what year it is, and how old I told him I was. I recall that when Dad got like this, it was always best to just talk about the old days. The older the better. Dad could then just concentrate on telling a story from his past. His favourites were from when me and Rachel were kids. Often stuff I could

hardly remember myself. So, for this conversation with Harry, the war it is. I studied this war too, back in my student days, but we always studied origins or consequences of wars, and rarely the wars themselves. I hope to be able to contribute to this chit-chat in some small way at some point, but I had better let Harry take the lead.

"No, Harry, I'm afraid I missed that one. Where were you, er, stationed then?"
"All over, son. From Normandy to Berlin and everywhere between. Landed on the beaches. D-Day they called it."
I know something of D-Day. Well, from a video game anyway. Don't laugh. I had read that it was supposed to be pretty accurate actually, the product of a whole load of interviews with soldiers from all sides. I doubt that this would count as sufficient knowledge in most academic situations, but I'm not here to educate. If anything, I'm here just to listen, as a respite from loneliness, and maybe understand a little, if I can. I could talk any old rubbish, I suppose, and get away with it. But even so, I shall try not to.
"Ah yes," I say. "Were you three-across on your boat? You know, the ones where the front swung down and became a ramp?"
He eyes me up and nods approvingly. "Yes, that was us. I can still see that ramp coming down now. Until then it was just noise. Dreadful noise. We couldn't even hear our orders. What they could have said that would have helped though, I don't know." He takes a sip of tea, looks at the biscuits, changes his mind and carries on. "It plays so slowly in my mind. Bit by bit the beach revealed itself to us. The guns, the bodies,

120

the defences we would have to get past somehow."
"Sounds awful."
"It was, but there wasn't time to think about that then, thank God. We just lived from one second to the next. No time to regret how we got here or what we were going to do even a minute later. Then the bullets started to come. The two fellas either side of me took one each to the head before they even got off the boat. They were my mates they were. Jim, Will. Good men. Went through training together."
"Wow, that must have been your lucky day." I chime in.
He looks at me like I'm some idiot, which I am. Fortunately for me, he won't remember what a fool I am by next time I see him. I hope for once that I don't keep reminding him, and make a mental note to say less and listen more.
"All my plans went out of the window then, you see. Just had to dive for some cover. Not that there was much. If you don't count the bodies. Didn't even think about shooting anything. I couldn't tell what to shoot at. Noise and dirt. And the smell of blood."
I'm way out of my depth here. I'm off to the Shakespeare even at the merest hint of a fight brewing down The Red Lion. Although normally you would be more likely to be ducking out of the Shakespeare in a hurry, scuttling to the safety of The Red Lion. This may well just be fascinating for some, but I don't think I'll be telling Harry any of this right now. He's carrying on anyway without me, as if in a trance.
"Somehow I make my way up the beach and a bit of shelter. There we had to take out a gun

emplacement."

"Gun emplacement, right." I say, just so he knows I'm still there.

"Took my first life at that gun placement. Young lad. Looked as scared as we did."

"Sorry. I wonder what he would be doing now if things had turned out different. Maybe having a cuppa in some place like this in Germany." This seems to be the best commentary I have to offer and, too late, immediately recall my own previous advice to stop saying things. Unexpectedly, Harry doesn't seem to mind what I have just said.

"I often wonder that, son. I often wonder that. I killed plenty more on the way to Berlin, had to, but the first one stays with you. If you were looking him in the eye that is. And I was. Yeah, I often thought of his Mum getting the letter, her going down the road to tell his sweetheart that he wasn't coming back, his Dad receiving a letter he didn't want to get, in some other battlefield somewhere, wondering what this was all for. That all came later though. I was just glad to get off the beach that day. My blood was up. It was almost like all this wasn't happening to me."

"Hmm," I say, not wanting to break my good run of conversational contributions, and hold up the plate of biscuits. He seems surprised that they are there. He checks his teeth are in, then takes one.

"Later, yes, I thought all those things. Never talked about it with the boys though. Wasn't the done thing. But you could see it in the eyes of some of them. They were thinking just what I was thinking, in the quiet moments. I didn't know his name though. Never stopped to check. I call him Hans sometimes when I

122

talk to him. He never answers back. I suppose I will see him soon enough now. I hope he can forgive me."

Harry's getting visibly upset now. You know, from the outside all this may look a little cruel, dredging up these painful old memories like this. But at least inside these memories Harry is himself once more, not the empty shell he is slowly becoming in here, day by day. Even on the beaches of Normandy, at least, Harry can be alive again. Harry can be *Harry* again. If I hadn't been through this with Dad, I would never have guessed that this was the case. You know, maybe I can be of some use in this place after all. I get Harry another cup of tea, and when I come back I'm not entirely sure he still recognises me. That's ok. We just proceed to talk about James Bond movies as if we were complete strangers. He's a Connery fan he tells me. I nod approvingly and pass him a biscuit. This all actually feels much better than it sounds by the way.

"Are you ok if I come by next time?" I ask, when I finally get up to leave. Harry just stares at me blankly and takes another biscuit. I shall take that as a 'yes' then.

Outside I rendezvous with Debbie.
"How was it?" she asks, with a smile.
"It was ok, actually," I say, a little unsure. "I felt like really nervous, but I don't know why. I'm way better off than these guys. But once I got into it, it was…ok. Learnt a thing or two about the war."
Debbie laughs. "Yes, and what I don't know about crochet now, isn't worth knowing!"
She pauses then kisses me. On the lips. Properly.

"Thanks for that, Dan. We need all the help we can get."

I think that's a compliment, so I reply, "No, that's alright. Thank you for asking me."

I look around. Matthew Hopkins is nowhere to be seen. For now. Which is the best I can hope for.

In a moment of weakness, or perhaps goodness if we are being kind, I have also agreed to help Ted out today. I'm all give and no take at the moment! I blame the guilt. It fuels all these good deeds you know. And just like with the visit to the care home, I feel distinctly underqualified for this job too. I feel even more underqualified here, truth be told. I have, you see, agreed to accompany Ted, for moral support, to The Greyhound pub. No, not that one. The other one. Yes, *that* one!

The Greyhound is so rough that you could throw a petrol bomb in it and it would be drunk before it landed. At least so Ted tells me with a chortle as we stand outside, readying ourselves to go in. I take a deep breath and just grimace at him in return. I had only ever been here once before, and that was years ago, by accident sort of, when we couldn't get in anywhere else on New Year's Eve. I had a remarkably good time as it goes, and everyone was warm, generous and welcoming. But that was New Year's Eve and I have learned on many an occasion that the rules are very different on that particular night, and certainly not wholly representative of the welcome you may receive for the rest of the year. It's a bit disillusioning really, the first time you come to understand that particular truth. That's because it makes you realise just how good things could be, and that makes it all the worse when things turn out otherwise. So, as I stand outside of this particular pub, I am not considering what pint I may have, just how I'm going to avoid getting beaten up. A low bar indeed.

"Remind me why I'm doing this again?" I ask Ted as he pushes on the door.
"Because you're my friend and I asked you to. Nicely," he replies, as he looks back at me and beckons me through the open door. I doubt that this is supposed to be a poignant reminder of quite how much I owe him, but it feels like it to me nonetheless. I put on my brave face, as close to alpha male as I can manage, (not all that close, as Amy regularly tells me) and stride in.

I take a look around at my new surroundings, not only out of curiosity but also out of self-preservation. If I'm looking at the fixtures and fittings, then I'm also not making any eye contact. Under no circumstances should I be making any eye contact here, not even with the pub dog. Especially not with *this* pub dog. The Greyhound is a bare old place, stuck in the 70's and not in a good way. Not a chandelier in sight, not even a dusty old grotty one. This place is the sort of pub that has a sign on the door for the ladies but nothing for the gents. Like the assumption was that there would only ever be blokes in here really, bar the most unusual exception, and they all know where the toilets are anyway. I check myself where the toilets might be. Ok, so there is a small and faded gents sign on one door, so I'm not literally correct in my predictions, but I am only talking symbolically here really. Continuing to look around, I see that there are indeed no ladies to use the Ladies, if you don't include the staff. There's two old blokes sitting either side of the bar, both reading the paper. One paper each I mean, not the same one. One is looking at the racing pages, the other the politics. We get to the bar and I have to suppress a sigh. Ted knows what I'm thinking and, in the absence of a proper pint, orders us both a Guinness, which is a fall-back routine we have used all too often before when 'playing away from home' as he calls it. By which he means in a pub without proper beer. The transaction continues wordlessly with some looks of suspicion from our host, then we sit at a table near the door. Good seating choice!

Ted looks at his watch. "Don't worry," he tells me, without conviction. He knows I'm a natural worrier at the best of times. "He'll be here in a moment. Then we'll be done, and our next pint can be at the Lion." I just nod, and sip my Guinness, and count the stains on the carpet. To be fair to the cleaners of this establishment, there are only two, so that doesn't take too long. It's the colour of the stains that worries me more though, not the quantity. Presently, the door opens again and out of the corner of my eye I see Ted getting up. The bloke coming in gives Ted a look of recognition and a three-part handshake, the individual movements of which I can't keep up with. The bloke raises a smile, but only with his lips, not with his eyes. I don't like those sorts of smiles. They both sit down, and Ted introduces me.
"Den, this is Dan. Dan, this is Den."

We both look at Ted curiously, to check if he is taking the piss or something. When we see that he is keeping a straight face, we look at each other and swap a brief, traditional, one-part handshake. "Alright, Den." I say tentatively. "It *is* Dan, for real. Jeez, I hope this doesn't get confusing!"
He smiles, this time with his eyes, then laughs, and for the first time in here I gain the slightest sense of relief. He nods over to the bar and then is brought a pint of something-or-other over to our table, seemingly without paying for it. I wish I could achieve that level of service!

Despite this decent start, I'm going to back off and let these two dictate proceedings for a while. You do need to work people out a bit first, especially when you are in a strange place. The normal temptation for me is to just jump in and chat, when I have a pint glass in my hand. But you don't want to do that and then get stuck with the wrong sort. So I have just one simple rule when I decide to talk to someone. They have to be *kind*. Actually, that is not strictly true. That is too high a bar. They just have to be *not unkind*. The unkind types cannot hide their true nature for long. These are the type who find sport in just winding people up. The type who thinly hide cruelty behind humour. You just can't win with them, so why bother trying? So, we'll have to see what sort of chap this Den is first, before I dare to converse too much further.

Turns out that Den is not the type to hold a grudge. No, he actually *nurses* one. The first ten minutes is spent with Den and Ted relating the whereabouts and activities of some mutual acquaintance, who Den is apparently going to mess up good and proper when he sees him next. I hope he's joking. I'm not betting on it though. I don't know what went on, and believe me I'm not going to ask. Something or other occurred at a wedding between someone or other and another, if you follow me. This was around, I don't know, at least six years ago from what I can gather. I will definitely have to make sure I don't get on the wrong side of this geezer then, I tell myself.

So I mainly just watch the pair of them and sip my Guinness for a while, as they dance around what must be the real subject at hand. I suppose I could tell you what Den was wearing, or his haircut or build, but then you'd just judge, so I won't bother. Sorry. I suppose that means I'm judging you. Forgive me. Finally, they seem to conclude their business and Ted excuses himself to the toilets, which are definitely the Gents, possibly to vacate his bladder, possibly to check the contents of an envelope he has just received. They were not being surreptitious at all by the way, so maybe there's nothing dodgy going on after all. Or maybe this is just because of the nature of this place that we are in, where suspicious stuff must happen all the time. Either way, that now just leaves me and Den. This could be awkward. Here goes.

"What's that you're drinking?" I ask for want of something better to say. It normally works as an opener down the Lion.
Den looks at me strangely, then at his pint, as if it was the first time he has considered the question.
"Dunno. Some piss or other. S'alright," he says, by

way of reply.

Hmm, that's not a great start. Just carry on Dan, no embarrassing silences that Den might fill by punching your face! I point to the remains of my Guinness.

"This isn't my usual pint, but it's ok when there's nothing else. Er, not that there's anything wrong with the selection here…"

"Right…" Den says, unsure. I panic.

"Which is a far cry from Top Deck, right?" I blurt out from nowhere. "Where it all began!" I have no idea where that one came from. It's as if someone else had just said it.

Den looks up at me and his face changes. In a good way, thankfully.

"Ha! Top Deck!" he shouts back at me, little too loudly for me to be entirely comfortable. "Man, I've not thought about that stuff in years. Limeade and Lager on the school bus, right? Thought we were so frigging hard. Drinking Top Deck. Oh god, what a bunch of tossers…and what was that other one?"

"They did a Lemonade Shandy as well but that was too hard core for me!" I tell him, suddenly buoyed by happening on some decent subject matter. "But Shandy Bass was fine. I could handle as much of that as I could get my hands on!"

"Brilliant," Den laughs, shaking his head in wonder. "Shandy Bass, yeah! Hey, remember those big cans?"

"Yeah, yeah, with 12 and a half percent extra free," I return. "But why 12 and a half percent anyway? What sort of number was that? I'd have been impressed with just ten!"

"Yeah, we thought we were double extra hard drinking those ones. Yeah, yeah. Soon got past that though. Was on the Cinzano Bianco by the time I was eight."

If I recall my personal timeline correctly, I hadn't even had a Top Deck by the time I was eight. And I think I've only ever had Cinzano Bianco once in my life that I can recall. And that was at the age of twenty-six. I'd best not inform Den of these facts though, now we are such kindred spirits and getting on so well. I look over to the door of the Gents but there's no sign of Ted yet. No worries, we've broken the ice.

"Another one?" I say, which normally goes down well wherever you are.

Den is busy telling me about the time he lost a friend's greyhound at a service station, when Ted re-emerges. The main factor in this story being that Den was not going to chase the thing in his new pair of Gazelles (which are shoes I'm guessing, or perhaps trousers) so was prepared to see the dog keep its new-found freedom. I remark that it is unlikely that he could have caught it anyway, even if he was wearing trainers, since it was a Greyhound rather than a Bassett Hound, which brings forth another laugh. Ted is visibly surprised to see a new pint waiting for him, if not a little perturbed. Methinks my friend has underestimated me! You know, maybe I was hasty about this place, and maybe Den isn't so bad after all.

Actually, scratch that last comment. As various past escapades are recounted during our next pint, the majority of which include some kind of violence or other, the pub starts to fill up and an impending sense of doom begins to descend on the place. There's a couple of groups in here now starting to have little snipes at each other, and Den is peering over, looking like he might want to get involved if things get any more 'naughty'. Something is going to happen here tonight, I'm sure, and I don't want to be anywhere near it. So, despite my early success. I sure hope that we are going to leave after this one. The look on Ted's face tells me wordlessly that he heartily agrees with me too. We down our pints at a polite but insistent pace and prepare to go. I would normally try the Gents at this point but decide to 'keep it in' this time. I can if I really need to.

"He's alright, that Dan," I hear Den saying to Ted as I head out the door a few moments later, having already said my goodbyes, and having let the door swing closed behind me. I wait for a moment out on the street and take a deep breath.
"Well done," Ted tells me as he opens the door again and strides through, rushing past me and looking much relieved. "I knew you'd be good with him. I owe you one."
"No you don't, Ted," I say, really meaning it, as I catch him up. "You really don't owe me anything."
"I might. What I neglected to say was that it was me who did that to him at the wedding. Nice to know he still has no idea!"
He whoops and hollers as I chase him down the street screaming and laughing at the same time. Both of us feeling very much like two school boys who have just escaped the bullies and are back heading home, safe and sound, for our tea.

We are both still out of breath when we reach the Lion, and give each other a man hug. We never said what was happening next, so maybe we will just go home. But I suppose I could do with a drink after all that excitement.

"Pint?" Ted asks, between breaths, grinning ear to ear.

Despite his flaws, and our history, I do really like this chap.

Thinking about this later though, I think I can find some dignity in The Greyhound too, yes even there. Not for me, but for its own regulars. Like the blokes with their papers. Don't get me wrong, I'm not about to go signing an ACV for that place myself, but I can just about imagine that there may just be about enough other people on this planet who might do so, and good luck to them if they do. I never found out what Ted was picking up by the way, and I'm not going to ask him. You can yourself, if you feel you must know. He merely assured me that nothing illegal was going on, so I wasn't being an accessory of anything. Well, not *really* illegal anyway, he said. Then, just in case I was going to complain about Ted and all his secrets, Ted gets in there first and tells me that there's a lot about me that I like to keep to myself too, so that's only fair. Boy, he's got that right.

Chapter 10

So, Debbie told me, I need twenty-one signatures.
That's my job. The signatures of twenty-one people,
each from a different household, who want to keep
this pub open. Shouldn't be too difficult for a man of
my talents and connections, Debbie also said. All of
which brings me back to The Red Lion, sitting like a
vulture from the vantage point of the middle bar stool,
surveying my territory. I say vulture, rather than
hawk, since it's pretty dead in here. Oh, the joy of
metaphor! For the moment, it's just me and Tom the
Landlord. And I can't ask him. I'm under strict
instructions not to ask him, or ask anyone within his
earshot. And he has an excellent earshot, does Tom
the Landlord. This is actually not going to be as easy
as had been previously been made out. This deserves
a pint of 'Double Dilemma' (4.3%).

Ah, here comes Gordon. He'll sign. But he goes and
sits at the bar. And that's very much within earshot of
earshot-range of Tom the Landlord. Perhaps I could
pass him a note. Hmm, but then Tom the Landlord
would see the note. Then he would ask what the note
was. And then I would have to say something like
"Well, Tom, you know that plan you had of selling up
and living your dreams and providing for your
retirement and your family and all that? Well we're
all going to stop you without asking. Is that ok with
you?" I really don't want to go there on one measly
pint of Double Dilemma. So I give Gordon a wave
and go and sit next to the jukebox. He doesn't take

the hint and stubbornly remains at the bar. I think of giving Gordon the eye, to beckon him over here. But he's a big lad, who may take exception to such advances, and I have a lifelong aversion to violence which I intend to carry on living by. Sigh. I need the cover of a busy pub to do my business. As I progress to the half-pint mark I consider that I may well have come down here at the wrong time. Oh well, I could just leave it until later, or… I could just stay until it is the right time!

A second 'Double Dilemma' later (that's four dilemmas!), along with some polite exchange of views with Tom the Landlord regarding the number of potholes versus the number of traffic cones on the High Street, I find myself on firmer ground. I realise that vultures may not be, in fact, bothered about the ground being firmer, spending most of their time perched menacingly from bare branches, but that's the problem with metaphors, right? They don't last too long until they break down somewhere or other. The jukebox, meanwhile, has a healthy queue, and the evening crowd are keeping Tom the Landlord busy and distracted. Plus there's a dozen or so people in now, with more arriving every few minutes. Thursday is the new Friday, for some reason I have never managed to fathom, but it suits my purposes now. Debbie starts her shift later and the form she gave me is still sadly bereft of names. She'll be checking up on me for sure. Oh, hang on. What a numpty. I haven't added my own name yet. There you go. One down, twenty to go. Result!

Gareth turns up presently. Oh good, he'll sign. I wave from my near-the-jukebox stand point, and he comes on over. He's drinking on a Thursday, which must mean he has had a bad day at work. I'll let him get that off his chest first, and then I'll show him the form.

"Bad day?" he repeats, after I enquire as to his status. "No, not really, Dan. In fact, I handed my notice in today."
"Oh," I say, helpfully, as I watch my arm, all of its own volition, raise my pint up to his for a chink of glasses. It's good to know that my instincts are more polite than me. "Cheers. Feels good, does it?" I add.
"Sure does," he confirms for me, after taking a healthy swig from his Guinness. "I really should have done it ages ago. I really should. But you just get sucked into what you do, and you put up with it, and then you think that what you are putting up with is normal."
"Hmm," I add, more to myself than Gareth. This could be me and my pathetic job. This conversation isn't about me though, so I let Gareth continue. I want to know more about his story anyway. It beats traffic cones into a cocked hat. Weird image. No, don't go there. Back to Gareth. He is a lawyer by the way, and by all accounts has always worked much harder than me, so this is a big deal for him.
I must be having my 'away with the pixies' face on, as Gareth pauses to look at me strangely for a moment before carrying on. "Yeah, then I just had this one case that was such hard work. We were told to put in a month's worth of work in just a week. I told them it would take a month. Then, when we sort

135

of got done, as much as we could anyway, they got
the deadline put back to a month! After we busted a
gut and worked all hours, just so we could show we
did our best. And no one said a single thank you…"
"No they don't," I agree. Well, honestly, they *don't,*
do they?
"…or even showed any appreciation. Then they just
kept piling on more and more pressure. All it would
have taken was for one partner to stand up and tell all
sides the situation as it really was but no, they
preferred to save their precious egos and let the rest of
us suffer the consequences. And I knew then, Dan, I
just knew deep in my bones, that I just did not have
another case like that in me. I'd break if I did one like
that again. And I really didn't want that. I wouldn't be
the first to break either. There's loads of us I know
from Law School have had to be signed off through
stress or exhaustion or whatever down the years. Not
all of them came out the other side quite the same.
Well, I'm not going to go that way."
"Quite right," I say, then notice he just has three
swigs left, all of a sudden. "And you deserve a top up
my friend." On my way to the bar I have to take a few
extra swigs just to catch him up, so I can get one in
for him and one for myself at the same time. He's
having more of a day than me, so he's drinking a lot
quicker. I had best not stay with him all night or my
job to get signatures will not proceed too well. Still,
I'm not going to get stressed about it. I ask Tom for
something special for Gareth then, when I get back to
where Gareth is sitting, he takes the newly poured
Guinness gratefully. He then stares curiously at the
top of the pint, smiling.

"What's that supposed to be?" he asks, pointing at the picture drawn into the head of the pint. You can do that with Guinness, just by the way you finish pouring the liquid into the head. You normally get a shamrock but some bar people, and Tom the Landlord is one of them, take pride in their work and will do requests if you ask them. Dad always liked to ask for the Tyne Bridge as I recall, and occasionally he would get a decent attempt at it.

"It's supposed to be a P45." I say, staring at the top of his pint from various angles.

"A P45..." Gareth says, also changing the angle of his view of this work of art, looking for anything that resembled the form you get when you jack your job in, getting nothing of the sort, but beginning to grin wider anyway.

"Tom the Landlord is good, but I may have been a little ambitious in my request. Look there. That looks like a 'P'. Sort of."

"Oh yeah... actually no, not really...oh well..." Gareth says, then takes a swig and destroys that work of art forever. "Thanks though, that's good of you. P45. You idiot."

We both have a little chuckle at that. We chit chat for a while, then I finally ask him what he is going to do next.

"Now, don't laugh," he starts.

"I can't promise that, it might be funny."

"Ok, so it's a slight change of scene, but I've always been into this and I want to try and make a living out of it..."

"Sounds good. Spit it out then," I urge him.

"Well, you know I've been into bikes since I was a

kid, right?"

I had no idea actually. But I get the nagging feeling that maybe I should have. But what sort of bike was it? I don't want to get all 'Grifter' on him when he's into 'Kawasakis', if that's what they are called. That's a lot of miles-per-hour to be wrong by. I'd better let him fill in the gaps.

"Sure," I let him know, "you love your bikes. Always have loved your bikes."

"Yeah, and I've built a few of my own from the engine up and helped with some of my mates' bikes. Won prizes at rallies and that for some of my custom stuff. And I know loads of people in the business…"

"Right," I say, relieved that I did not try and join in with him in his supposed love for pedal power, "and you can do this for a living, can you?"

"Yeah, I think so. Well, I've worked it all out. On a spreadsheet. If I get a fairly regular supply of work, I'll be able to pay the bills. And I can live a simpler life anyway. Most of the time I was just spending money to cheer me up about going to work to earn that money I was spending because I hated it in the first place. You know what I mean?"

He catches me in mid-sip, staring into my glass. Oh, golly yes, I know what he means. "I believe I do," I agree, "it is a vicious cycle indeed."

"I don't know why I didn't make the change earlier. I mean, the only time I could stop thinking about work was when I was working on a bike. Or when I came in here…"

"To be fair mate," I say, "you talk about work a lot when you are here too."

"Do I? Damn it, I probably do, don't I? Well… no

138

more!"

"Oh don't worry. It was never a problem. Don't stop now, just when you are starting to do something you actually love…"

"Ok, I won't then." Gareth tells me through a grin. "So, how much do you know about bikes, Dan?"

"What you've just told me. I suppose that means I have some scope to enhance my knowledge on the subject, should you choose to educate me on occasion."

"Well, I may find it hard not to, mate. I'm so pumped up about this. It's such a big change, but I can honestly say I've never been happier. Got my first job on Monday. Can't wait."

"Now that *is* a change of attitude. Radical even," I tell him.

"Cheers. You having another?"

I nod. "Double Dilemma for me tonight buddy."

"What the hell *is* that? You're on something different every time I see you. Ok, no problem. I'll ask at the bar." He stops and looks at me. "Enough about me anyway. When I get back with these next ones, you have to tell me what you would like to leave work for, and get up to instead."

As I watch him weave his way through to the bar, since the Red Lion is now filling up nicely, I'm glad he gave me a few minutes to think about that one. I rack my brains to dislodge some previously ignored passion, but before I know it Gareth and two fresh pints appear through the crowd, and I have no answer for him. I don't even know if there *is* any answer in there at all, to be honest. Maybe Jen is right. Maybe it is best to run away, and leave it all behind.

But "Thanks mate," is all I say upon receipt of the glass.

"No worries. How do you choose which of this stuff you like? That's the great thing about Guinness. Once you are on it you never have to think about what you are going to have next."

"I suppose so", I say. "You do have to wait around for it to settle though. That can take a big chunk out of your life, if you add it all up."

"This is true. Especially when the bar person forgets to top you up. Drives me nuts."

"Ha, yeah. Tom would not allow that in here though. Cardinal sin."

"Yeah, he's a good one," Gareth says through another swig. "This is a good place."

"Hmm, about that, Gareth. Don't say anything, but we have a problem."

"Do we?" he says, suddenly a little confused.

" I mean the pub. The pub has a problem."

"Ah, how so?" he asks.

"Tom's leaving. Don't look round! He's selling up. But it's a secret."

"Oh no. That's a shame. How do you know then, Dan?"

"I have a secret source…" I begin.

"Ha, yes I know. You dirty dog." Gareth grins at me like a schoolboy.

I let that one pass. "Tom the Landlord is not just selling up," I tell him. "He's going to sell to developers and they are going to turn this place into flats."

Gareth looks around sullenly, as if trying to imagine this place after the conversion process. "He can't do that, can he? I mean it's *our* place too!"

"Well, I'm no lawyer, but it is his place more…"

"Well, putting *my* lawyer hat on, I'm thinking there must be something we can do…"

I whip out my piece of paper. "There is, Gareth. You can sign this."

He takes it from me and reads it carefully (he is still a lawyer for one more day at least) then looks up and smiles. "Yeah, this stuff might well work," he tells me.

"So I am lead to believe. You going to sign?"

"Damn right I am. Have you got a pen?"

I pat my pockets ineffectually. Unsurprisingly, I have lost my pen already, don't ask me how. "Ah, no I don't. Stay there. I'll get one at the bar."

"Jesus, Dan…" Gareth is now laughing.

I return with a pen, procured from Tom the Landlord for God's sake, and hand it to Gareth. He signs it and hands to back to me.

"Two down and nineteen to go," I say, and start looking around. I beckon over Gordon with way more confidence and authority than I could have mustered earlier. He quickly signs for me and pledges to keep quiet for now. He flicks an angry look at the bar, but relents when I admonish him further and plead for secrecy. Once he drifts off again, Gareth leans in and says "That Double Dilemma is powerful stuff! You just took charge of Gordon!"

"I know. Magic! Imagine what I would be like on Dutch Courage…"

"Yeah, that's what I meant…"

"No I mean 'Dutch Courage'. It's another beer on, over there…oh never mind. What are you grinning at

141

anyway?"

"Well I was going to ask you what you would like to do if you left your job, where *your* passion lies…"

"Yes, so?"

"Now I think I know," he says, and he flicks the back of the form with his finger.

Case closed. He reckons.

Debbie pops by later, checks out my form, adds the fourth signature to the list, then kisses me on the forehead, much to Gareth's delight. He is in such a good mood tonight. I should be jealous really, but somehow, I'm not.

I try and stay away from the pub for a few days and am managing manfully until Jez sends me one of his 'cheeky texts'. I'm not saying he is presumptuous, but he is waiting down the end of my street two minutes later when I leave the flat, still putting my jacket on. I give him one of what I think of as trademark quizzical looks, although I'm not sure, as no one else has ever taken care to comment on them. Anyway, he stops me saying anything from ten yards away with:

"I'm not saying you're predictable, but…"

"I *might* have been busy, you know, doing something else!" I counter, in my defence.

He chuckles in response. "Well, ain't I lucky then," he replies in what he thinks is his American accent, but which is more like Cardiff. I wonder if I should tell him? Who am I kidding? I tell him every time.

"Thank you, Jones the Steam…"

"Hey, it's nothing like…"

"Toot, toot, lets shunt over to the pub and get that pint then, boyo!"

"No one appreciates my talents," he moans, as we swap a brief man-hug and trundle down the road to The Red Lion.

"So, what's the plan?" I ask, once we are sitting down and staring at our pints of 'All Bar the Shouting' 4.3%, prior to the all-important first sip.
"As it happens, I've been reading up on project management..." he begins.
"Really? You? Whatever for?"
"I had to wait a while at the dentist and my phone battery ran out. Seriously, it was that, celebrity weddings, or thinking about the hole in my tooth so..."
"Ok, ok that is explanation enough already," I assure him, wondering if I was supposed to know if he had a dodgy tooth or not. Maybe he told me the other day and I forgot? Maybe he never bothered saying. Who knows. So I stick to the subject in hand, just to play safe. "What was your conclusion in regard to said project management, dare I ask?"
"That we, in fact, are rather excellent project managers!"
"Us? Really? How strong is this pint?"
"Yes. We are particularly good at structure."
"We are?"
"We are. We specialise in structured fun."
"Sounds awful. Also, doesn't sound like the sort of thing we actually would do."
"Ah, but that is where you are wrong. We do structure every time we go out."
"Really? Well, so what exactly is this 'structured fun' we do then?
"Go out..."

"Uh huh."

"Get pissed…"

"Er, right…"

"Get a kebab…"

"When applicable"

"Go home…"

"Um."

"Structure!"

I think about this preposterous notion for the time it takes me to take two pensive sips of my 'All Bar the Shouting'. And two sips are all it takes for me to reply "Fair enough. Genius observation, Jezza. We must be more professional than we thought."

"Damn right," he agrees, looking a bit proud of himself. I can't work out if either of us are being sarcastic anymore to be honest, but I don't rightly care either. We then somehow manage to find more to say about this for a while, until this thought occurs to me.

"Trouble is though…" I sigh.

"What?"

"Doesn't the structure take all the fun out of 'fun'?"

"Nah, not the way we do it. Drink up, my project plan says it's time for another drink. Cheers!"

"Ok, maybe all this planning could work out well after all! Cheers. But can I just ask, Mr. Project Manager…"

"Yes? What would you like me to opine on next?

"…where does Amy fit then, in all this structure?"

The smugness deletes itself from his face all of a sudden. "Oh bugger, I forgot to text her! Hang on…just a second, I'm doing it now. Don't you dare tell her!"

I hold my hands up in solidarity to the Management Structure.

Amy's turnaround time, from cheeky text to actual arrival, is occasionally impressive, but nowhere near as quick as mine, so over our next pint of 'All Bar the Shouting', as yet not threatening to raise our own personal decibel levels, Jez starts talking to me about *his* Dad, perhaps as a payment back for me finally talking to him about mine, and the funeral and stuff, a while back. Friendship can be just like an emotional round system sometimes, I guess.

Jez's Mum and Dad are still around, by which I mean alive. Unlike his sister Tina. It's still Tina who defines all of them who are left even now, and Jez finds another way to tell me this again.

"Dad was never that chatty about emotions and stuff when we were kids," he sighs, "such is my role model. Mainly, at least what I remember anyway, our interactions were just small talk and instructions. Mum did all the, er…touchy feely stuff, you know?"

"Yeah, I know," I reply. "I don't think men were supposed to show their feelings back then. I think my Dad wanted to a bit more back then, but maybe felt he wasn't allowed…"

"Mmm. Well I think for my Dad, he was happy that society let him off the hook on that one. Didn't give us much to work with when Tina died, though."

"What? He must have let himself go even a bit then, surely. That was such a terrible…"

"I don't think so," Jez tells me. "I wasn't really thinking straight but I just remember hugging Mum really, with Dad just standing around not knowing what to do."

"I always assumed you got your laid-back attitude from your Dad. But I guess I never got to know either of your folks that well."

"Hmm. I guess you can confuse laid-back with emotionally repressed if you don't look too closely. I am what I am because of me, I think, not through either of them. As much as I love them, I've never gone out to copy either of them."

I start thinking that's maybe a shame, as I take another sip. I enjoyed taking on Dad's obsessions and sharing them with him. They were one of the last things that survived in his brain before the real him disappeared completely. That made them the most precious things, to me at least. I've got nothing to say to help Jez though, so keep that thought inside.

"I always got the impression that Dad didn't think I was man enough," Jez continues reminiscing. "He was always saying I cried too easily. So I just pretended to be the strong silent type…"

"Pretended?" I quip sarcastically, unable to resist the moment. Jez merely acknowledges with a wink and carries on regardless of this intervention.

"…when he was around. I guess he made me into two different people."

This stops me in my tracks. I know that feeling all too well now. But my Dad only did that to me after he was gone, and it wasn't him who did it anyway really. I'm not going to say any of this though, and no quipping would be suitable here. So a sombre "That's no good, mate," is all that falls from my mouth instead.

"Ah, well," Jez says, finishing the last third of his pint in one, and forcing me to quickly catch up, "I gave up

146

on the strong and silent type a long time ago. At least I hope I did!"

"I'm pretty sure you did," I assure him. "Thank God that phase didn't last. We may not have become friends." We are not thanking God here by the way, or having a religious experience, it's just a thing we say.

"And another thing," he continues seamlessly, even though three minutes have since elapsed to procure a more relaxed pint each of 'Dock of the Bay', 3.4%. "I'm not going to be like that with mine, if I ever have kids. Open, honest and emotional. That'll be me."

"Me too," I say forcefully in reaction to this, before I have a chance to digest the implications properly. It's all too easy to be like this after a few beers. Another thought soon follows though, which prompts the question "When are you ever going to have kids anyway, Jez?"

"When are *you*?" he retorts amiably with a raised eyebrow, fully in wind-up mode, which is standard between friends like us.

We continue to imagine what each other's kids would be like as we wait for Amy. Ted can't come tonight, by the way. We both knew that as it turns out, but each of us has a different idea why. Fencing lessons, Jez says. I thought he was off buying his mate a greyhound. I have no idea if I'm misremembering what Ted said, or whether he just likes to mess with our heads. Both are equally possible in this universe.

We have not been sitting too long at the 'Dock of the Bay' (sorry, couldn't resist it) before Amy gets here.

She procures a 'Liquid Sarcasm', 5.375%, to help catch up. Since we are not past our own half pint markers, there is no requirement for her to furnish us with another just yet. Once she gets comfortable, she quickly informs us that Ted can't make it, as he is hosting a bicycle maintenance class, then reveals an idea for a short story that she has just had while on her way here. This is a welcome surprise!

"So," she begins excitedly, impatient to get the idea out of her head, "this is about a man…"

"Good start," I say.

"Could have been a woman," Jez responds. Amy just ignores us, well used to the rhythm of pub banter.

"…who keeps seeing pictures of himself in magazines and books. Pictures that could never in fact have been taken....

"Ooh, ok then…" we both say, there or thereabouts, shuffling into a more comfortable position to enjoy the ensuing tale, and taking a cheeky sip at the same time.

"It all starts innocuously," Amy continues, "with the front of his house appearing in an advert. 'That's nice' he thinks at first. 'Someone likes the front of my house, and thinks it has the sort of style to sell more coffee'. He smiles as he turns the page of the magazine, even this occurrence only holding his attention for a few moments."

"Yeah, we sure are hard to impress these days," Jez agrees. "Mum would have had that picture framed and put up in our front room for all time if that had happened to us!"

Amy nods in agreement and carries on resolutely, for once not eager for digression. "Then, a few days later, he spots another advert on a billboard as he rides along on the bus. This is of a family enjoying their back-garden with lovely flowers, a pristine lawn and a smoking barbecue. 'Looks nice' he thinks as the bus rides past. I might go to that garden centre next time'. Then, as the bus carries on down the road, he realises that the picture is of his own back-garden, his flowers and his barbecue. But then the bus rounds the corner and it is too late to check if that is what he actually really saw. Later, on his way home, he buys a padlock, at that very same garden centre as it goes, and puts it on his back-garden gate."

Amy pauses for a sip of 'Liquid Sarcasm', to fuel both the story and our anticipation. We both just let her pause without interruption, keen to hear the rest of the tale already, limiting our critique to an approving smile and a raised eyebrow to each other.

"A few days after that, he's at the doctors for an infection that has developed on a cut on his arm, and he picks up a magazine in the waiting room. Already, part of him has a bizarre curiosity as to whether he will find anything else familiar. But all he sees is an advert for beer."

"Yay!" we both say. Had to really.

"The pub in the picture does look familiar though, but he can't quite put his finger on it. Then, just as his name is called impatiently by the receptionist, and he is putting down the magazine, he thinks he spots himself in the picture, sitting alone at the table in the corner. But his name has been called, so he has to go. He resolves to check the picture again when he comes out, but when he does, unfortunately the magazine has gone."

149

"Ooh, yes this is mysterious!" Jez claps his hands in delight. "That would totally freak me out." Amy tries to look implacable but is visibly pleased with this reaction nonetheless.

"So, as he walks home from the doctor's surgery he looks nervously at the street around him, trying to spot anyone with a camera, or holding out their phone. He's looking for anyone suspicious at all really, but he sees nothing unusual. Once he gets home he closes the curtains and double-locks his doors."

Our pints have now descended beyond the one-third mark, and it is arguably my round, so I ask for a pause in the proceedings to get the next drinks in. It is a rare conversation indeed in here where this is inappropriate, and although I have effectively cut Amy off in mid-stream, this is entirely acceptable under these circumstances too. However, since we are all keen to resume the tale, I dispense with the usual debate on the subject of the choice of the next drink and just repeat the order. Such is this silent compromise of a well-oiled friendship. Once I am back, Amy and Jez have just emptied their glasses and we resume as if nothing had happened.

"He rings in sick from work the next day and decides to stay indoors all day, TV off, and just read a book. That way he has no chance of seeing any pictures anywhere. This is all fine for a tense hour or two, but then the letterbox opens and closes with a snap."

"Oh no!" Jez exclaims, now immersed in the moment. I'm enjoying this too, but something is making me wary. Maybe it's just that everything makes me wary these days.

"For a full thirty minutes," Amy tells us, "he ignores the fact that he has heard the sound of the mail falling from the letterbox onto his hallway floor. But part of him needs to see what is lying there. He slowly gets up…"

Amy is starting to milk this a little now. This is not a criticism – we are loving it. Plus, I would imagine that it is hard not to milk things after a pint and a bit of 'Liquid Sarcasm'. I would be much worse for sure.

"…and looks around the door into the hallway. He audibly breathes a sigh of relief, if anyone was there to hear it, as he sees that all that was put through the door is just junk mail."

"I normally react with distinct disappointment to that scene," Jez muses briefly, then gives the floor back to our storyteller.

"So, he goes to pick up the junk mail, in order to put it straight in the bin. But then he sees…"

She pauses for another sip now, for dramatic effect. Well, dramatic for this place anyway. This sort of thing would barely pass as noticeable in The Greyhound, or indeed The Shakespeare, of an evening. Jez is now physically curling up in anticipation, which, despite similar feelings myself, I'm finding most amusing. After another sip and a smile, the tale continues.

"…his own face smiling back at him from a leaflet, holding a form in an advert for Life Insurance! He stares at this aghast. He never had this picture taken! He checks every part of the page for clues or signs of Photoshop but every little thing about it confirms that this is him, from the hairs on his nose to the freckle on his cheek. Even the way he is smiling, a little bit

151

too self-assured, cocky perhaps, if he truly cared to admit it. He fearfully scrunches up the page and pushes it into his bin. Then, even though he knows it has been a long time since the mail was delivered, and he is still only in his dressing gown, he rushes to the front door and flings it open. Of course, the postman has long gone. Outside, the world is just carrying on as normal."

"Aggh!" Jez cringes. "What is it? What's going on! I need to know!" Despite knowing that not only has this story just been made up, and not only that, but also has been made up by someone he talks to almost every day, this particular fiction has taken him over and consumed his moment. We all love the escape of this type of thing, I guess, but not only that. We also crave the tidiness that is inherent in a story. We know what the agreement is between writer and reader, the agreement that once we have set up a situation, we will find resolution in the eventual conclusion, and hopefully satisfaction. We crave this, I think, because it is so absent in our own lives. Jez has never received any resolution from losing Tina so pointlessly, that much I know. Myself, I can find no comfort from anything that has happened since losing Mum, and then Dad. So it's hard not to look for sense elsewhere, even if it isn't real.

"A bus goes past his front door just at that point," Amy carries on, now with an extra cider-fuelled dramatic flourish, "and on the side he sees a picture of a red sports car, driving off into the distance, top down, the road clear. And sure enough, in the picture there he is, in the driver's seat, shades on, looking all assured, smug even. He has never been there! He has never been in that car! He is possessed by fear now and can't help but chase the bus down the road to get a closer look, then..."

"Then??" Jez cries, now bouncing up and down on his seat.

"Then..." she adds, adding very little.

"Amy!" I interject, for poor Jez's sake mainly.

"He gets hit by a red sports car at the crossing and is killed stone dead!" She laughs and sits back for a moment, giving us the floor.

"What?" is all I can manage as a response "Is that it? That can't be it!" I jump in to fill any potential gap in the conversation, and the resulting tension, brought on by the fact that Jez's sister Tina herself was hit by a car, all those years ago. I guess Amy could have chosen a more sensitive demise for her character, but we can't wrap our friends in cotton wool forever either, or we wouldn't be their friends, would we? Looking at Jez though, he doesn't seem too fazed, fortunately.

"Turns out," Amy relates calmly to us, "that our hero was not so heroic after all."

I can relate to that, but I let Amy continue without any addition to the conversation.

"As the police turn up to survey the scene, they find some suspicious blood stains in his house. Then, after further investigation they discover that this man had, in fact, recently killed his wife."

"No way!" Jez is back in the room thankfully.

"He had written a confession too but had hidden it away in his chest of drawers. Turns out that he had killed his wife for not making him a coffee..."

"Ah..."

"Then buried her in the flower bed..."

"Aha!"

"Went down the pub as an alibi…"

"Ooh!" Jez exclaims in delight. My heart just skips a beat and a take a deep swig to regain my rhythm.

"And then…" Amy teases us.

"Cashed in the life insurance!" we all say together, much to the confusion of those at the table next to us.

"Then, of course," Amy concludes herself, "his tale is ended by the red sports car."

"Yeah, that's a totally cool idea!" Jez tells her, chinking her glass in additional approval. "You should write that up!"

"Yes, yes, totally cool," I agree, "but what's the story behind the story? I mean, where did the pictures come from?" The resolution as it stands seems enough for Jez, but I can't relax with the continued mystery back story hanging over our heads.

"Well…" Amy muses, "I haven't quite decided yet. Maybe it's the wife's friend or sister or something, who is an advertising executive and uses what resources she has to exact her own brand of justice."

"Yeah, that might work…" I begin.

"Or it could be just in his head, his guilty conscience creating this illusion."

"Yeah, I like it," Jez chimes in. I add absolutely nothing to this.

"Or it might be just the universe, you know? It will always find a way to bring out guilty secrets in the end, one way or the other."

"I think you should go for the advertising executive," I firmly tell her. All of a sudden, I'm finding this

154

particular story a whole lot less satisfying, and my stomach ties into ropes without any warning.

I have to stop talking for a moment. I look at the table and say this word in my head. Safe. I look at the empty glass. Safe. The bottles. Safe. Here. Now. I am *safe*. I know all about what lies beyond these walls and beyond this session, but if I try I *can* make it stay beyond, if only just for now. I can do this. I can. Deep breath. Then I turn back to the conversation with my friends. Here especially, I am *safe*.

It only takes me a short while to recover. I am in my safe place with good people, so the dip in my mood is brief and hopefully unnoticeable. We get in another drink, start talking about something else or other, and soon we have ascended to what we like to call the Happy Plateau. Yes, the hallowed Happy Plateau. This is the state of existence you could describe as being 'As drunk as you need to be on any given night'. It's a happy place, and I enjoy it while we are there. But it is also a sadly fragile state. All it takes is one pint too many, or a certain thing being said, and you are either flying too high, or falling off the cliff.

I've been gripping onto the Happy Plateau for as long as I could, and felt I had been doing pretty well lately. But I always knew that I could not hold on forever. And as I spectacularly fall off the cliff, later when I get home, I imagine myself reaching out to these two lovely people, and unburdening myself of all my guilty secrets before the universe hunts me down. I imagine the scene playing out in a hundred different ways. I start with the good ones, with the hugs and

155

the tears and the sheer relief, but then descend to the reactions of shock and disgust that change my life forever. At that point I have to force myself to stop these thoughts. But they don't stop. They only begin to churn around faster and faster in the back of my brain, now not even pretending to be under my control. I sense Matthew in the room with me, watching, no longer feeling the need to say anything. He just watches as I torture myself. It is only the beer that eventually brings unconsciousness, not even sleep, and precious little of that.

And when I wake up, nothing has changed. Of course it hasn't, Dan. Why the hell would it?

Chapter 11

It's D-Day. Or maybe J-Day. You see, I've arranged to meet Jen again after she dropped her travelling bombshell the other day. I just didn't feel strong enough to do anything else. Typically for me though, I am preparing by having a drink with someone else, rather than thinking things through by myself. This occasion requires Ted's magical brand of advice, even considering his past record, so he has kindly agreed to beat me into shape before the summit meeting. Debbie is not here. I did not tell her about Jen's offer. Is this wrong of me? I don't know. It certainly isn't brave, but then I have never previously given anyone the impression that I was likely to be brave about anything, have I? Anyway, meeting Ted also means that I have procured signature number five. Almost a quarter of the way there, for those who like a bit of maths. Matthew Hopkins is not invited. I do not need his signature. Of course, we can't jump right into the subject of Jen. That just isn't the way things get done around here, and certainly not over a pint of 'Up Yours', 4.0%.

"I'm not happy about *this* pub disappearing," Ted says, shaking his head, still holding the pen over his signature. "Some pubs have got to go, maybe, but not this one."
"Hmm. What do you mean? Corkscrews or something?"
"No, that can stay. Don't like it myself, but it keeps other types of folk out of the community pubs like

this one, and that helps make us be more of a community." He looks around at the odd mix of folk around us, then back at me. "Well, sort of," he adds limply.

"Well, what pub should go then, if not Corkscrews? Personally, I can't think of anything worse!" I exclaim loudly. Don't worry, I'm only being overdramatic for the purposes of entertainment.

"Well…" Ted muses, dredging something up from his ample store of stories, "there's always the story of The Mariners Arms…"

"Sounds lovely," I say to buy some thinking time. I've never heard of the place. "What's so wrong about the Mariners Arms?"

"*Was* so wrong about the Mariners Arms," Ted corrects me. "The Mariners Arms is sadly no more."

"I'm sad now. Whatever happened?"

"I'm glad you asked. The Mariners Arms was in Slaughter…"

"I think I'm starting to see the problem…" I tell him.

"No you're not," he tells me. "Unless you know in fact where Slaughter is…"

"No idea. Not a one. It was more the name of the place really. Sorry, over to you."

Ted resumes unabashed. "It was probably pronounced 'Slur-ruh' or something like that anyway. Anyway, the problem was not the name so much, as the geography…"

"Ah, do tell…"

"I shall. Do you know Aldeburgh?"

"East coast somewhere?" I offer uncertainly.

"That will do. It's on the Suffolk coast."

"Which *is* the East Coast…"

"Yes, well done Dan, but more specifically the part of the East coast that is the Suffolk coast, and even more specifically the part of the Suffolk Coast that is subject to a great deal of erosion and loss of land. People are losing ten metres a year from their gardens and the like around there. Anyway, Slaughter was a thriving fishing village with a popular pub…"

"The Mariners Arms!" I declare proudly, with all the enthusiasm that a couple of beers can muster.

"Glad to hear you are keeping up, Dan. Indeed, the Mariners Arms. The thing was though, that during a flood, the sea was coming into the town, and even into people's houses, for years and years and they just put up with it. Part of normal life as it were."

"Not sure what to say about that. Stubborn is the word, but I don't want to sound too critical..."

"Hmm, so when the sea came up they just opened up the front door and the back door so all the sea water flowed all the way through that house, or the pub, without taking it down." Ted pauses a moment to consider my last sentence, a little delayed. "Actually, I think 'stubborn' does cover it, yes. But then, then came the final straw!"

"Whatever could that be?" I ask him, now genuinely intrigued.

"One night, one fateful night…"

"Ok, ok, don't over-egg it, Ted…"

"Says you! One fateful night the sea washed the entire pub away…"

"Tragedy! Who forgot to open the doors!? Public enquiry!"

"Well, after that, enough was truly enough. Without the pub the locals just decided to ship on out. They

159

were gone within weeks and the town closed for good," Ted concludes.

"Right. No point staying anymore right? Very sad."

"Right, but that was years and years ago now. Before the war I think. The whole area is under the sea now as is goes."

"Oh dear. Well, you can't stop progress," I add, admittedly a little too flippantly.

"No Dan, you can. You can stop progress. You just can't stop the sea. Get all your signatures then we'll see about stopping this particular attempt at unwelcome change."

"So," Ted says a little later, changing the subject, but noticeably still not onto the impending meeting with Jen. Instead he eyes me up with a challenging air and asks, "How else can you edify me about the English Civil War then? From your ever so *large* book."

"Ah, size is not everything" I say, to buy myself yet more thinking time. All of about half a second of it. Then I take a thoughtful sip of 'Up Yours', which is exactly as friendly on the palette as you may expect, to buy myself another second and a half. Then I take another sip. Then say "Ah, yes" again.

"You haven't read any more, have you?" he accuses. He knows me too well already.

"That's not *entirely* true, I've read a *little* more," I counter. "Did I tell you about the beer taxes?"

Ted replies merely with a silent sip of his own and one of those looks.

"Yes, I did, didn't I," I continue. "Hmm, ok then…well I have been reading about some book burnings…"

That causes a raised eyebrow, which is enough for

160

me, so I plough on. "You see, even prior to the war, The English Civil War I mean, there was a rich tradition of book burning."

"You don't say. I always kind of thought of it as a Nazi thing…" Ted muses.

"I know. Well, I suppose that we've been burning books as long as we've been printing them, knowing what us humans are like."

"Well, *almost* as long," Ted corrects me, smiling. "Otherwise that gives me an image of books coming off the first printing press and straight into a bonfire. Hilarious!" Sip. Pause. "And also depressing."

"You're not wrong," I agree. "There was also a rich tradition of burning the author of the book along with the books as well…"

"Oh dear. That's a bit harsh. Well it's good to know that conditions for authors have improved since…"

"A little, yes. Anyway Ted, these burnings would attract huge crowds, particularly if there was a writer on the menu, as it were…"

"Not literally I hope," Ted quips. Someone had to.

"No, not according to my research. These were often at popular public places like Cheapside in London, like they were some form of public entertainment…"

"Well, yes," Ted agrees, "I bet there was the odd slow day, you know, before television…"

"Yeah, but get this," I say. "In the chapter I was reading, it said that book-burning actually worked to create a boom in the printing business, because the printers just had to work harder to keep ahead of the burners. And they managed it!"

"It's just like that today. As soon as something gets banned everyone wants a piece of it."

"Relax."

"I'm quite calm, Dan, despite *this* travesty of a pint. Aha, yes, I do know what you mean! Frankie Goes to Hollywood. Straight to number one right after Radio 1 refused to play it."

I knew he would know what I meant. Ted is good like that. I can't say we are exactly on the same wavelength, but we at least have a significant wavelength overlap.

"Yes, that is a kind of parallel," I agree. "So the book burnings were good for sales…"

"But not necessarily good for the author…"

"Oh no, not so good for them. At all. This could explain why sequels are a relatively recent phenomenon."

"Rough times," Ted muses, swilling the remaining three swigs at the bottom of his glass thoughtfully. He then looks up at me quizzically and asks, "Same again?"

I look down at my glass in contemplation too, then screw up my face and say, "No, I think I may try something else this time. 'Up Yours' did not go *down mine* so well!"

"If this beer was brewed in the Civil War they may have burned the brewer for that one. I'll pick out something else then." Then he leaves with a cheeky grin.

He comes back shortly with a pint of 'Something Else', 4.2%. It took a few enquiries to establish that 'Something Else' was in fact the name of the ale in question, and from the same brewery as 'Up Yours'. That particular exchange must be being repeated in pubs county-wide as we speak. The slight extra kick in this particular ale convinces me to mention my other topic of historical research, which I was oddly scared to vocalise until now, as if it would make it more real than it already was.

"Ted," I say.

"Yes, Dan?"

"It wasn't just writers that had it bad then you know. The war, the English Civil War, it was a really turbulent time for society as a whole. A huge proportion of the population were killed or otherwise affected, compared even to the world wars. Less people then, I suppose."

"I can imagine," Ted, says, which is really just an encouragement for me to continue, and also serves to give me an opportunity to try another sip of 'Something Else'. Hmm, it really *is* pretty good, much to my relief. I am now feeling compelled to turn the conversation this particular way, even though I've been fighting it for weeks now. But it's been trapped in my head long enough and I think I need to get it out. Ted is good for these moments I have found. Here goes.

"And you know who had it worst?"

"Life insurance salesmen?" Ted laughs, then concedes the floor to me with an apologetic "Sorry, do carry on."

"No, it was the witches. I've been reading about the witch burnings you see…"

"Most people read about battles, treaties and kings. Trust you to pick out beer, books and witches, Dan. I must say my friend, this is becoming quite an education, this session."

"Aren't they always? Well, I *say* witches, but you

know, I'm not saying that all these women actually *were* witches. They were just *accused* of being witches. Which, to most people then seemed to be one and the same thing."

"Ah, yes", Ted says, nodding. "Is this the Witchfinder General and all that stuff? I think I saw that movie. Years ago. Was that stuff real, then?"

"Yes, I'm afraid to say it was real. He was a real man anyway, the main one. Er, Matthew Hopkins was his name…I think. During the Civil War. He went around Essex, Suffolk and other counties round there taking advantage of the fears of the population, already heightened by the war. Right after the battle of Naseby…"

"Naseby. I did read about that one."

"Yeah, Ted, it was one of the big ones so even I got to that one. Anyway, after that battle, which was a decisive win for Cromwell and the Parliamentarians…"

"Roundheads right?" he interrupts again. Which is all fine. It is what we are here for, after all.

"Yeah, but they never called themselves that. That was a disparaging term. Anyway, they all but destroyed the King's Army at that battle."

"So you *do* know about battles then?"

"Well, that's about it really for battles I'm afraid. Anyway, in the confusion following that victory, in the following three days after it in fact, thirty-six witches were put on trial in Essex alone."

"That's a lot of witches. Puts the opening scene of Macbeth to shame." Ted can't help but keep butting in. I understand this. After a certain number of drinks, it becomes like a rhythm you just have to follow,

164

whichever side of the conversation you are on.

"Indeed. And of those thirty-six, nineteen were executed, nine died in prison and six were still known to be in prison three years later."

"What about the others?" he asks.

"Well, one was acquitted…" I begin to reply.

"Blimey, she must have had one hell of a lawyer. How did she get off I wonder?"

"Can't imagine. She probably had some money. Or a big goat or something."

"A big goat, ha. And what about the other one?"

"What other one? Another goat?"

"No, you numpty. Nineteen, plus nine, plus six, plus one makes thirty-five. There were thirty-six you said. So what about the other one?"

"Oh, I never noticed that, actually," I apologise. "Er, my research did not go so far to work all that out I'm afraid, Mr Mathematician."

"Shoddy work, Dan, as ever. Hey, maybe *she* was the real witch and she used magic to get herself away. Eye of newt and all that."

"You know, I like the sound of that, Ted. Shame for all the others but good luck to her. Hey, cheers to her then!"

"Yeah, cheers to her!" We chink glasses. Somewhere back in time, this statistical anomaly was actually a real and actual woman, and to think we are now raising a glass to her, all via the magic of reading books! I would like to think she can somehow see us now, having this conversation, and is finding this most amusing, if not entirely perplexing. I also am really liking the thought of someone else out there getting the better of Matthew Hopkins, if only just the once.

"You know," I continue, "I reckon it wasn't a religious thing at all, all this witch stuff. Ninety percent of these women were of lower social status apparently, so I think people were just looking for scapegoats when things went wrong, like illness spreading or crop blights and the like."

"And it's the poor that always get it, right? As it ever was."

"I reckon so, Ted. And you know what else? It wasn't even a sexist thing. It was mainly other women who were the prime accusers. You had to get your accusation in quick when Hopkins came to town, before someone accused you."

"Hmm. Sounds like Russia under Stalin," Ted says soberly. Well sort of soberly, you know what I mean. Then he chuckles and continues. "Ha, also reminds me of when someone farts in a lift. That's human nature for you!"

"How, Ted, how on earth did we get onto that? Anyway, yeah, it *was* like that. But the witch-finders themselves were even worse. They would come into a village or town and get the accusation in quick, eager to bolster their own position. They made a lot of money out of providing this service too. And Matthew Hopkins was the worst of them all. And all of this based on fear and ignorance. I suppose this comes under the headline of 'some things never change'." I sigh, and we both pause for a moment, me having suddenly killed the atmosphere, as I am wont to do on occasion.

"I went out with a witch once," Ted throws in suddenly, to lighten the mood. 'Ok', I think, 'here we

166

go again.' "True story," he continues, which, as far as I can tell, means precisely nothing at all when it comes to Ted. Nonetheless, I enjoy the ensuing story immensely, involving cats, mild mind-reading and hot hands. It really felt like such a weight off my mind, to get Matthew Hopkins out of my head briefly and into Ted's, just by mentioning his name. Like he was the Candyman or Mephistopheles or something. Sorry Ted, needs must. We continue to chat on these lines, Ted and myself I mean, until it is finally time to turn the conversation onto the imminent arrival of Jen, and the offer she has given me.

"Ooh, that's a tricky one," Ted advises me wisely, once I have filled him in with the full details of the 'Jen situation'.
"Stupidly, Ted, I was hoping for something a little more useful from you." I reply.
"Were you now? You were? Oh, for real? Right, ok then. Hmm, let me think..."
He has a think. I have a sip. Then he puts his glass down on our table, so he can make his hands into a kind of weighing scales. Weighing up my potential happiness, I'm guessing.
"So on one side…" he begins, lifting the right hand. His right, not mine. "…so on one side you have the old girlfriend. I have heard very much enough about this one, mostly within these very walls, to know that you sure did love her, despite what she did to you. Plus, there's a trip around the world on offer. That is something we should all try and do at some point in our lives, if we can be so lucky…"
"Have *you*?" I ask, defensively, instantly regretting this. Jen is due here in half an hour and one of Ted's

life changing stories, be they true or otherwise, can easily consume a couple of beers on any given night. And a couple of beers, as I may have explained before, would convert into time as approximately an hour, within a standard situation, and therefore we really do not have time for this just now. Ted, bless him, is thankfully mindful of my current state of mind, and also the challenging timeframe at play here, so passes up on an opportunity to edify me for once.

"What do *you* think?" he asks smiling. "Anyway, great girl, the whole world, getting away from your, um, recent, er *situation*…that all sounds good on the plus side."

"Yeaaaah…" I say, stretching out the syllable while waiting for some kind of inspired response. Talk of 'the situation' is still far from comfortable for us yet, even when being wilfully ignored.

"But on the other side? The staying here side?" Ted starts, raising his left hand.

"The other side? What about it?" I ask, cajoling him into revealing further details. I would love to know what he thought exactly *what* was so great in my life at the moment.

"No, why don't *you* start?" he suggests. So much for him helping me, I think.

"Well," I muse, "There's this place…"

"Really, that's first on your list?"

"Not first. I'm not listing them in order here. Honestly. Then there's you…"

"I'm *second* on the list?!"

"*Not* in order, Ted. Hang on, then there's my family. You know, what's left of it."

168

"I know, Dan. I know."

"Rachel and that. Well, just Rachel really, if I'm being honest. Amy and Jez too. Then, well I think then there's Debbie."

"At last! At last he gets down to the top of the list!" Ted exclaims to the chandelier above. Yes, there really is one here. It needs a dusting, plus other things an old chandelier might need, but it's still hanging in there. I am the 'he' here, by the way. Ted sometimes refers to me in the third person when I'm in trouble or being particularly dense. Just like my mother used to, as it happens.

"Are you sure?" I enquire genuinely. "I mean, we've had a few dates and that. But I don't know if she *really* likes me…"

Ted chokes into his beer, or at least pretends to, since that's one of our running jokes these days. In fact, I think he initially meant to pretend to, then he actually did do it. That can happen remarkably easily, as I'm sure you know yourself, if you've ever tried it.

"Of course she really likes you, numb-nuts," he replies eventually, through the fading remains of a choke. "The way you two look at each other when you meet up, all grinning from ear to ear. Honestly, it makes you sick." He clears his throat finally then smiles back at me. "So, there's Debbie," he says, with a certain finality.

"Yes, and I've started going volunteering to visit at the retirement home too. That was good, in a way. And then there's my job…"

"Don't make me choke again, Dan…"

"Well, there's the money anyway. That sure comes in handy."

169

"Ok, well we'll put the job on the list then, but near the bottom. What else?" He has both hands in the air now, bobbing up and down like some finely balanced scales of justice. Ooh, the symbolism!

"What else…what else. Did I mention this place?"

"You did, Dan, you did."

"Yes, I did, didn't I. Um, well I quite like my flat."

"When you are in it, mate. Which is not that much. Anything else?"

"Right, well, um, what else…" another sip is taken to inspire me. Ted takes score in the meantime.

"So on one side you have the old girlfriend, who was the love of your life," he says, "but did leave you in a mess by all accounts, plus a trip round the world. On the other side you have the new girl, who may be the next love of your life, but you are patently not sure yet, and staying here, in this pub, with some old geezers and me, your mates and anyone else who comes down The Red Lion,"

"While it is still here," I say, taking another sip. What else is there? There must be something. Oh right.

"…plus beer of course! I couldn't get a beer like this anywhere else in the world."

Ted laughs and declares, "We have our answer! The beer tips the scales!" The right hand, his right, falls dramatically.

"Ted," I respond, "I'm not that shallow." Ted is still laughing as we both think about this. "I'm *not*," I insist, feeling less sure of my conclusion at every sip. Each lovely sip.

"I know you're not, mate, I know. You could handle a Thai lager if you were in Ko Samui for sure, at a stretch anyway. You would probably moan, but you

170

would drink it."

"Thank you," I reply, "thank you for that vote of confidence."

"Really though, Dan…" he says, pausing to fix me in the eye. I fix back.

"What?"

"It just boils down to this. It's not a 'what' or 'where' question. It's a 'who' question."

"What do you mean?" I ask, knowing what he means.

"Where you are, what you do, what you drink. It doesn't count for all that much in the end, Dan, does it? It's who you do it with." I nod in response as I notice his face turning sad, the facade crumbling for once, briefly. And I have no idea why, I suddenly realise.

"Right then, so…" I say, to show I didn't notice, or at least allow him the dignity of thinking as much.

"So," he states clearly, recovering himself, "is it Jen, or is it Debbie? That's entirely all you need to think about, my friend. And you do have the power to choose. It's your choice, not anyone else's." He then drains his glass, says his goodbyes and leaves me to it, Jen's arrival being now imminent. As I sit alone and wait for her to arrive, I consider that Ted has really hit the nail on the head, once again. All that other stuff, holidays, jobs, friends and pubs and all that, was just confusing me. It is a simple choice really. Which *really* doesn't make it any easier, I ponder sadly, as I go to the bar and order another drink. I don't get Jen one yet, as I know she will be late.

Thirty minutes later, I'm finishing that next pint, a 'Drop in the Ocean', 3.6%, as Jen breezes through the door, a 'reasonable' half an hour late. Reasonable by her standards, not mine, as I now recall from the dusty relationship archives of my brain. I have always considered myself to be 'late' if I was actually on time, if you see what I mean. I check her out, up and down. She looks...she looks…sober. I doubt I do, I consider, as she checks me out in turn from across the pub, while providing a cheery wave. Nice smile. She always had such a nice smile. Oh god, I'm in trouble.

Without asking, I get her a challenging cider, 'Punk Lady', 6.8%, so she can catch me up a little. We need to be on the same level to have this conversation, whatever it turns out to be. I have now moved onto a speciality lower alcohol, higher hopped beer, that still is supposed to taste like it has the normal amount of booze in it. It is called 'Hop Damn' and although it comes in at a limbo-low 2.8%, it does the job nicely. Right then, we are all ready. Let us begin.
"So, have you given any more thought to our plans?" Jen begins.
"Well…" I inform her.
"Because I've been looking online and there are some great deals if we book up together. It's a fair bit cheaper than booking for one, I must say… Anyway, we can still do Italy as well. Venice, Rome, Florence. On our way back. Acclimatise us back to Europe before we have to go home. We always said we would go to Italy, didn't we?"
I resist the temptation to remind her why we never ended up going to Italy ('because *you* left *me* before we got the chance, Jennifer' I whisper instead, into my 'Hop Damn', 2.8%), but I can't help but admit to myself that is does sound rather nice. And a million

miles from what I've just been through. Sip. I deserve a break, don't I? *Don't* I? I do need to turn my life around, don't I? Well, *don't* I? And what if I don't go, and the pub closes, and Debbie dumps me for no reason, or some reason, then I'd sure be wishing I was off round the world, wouldn't I? Wouldn't I? Oh, I don't know. The answer is not at the bottom of this glass anyway. Oops, I'm drifting away, and Jen is still talking away, unabashed. She is getting something out of her handbag, I notice.

"I had to check this wasn't out of date. You should check yours. You need at least six months more than the end date of travel just in case," she says, flashing her passport in front of her face. "This one is old, but I've still got a couple of years on it so I'm ok. See? Look at that photo! I'm so young!"

I look at the photo. It is an old one. She hasn't changed that much really, but the Jen staring back at me from the page is the exact same Jen who was with me all those years ago. I may even have been right there, just outside the photo booth when that photo was taken. I should remember really. But I don't. When you hide so many memories away, some must get damaged while in storage. Shame, but at the time it was them or me.

"Yeah, that's you alright. Not that you've changed much, mind," I observe. "Er, right, I would have to check my passport, I think I'm ok, but that's the sort of thing I can lose track of. I haven't travelled that much recently."

"You do that. Anyway, as long as we book around Christmas-time, we should be ok. That's what Stephanie told me anyway. She's been away loads.

That's why she kept coming back to see me for jobs at the recruitment firm. She would work and save up for half the year, then travel for the other half. I think that's where I got the idea to go from. Every time I saw her again, something amazing had happened to her, and there I was, just stuck behind the same desk, doing the same thing. If we are lucky, and time it right, we might bump into her in Thailand. Oh, and she said that there's this *amazing* place…"
And off she goes into a lengthy story about Stephanie's adventures in Thailand. You don't need to know the details. If *you* time it right, you might bump into her too and she can tell you herself. They were good stories though, I will say that much. That girl sure knows how to live.

"Yeah, it sounds lovely. I would have to sort things out first, you know. The money might be an…er…an issue you know? But yeah, it does sound lovely…" I tail off, trying desperately to leave things up in the air, to maintain a way out, in case things look different in the morning. But the joyous, or perhaps victorious, look on Jen's face tells me that perhaps I have not been successful. Why can't I ever just say what I mean?

Its official. I have drunk too much this evening. And not even 'Hop Damn' could save me today.

There is a moment, as Jen is leaving, that might have been awkward if I had been more sober. I either go for the wrong cheek when we say goodbye, or by some old-forgotten ingrained habit absent-mindedly go for the lips, but we clash noses a bit before laughing nervously and then finally find the right cheek. I take a deep breath as I then watch her disappear in her taxi. What just happened? I didn't say yes, but it felt like yes had been said somehow regardless of that. My plan was that I didn't say no, but that didn't feel like enough anymore. Bloody hell, Daniel, you are such an idiot! I am busy trying to congratulate myself for not actually *saying* yes, when Matthew Hopkins joins me. He is waiting by the tree at the end of my street.

"Thought you could get rid of me that easily?" he asks, contemptuously.

"Whatever," I reply dismissively, but not out loud as far as I can tell.

"Don't think running away is going to help. Thailand? You think I can't get to Thailand? I can get anywhere I choose, fool! You know, I think I would actually enjoy a trip to the Orient. Plenty of witches there for me to play with!"

"I didn't…" I begin, but tail off. Because I guess I actually *did*, deep down.

"And as for your friend. I will get to your friend in due course. Ted!" he spits. "Don't think for a moment that I have forgotten about him…"

That's enough. I drunkenly stop in my tracks and turn to my tormentor. "Don't you dare. You leave him alone, you hear me!"

Oops, that was definitely out loud, that one. I look around. But it's ok. No one is there. And now, not even Matthew Hopkins. The spell is briefly broken by nothing more than my embarrassment. I fumble for my keys and hurry towards my front door, for once not only to appease my bladder.

175

Chapter 12

I've taken to putting flowers down. Not at cemeteries. That particular act, I have found, does no good for me whatsoever. And what it does for Mum and Dad, when I do occasionally do it, remains a mystery. No, instead I put flowers down wherever I see a bee on the ground. Maybe the bee in question just needs a breather but you never know, it might be in trouble, so I act like a pop-up bee service station, or something like that, and put some flowers down for them. I know, this is a pathetic attempt to make the universe right with me again after what I have done. But it's a start I suppose. The bees generally perk up and have a root around the flower when I do this, which is gratifying. If they are gone when I come back later, it makes me feel good. But if they are still there, inert, it makes me feel sad. Some situations just can't be fixed. Or at least I can't fix them. It really doesn't help to find that out though, does it?

I'm staring at one of my miniature flower arrangements, by a tree near the end of my street, when Debbie unexpectedly taps me on the shoulder. "What's that you are looking at? It's like a flower arrangement for bees!" she says. It would normally be my nature to congratulate her on this observation, or use it as a launch pad for some entertaining banter, but I am slightly taken aback by her sudden presence, and still preoccupied with wondering quite how that last meeting with Jen ended like it did. So I just smile back at Debbie and shrug in a jovial but non-committal way.

"So what you up to?" she carries on breezily. "Off to work?" Since this is 8.45 on a Friday morning, it's not a bad guess. "Hangover?" she continues. Four questions in a row now. I'll have to answer one of them soon. And since this is still 8.45 on a Friday morning, this last enquiry is not a bad guess either. Debbie knows I like a Thursday night out.

"Morning," I reply, which is short for 'Good Morning' for those who like to be efficient with their use of syllables. "One of those may be correct, Deb. Just the one."

She raises her eyebrows at me and smiles, her hand still on my shoulder. Then she leans in and gives me a quick kiss on the lips. It feels nice.

"Oh dear," she says, "I'm not sure which one I wish were true. What should I wish on you, a day at work or a hangover?"

This is not the most taxing dilemma. "A hangover, for sure," I reply. "It goes away quicker than a day at work, and it's more fun getting rid of it. Bar a few legendary exceptions I admit. Anyway, I'm afraid I don't have a hangover but indeed, yes, I am off to work."

"Ah, what a shame. Well, we can walk together for a bit. I've got to get some shopping in before I start the lunchtime shift." We set off and her hand moves down my arm until it takes my hand. Which unconsciously accepts it before I can consciously worry about the situation. Which should be a blessed relief for all concerned, knowing my conscious brain's tendency to worry.

"Ah, you are doing the early shift today," I offer. "I

177

forgot."

"Yes, what a bonus! You get a much better class of customer during the day."

"Is this some barely veiled comment upon myself and my fellow evening-drinking compatriots?" I ask, now feeling a little more playful. "Surely we can't be as bad as the afternoon crew? It's not like anyone comes to The Red Lion for the food. It's mostly professional drinkers there on an afternoon."

"Well I have seen *you* there before. How professional do you consider yourself?"

"Semi-professional I think. Or maybe an enthusiastic amateur…"

"Very enthusiastic!" then she laughs, causing a few downcast fellow work-bound pedestrians to turn their heads and eye us up, possibly jealously, I don't know. My conscious brain causes me to pretend to bristle at Debbie with indignance. My sub-conscious brain, I notice, just causes me to squeeze her hand gently. As usual I'm glad that it is the sub-conscious that is really in charge. True fact. If you don't believe me, just ask Ted. He's read up loads on the subject.

"Can we agree on 'committed enthusiast'?" I venture.

"Ok, I can live with that," she laughs, and squeezes my hand back. "And no, don't worry. You are nothing like some of my professional drinkers on the afternoon shift. However, they tend to drink quietly. They drink a lot I grant you, but they do behave themselves on the whole, so things don't get out of hand much. It's not as scary as the evening shift. A bit sadder maybe, but not as scary."

"Yeah, suppose you are right. It is like a different place during the day. Evening is not really that scary though!"

"Not usually, but I have noticed that you have just upped and left before if things look like they are about to kick off. I don't have that luxury, unfortunately."

"I never thought of it like that. If I just slink off and miss the trouble I can pretend it never happened. Then I can still feel comfortable when I go back to the place. Trouble is pretty rare though, right?"

"Yeah, it's a good pub really," she admits. "Good sorts in there mainly. Which is why it would be a shame if it were to close, Dan." She then fixes me in the eye and raises her eyebrows expectedly.

"Ah, yes I had been meaning to mention that. I have twelve signatures now. Just nine to go!" I dig out the form from my jacket pocket, now with an inevitable beer stain in one corner, and show her. She nods, not approvingly I think, but she does nod. I'm glad I remembered to get a few more last time I was in.

"Not bad. I would prefer 'none to go', but not bad. These are all regulars, right?"

"Right. In fact, there are a few there where I didn't even know the name of the bloke until they signed it on here. I've just been calling them 'mate' for years. This has been a useful exercise in that way. Don't worry, I'll get the rest at the weekend."

"Great. Well done. What would we do without you?" Then, ahead of me as usual, my guilty sub-conscious takes my hand away from hers. As if she would sense my potential betrayal through my skin. That I may even leave her, the pub, and everything, for the old flame. This time it is my conscious brain who saves the day for once, hastily sending a message to my

179

hand to run my fingers through my hair with the offending hand. 'Without you' she said, I'm repeating in my head, the thought suddenly coalescing into a version of reality for the first time.

"Then what?" I ask, to keep the conversation flowing as I press the 'Wait' button at the crossing with the same hand, even though it's the wrong one.

"We put the form in and the rest of the ACV application to the council," Debbie explains. "Then, and only then, I'm going to tell Tom."

"Rather you than me," I say. "Sorry, just me avoiding trouble again." I grin sheepishly by way of apology or distraction, not sure which, as the lights change.

"Don't worry about me," Debbie says stridently. "He's planning on doing me out of a job, so I'm not going to be shy about that. Just need to make sure it's all official before we tell him, so he can't scupper the application." As I look left and right for the traffic, despite us having the green man, I notice her face (on the right) looking determined, impressive and not a little scary.

Once we get across the road, she looks over at me again, the look on her face only partly receding.

"So, this Jen is still around I hear," she tells me flatly. 'This' Jen. Not some Jen or other but 'this' Jen. Her radar is up on this one, despite my previous resolute assurances that Jen is all in the past, etc etc. Probably because I was being too resolute at the time, I'm guessing. I'm now trying not to look nervous or guilty, and will therefore be failing miserably. My saving grace is that I think I look pretty nervous and guilty most of the time, these days, when I'm sober anyway. So I can only hope that she might not recognise any real feelings underneath this time.

"Yes, she's here until early next week," I find myself replying. "Still seeing her parents. I might see her before she goes this weekend. Just down the pub, you know."

"Right. Then she's off right?"

"Oh, yes. She's off round the world in fact. A year long trip or something like that."

"Ok then, good for her. Good. So, nothing to worry about then?"

"No, she'll be a long way away!" I assure her. What I neglect so say, as you may have noticed, is that *I* may be a long way away too! But at least, because of this omission, her face softens as we stop on the pavement. This is where I turn left for the office and she carries on down the High Street. She places my hands around her waist and she kisses me again. Extremely nice. I hug her tight, mostly because it feels great, partly to silently say sorry, partly to avoid looking her in the eye. We then part, but I do stay and wave at her when she turns around again, forty-two steps later.

I find myself mulling over this, as I turn and amble towards the office door. One good thing about having low self-esteem, if you choose to see it that way, is that you can just blithely assume that you are worthless. The result of which is that you can then choose to believe that you can do whatever you like, because no one is going to care what you do either way. You can go away, because no one will miss you. You can stay, because no one is going to notice that you are still here. Wallowing with low self-esteem is no fun, don't get me wrong, but it can sure make

181

things easy. You can just wallow away on your own, be an island. But we're not ever really on our own for long, are we? And I am starting to admit to myself now the obvious fact that I am not on my own anymore, as I reach the door of my building. Bloody hell, Dan, trust you to spoil this, you idiot. This *should* be a nice feeling!

But this feeling, in fact, is something else. It means something else. It means this. I realise that I now have the power to hurt people again. Which is the last thing I want.

It feels like a long work day, as most of them do, but I got my head down and eventually it is all over without much cause for comment. I received a text from Rachel at lunchtime, asking if I wanted to meet for a coffee after work, since she would be in the area. She did not say why she wanted to meet. But there doesn't need to be a reason to meet my sister even at the best of times. And these certainly are not the best of times, so I could not say no, even though the location would not be of my choosing. You see, Rachel has recently taken to calling on me when she is missing Dad. It's not like I even look like him, or act that much like him. I get what she is trying to do though. I sort of feel closer to him when I'm with her too, in a weird way. In terms of our part of the family, each other is all we have left, a sad truncated leftover of the unit we grew up in. Watching her suffer makes me feel ten times worse than usual though, so I confess I have mixed feelings as I leave my desk for the day.

And so, because of this, I seem to have found myself in a café for God's sake, and somewhat out of my comfort zone. Rachel texted me again to say she was running a little late, so I'm sitting on my own on a table next to the window. I'm staring at the menu, if that's what you call it, but nothing is leaping out at me. I'll need to order something soon, before the nice lady comes around again. Otherwise this could get embarrassing. I just wish there was 'coffee' and I would pick that. Ah, looking down the bottom I see that they do tea. I'll have a tea then. But which tea? Jesus! Maybe I'll just have the English Breakfast. It's the afternoon but what the hell. Ooh no, hang on, they've got Oolong. Oolong is awesome!

I bumped into Oolong tea a couple of years ago at a work conference. It is without doubt the only thing I took away from that conference. Well, that and a free pen that lasted but a month. I was about to put a splash of milk in it, purely out of habit I guess, but I read on the packet that it was best without milk. Later on, when I had bought a box myself, I tested this out. Wish I hadn't. Take it from me, just put the milk down and walk away when you are having an Oolong. It's made from the tea plant just like tea is, but the leaves get twisted and bruised in a particular way then baked, again in a particular way. There's something about it being fermented too but I got a bit lost at that point and just drank the tea. Anyway, it comes from China and there's lots of people there who will do all the growing, bruising and baking for you just right, so you don't have to. Which is just as well, as it sounds like an awful palaver to me, despite the excellent final results. This is just one thing in a long list of things that make me wonder how they ever got invented at all. I mean, who was the first guy who decided to bruise some tea leaves then ferment and bake them a bit and maybe try that a hundred times until something came out that didn't taste like grass juice? Beer is also on this list. Who decided that adding barley, malt, hops, water and yeast together, then leaving it for a bit, was going to be a good idea? Must have been a slow day. And football, how did that all happen? Anyway, I hope you found that little tea tip useful. Hey, I'm not just about beer you know. I have hidden depths, me.

The tea itself comes along, in a lovely large round, and very white, cup, in about the time it takes me to think about the above. Rachel comes in shortly afterwards, waves at me from across the shop, then effortlessly orders some coffee or other from the bar (which I did not know you could do) with barely a thought. This is clearly home territory for her in a way that The Red Lion probably isn't. In a sudden wave of empathy, I realise that maybe this is how she feels when I insist that we meet down the pub. There are some awkward minutes as she waits for what seems like an age for her coffee to appear, and I remain at my seat, not knowing whether to come over to say hello, or whether she is about to come over to me at any moment. Like I said, I'm out of my depth in here. Rachel must have looked over and waved about three times before her brew finally arrives and she wanders over. At that point, finally, I get up and give her a hug by way of a greeting.
"Hi sis. Had a good day?"
"Yes, busy busy! I've been…whatever is *that* in your

184

cup?"

"An Oolong!" I reply.

"Oolong?"

"It's a tea. It's nice. Felt a bit intimidated by the coffee menu to be honest, so plumped for this instead. Is it bad form not to have a coffee in a coffee shop?"

"No, it's fine. Of course it's fine, Dan. How are you anyway?"

"Just got out of work. Same old. Otherwise, fine," I inform her, in a way that tells her I'm not fine really. You know the way.

"Hmm," she says, letting me know she has picked up on that particular contradiction, as she gets herself comfortable. "I'm 'fine' too, today. Trying to keep myself busy, with other people's jobs." A sigh, a brief pause then she starts up again. "You know, just for a moment, a brief moment, I forgot that Dad was gone. Stupid I know, but I was rushing around and got all distracted, and then the thought just popped up that I should go over and see him since I was in town." She sips her coffee and looks up at me as she continues. "But then it hit me that I couldn't. And never would. Silly, isn't it?"

"No, no, not silly at all, sis. I get that all the time. Especially after a few beers."

She's beginning to tear up already. She must have been holding this back all afternoon, just waiting to talk to me. Poor thing. Oh God, she's going to set me off too if I'm not careful. And I don't want to start diluting my Oolong, which is a phrase I did not think I'd be using today when I woke up this morning. I am, of course, feeling guilty again because my 'not fine' was actually about the Jen-Debbie thing. It

185

should have been about Dad too, but it wasn't, not this time anyway. Maybe that's because I'm always missing Dad and I've just got used to it? Yeah, let's run with that.

Rachel continues. "Then I got to thinking about all the times I didn't go and see him. Always had something else to do. The boys needed picking up or something. Something that seemed important at the time, but seems so damn unimportant now. Something that I never got thanked for and kept me away from my own Dad in the last days I had with him! You and me, we argued about that sometimes, I recall…"

"Oh, now now, I wouldn't say 'argued' per se. I just wanted some help sometimes, you know. When you could…"

"Yes, I remember. I just don't get why those other things were so important. On the day they seemed like they were more important. But now? How could they have been? How? Jesus, what I wouldn't give for an hour with him now!"

I didn't know things could get this emotional in coffee shops, as well as in pubs. She's right though. I've had those same thoughts and it does indeed feel awful. But at least I was there with Dad for most of it all, so that is one thing I don't feel guilty about.

"Yeah, well, don't beat yourself up about it," I say, without a hint of the irony that usually accompanies that arrangement of words. "We were all trying to balance everything. It's hard to know what to do for the best. And there's no manual for this. No rules, Rach."

She sighs, and leans in to take the hot coffee steam up

186

her nostrils. Which looks more appealing than I'm making it sound.

"Yeah well. I miss him now, that's all," she tells her coffee.

"Yeah, me too. Sorry."

"Don't be daft 'lil bro. What have you got to be sorry about? You were an angel!"

Time to change the subject. We start talking about Dad, and Mum, for a bit, but from when they were alive, back when we were kids. Rachel reminds me of one particular time that I had completely forgotten about until now.

It was the day that Jasper went missing. Well, maybe not *the* day. It takes a couple of days, maybe even three, when you finally accept that your cat is not out on a feline bender and may in fact be in a bit of trouble, or worse. It's a gradual realisation, but, at some point, dread hits you regardless. He had been gone for a day or two on occasions before, but not for some years by this time. No, by this stage in his life he had pretty much settled into his daily routine, and we now took those habits for granted. I was still a kid, so didn't know what I could do to help. I tried looking around the garden for him, then tried ignoring the fact that this was all happening, holed up in my bedroom, willing that all would be well when I reappeared downstairs. Like my absence would work some kind of magic, or something equally dumb. Even then I must have had the idea of observation affecting the outcome again, like the quantum physics enthusiast I eventually became. Anyway, neither worked. Dad was gone when I came down the third time. Mum was pacing the kitchen but had nothing much to say. I did not dare ask where Dad was. Had he too disappeared like Jasper did, never to return? Rachel had no such misgivings however.

"Where's Dad, Mum? Why isn't he looking for Jasper?"

"He *is* looking for Jasper, hun," she replied, trying to affect a calm demeanour, but cracking towards the end of the sentence. "He's gone out in the car, in case Jasper's been run over."

"Mum!" Rachel bellowed. "Don't say that! You'll make it happen. When did he go? When is he back?"

"Er, twenty minutes maybe. I don't know when he's coming back."

"Is he going to find Jasper?" she said, continuing her insistent line of questioning.

"I don't know…" Mum faltered.

I just stayed quiet, next to Mum, and stared at her apron from a distance of about an inch, waiting for something to happen. I focussed on the tiniest part of a picture of an onion, or at least that's how I remember it, while this exchange carried on in the background, in much the same manner as it had begun. Rachel must have thought that more information, rather than magical absence, would solve this problem. I assume that, by then, I had discovered the lesson that more information usually just brought you more worry. Not the trivia, you understand. Trivia is just fine. I mean the real stuff. Like people dying, or leaving, or changing. That stuff.

Then the door suddenly opened, and banged shut again. Dad always shouted through a hearty 'hello' when he got back home, but there was silence this time. We all had to turn and look down the hall to check whether it was actually him who had come in. "Did you find him?" Rachel asked, running towards him, as I continued to grab onto Mum's apron tightly and stare at the onion.

Dad just shook his head, and exhaled loudly. Then finally he shrugged, and stared at us blankly with tired eyes. I thought Dad knew everything, right up to that point. I thought he could do anything. But now I could see he was as lost and bereft as the rest of us. As lost and bereft as me.

Jasper, as it turned out, was in our neighbour's shed all that time. He had found a gloriously sunny spot next to the window and presumably was enjoying it immensely when the neighbours locked up and went away for the weekend, unaware of the presence of an additional guest. He was a little chatty, and very hungry when he finally returned on Sunday evening, having been released from his weekend prison, but he still managed to keep a certain nonchalant coolness that not one of the four humans in the house could muster. Not then, and not for days afterwards. Mum even let me and Rachel stay up late that evening to be with him, and Dad was even late going down the pub.

"God, you were insistent at that age," I tell Rachel, once the story is retold. She just laughs, proud of her former self, so sure of everything. Jealous too I expect, of the girl she was before real life and all the resulting doubts inevitably kicked in. Then she looks at her watch and says she has to go and pick up…er, one of the men in her life, husband, son, whichever one that was today. There's always someone she has to pick up.

189

"Oh, I nearly forgot," I say, as she hugged me goodbye. "You drink down The Red Lion occasionally…"

"Only when you make me, Dan…"

"I never made you when you were seventeen…"

"Ok, fair enough, what about it?"

"Would you sign this form for me?" I ask her. "We are trying to keep the place open."

She reads the form and then signs it. "No problem," she smiles as she hands it back to me. "I would surely not like to see the state *you* would be in if you lost The Red Lion too. You've been through enough, little brother."

That innocent enough statement fair cuts me in two as she hands the form back to me and gives me a goodbye kiss on the cheek. A lot of innocent enough statements are doing that these days. I can't even handle it when someone is nice to me now. I don't deserve it, you see. But I can't tell anyone that, can I, so don't they just keep on being nice. And yes, because of my silence they will continue cutting me in two, blissfully ignorant of the wounds they make. It is one type of price that I have to pay, I suppose.

"What?" states Amy, to me, over the top of her pint glass that evening.

"What *what*?" I reply defensively, into my glass, then proceed to empty it.

"What…" she continues, "is going on with you?"

"Nothing. I'm good."

"You're '*good*'?"

"Well," I reply even more defensively, "considering…"

"Considering what?"

"You know…"

"Argh! God!" she grabs my glass roughly and takes it over to the bar, leaving me to wonder what I have done. Or indeed not done. She was going to go anyway, it is her round after all. She didn't ask me what I wanted next though, which is sometimes bad form. Soon enough she brings me back what looks, smells and tastes like my last one, a 'Verbosity', 4.5%. Somewhat over the usual strength but needs must.

"Men!" she resumes, unabashed, but without further clarity.

"*All* men?" I check cautiously.

"Men," she continues, "are totally rubbish at talking about their feelings."

"Er, *I* talk about my feelings…"

"Only when you are really drunk, you do," she responds, "and even then you don't make much sense."

Hmm, she may have a point. "Well, that's better than nothing," I assure her, somewhat weakly.

"Maybe, but Dan, you know you can talk to *me,* right? About anything. You've been through so much recently and you've hardly said a thing. You hardly said anything real about the funeral, or Jen coming back, or anything real. All this internalisation you do, it's not, I don't know, *healthy.*"

I take a swig of 'Verbosity'. Wow, this brew hits your taste buds between the eyes, if you see what I mean. She's right of course, she most certainly is right. But that alone is not going to be enough to open *me* up. I mean, what would she say if she knew everything? I mean *everything*. Even more than I've told you.

191

Would she still want to even know me? Would she just give me a hug and tell me I did the right thing? But does she deserve the chance to choose? Do I, on the other hand, deserve to be judged by everyone who knows me? Who the hell has the right to know all that about me? Yeah, yeah, yeah, this conundrum will keep me silent for a good while yet, knowing me. Which, inevitably, will keep Matthew Hopkins as my sole confessor. And you don't need to tell me how unhealthy that is. However, looking over at her, as I ponder this, I know that I should at least give Amy a little something.

"I suppose so," I admit. "Yeah, I have been through a lot. And I do miss Dad. I miss him all the time." I take a swig. I have to be careful here. I'm scared that if I start to say anything real I might not be able to stop. But I can carry on just a little more. "Actually, I miss how he used to be you know? Not how he was at the end, or when he got really ill. There was, er, some relief mixed in there at the end to be honest." There really was too. If I'm being honest, it was the thought of the relief that kept me going right at the end. Oops, 'Verbosity' is taking me too far here already.

Amy nods at me kindly. "Oh yes, I'm sure there was. For all of us, in a smaller way. But you shouldn't feel guilty about that, you really mustn't. It was terribly difficult on all of you, and you are bound to feel some relief. You're only human. Relief for your Dad too. He wasn't having much of a life by then, was he? Very sad…"

I look at her eyes as she says these words, unknowingly inflicting another wound upon me. Would she understand, if she knew everything? Could

192

she *really* understand? I take another swig but I back away from a response, just nod instead and purse my lips. I let her speak next.

"Ok, ok," Amy says. "I'll leave you alone. But be careful, will you? It's a real problem, you know. I've been hearing about this so much recently. You know, that so many men can't express themselves properly these days, and it's cited as the main cause of male suicide. I'm not saying that *you* would, it's just that you just don't look well sometimes, and that's the main cause of death in men under 40. That's crazy. Just for not opening up? I mean, who said that opening up is a sign of weakness!"

"It isn't. I know it isn't, Amy. Yeah," I sigh. "It does seem crazy now you put it that way. But a lot of people do say that. A lot of men anyway."

"No wonder there is so much loneliness out there," she continues to rant. "It's a mental health time bomb! How did we all get so bloody repressed? How did we all get so bloody distant?" 'Verbosity' is taking effect on the other side of the table too, it seems. Appropriately named stuff, that. But Amy now seems to have run out of steam having reached this point, and she then begins to swill her drink around the glass in frustration. I hate to see her like that, even for a moment. She is my *friend*. So I reach over and take her hand.

"I *am* ok, Amy. And I *can* talk to you, I know that." Jesus, I wish just one of those statements was remotely true.

Chapter 13

I cannot tell a lie, I *was* worried about the coroner and the police and all that. Really worried. I'm somewhat paranoid at the best of times after all, and I've watched enough cop shows and movies to know that this sort of thing always dominates the narrative of any story. But, in reality, all that stuff went by in a flash without much incident to report. By the time my heart had stopped pounding, my head had stopped spinning and my nails were all chewed down to minimal levels, it was all over. The system went off to deal with someone else's problems and left me alone to my own. I'm listening to a story on the radio now about a series of stabbings in the area. One of the victims died. That will be keeping people busy instead I suppose. Sorry if all this bursts the dramatic tension for you here.

Inside my head though, it has all been happening, and it's not just the memories of things that actually happened that I can't get rid of. Every dark possibility has been invented, embellished and relived by me, again and again. Then Matthew Hopkins introduced himself and has been informing me of my certain fate ever since. I've told him to bog off, but he's a persistent blighter for a configuration of electrical pathways in my brain. Which is all personal demons have ever been throughout history, right? Knowing that should help I suppose, but it doesn't. It seriously does not.

So yes, I have been suitably plagued by worry, if that makes you feel any better, while I have been quietly pretending that I am not. All fair enough. What I had not been worried about, however, until just now, was the visit to the Probate Solicitor, the guy who has been taking care of Dad's will and estate. Rachel and myself are currently sitting quietly in the solicitors' waiting room, worrying. After a manic bout of chit chat on the way here we have now given up to a nervous silence. So has everyone else in the room, as it goes. They are all here for various reasons, all of them bad, in one way or the other. If I met any of these people down the pub I might find out what some of their stories were. But I won't find out here, this is not that sort of place. Presently, the Probate Solicitor, Mr. Charles, comes out to greet us. He knows me and Rachel already, since he sorted out the Power of Attorney for us when Dad realised he was getting ill. Therefore he greets us warmly, while maintaining a professional distance, using our surnames. He shakes our hands, escorts us to his office, then offers us a drink, which we both politely refuse. It was only water after all.

So why am I worried today? Let me tell you. I'm now worried that something *good* is going to happen, that's why. Here goes.

"Well, as you know we have been administering the remains of the estate of your father as per the provisions set out in the will, and following settlement of various expenses, funeral, care costs, donations as per the will, er, our costs etc, we are now in a position to divide the remains of the estate equally between the both of you, according to the wishes of the, er, deceased."

I glance over at Rachel at this point, who is already glancing over at me. She just looks like she wants this over with. She looks guilty too, even though she has nothing to feel guilty about. I know she could do with the money, with Don's business not doing so well, I gather, and with two voracious consumers in the shape of my nephews. But no one wants to have money come to them in this way, not really. You would swap it all in a heartbeat to have your loved one back again, as long as you had a semblance of a heart to be beating. But things are as they are, and so we carry on and make the best of it. We're just not going to feel good about it, that's all, and me even less so.

"Firstly," begins Mr. Charles, "there is the schedule of personal items, much according to our previous conversations. He hands us a piece of paper each. In it are photos, paintings, records and the like. And books of course. Some for me, some for Rachel. I notice that near the bottom of my page a box of concert tickets and programs is mentioned. In that box should have been the ticket that I have already taken for myself, the one that I took that night and has ever since been tucked away in my jeans pocket. It seems to burn my leg as I see it mentioned on the page. I shouldn't have it yet, but I do. My leg is not really burning, I know this. This is just my neurons misbehaving again. But this changes the feeling not one jot. Everything is experienced through the neurons after all, real or otherwise.

Mr. Charles pauses, then raises his eyebrows and

clears his throat, to give the next moment a little more gravitas perhaps. "There is some, er, good news, if you forgive me, here, in that your father's estate has not largely been swallowed up by care costs. This is so common nowadays…" He looks to us from over the top of his glasses. I just see Matthew Hopkins staring back at me. The Witchfinder knows why we did not incur such huge care costs. 'Don't judge me, Hopkins. This was not why', I think back at him. "…I always hate to see the look on the faces of the beneficiaries when they realise nothing much is left…" Mr. Charles continues with a shake of his head, then pulls back, realising he is close to losing his professional veneer. "Anyway, I have written down the amount for you here."

He passes us a piece of paper. Four eyebrows achieve a position slightly closer to the ceiling than before. Then comes the guilt again, stronger than before. Rachel doesn't know what to think, her face keeping changing between what the subconscious is showing and what her conscious wants to show. I look away, so she can perform this facial dance unobserved. Then, once we finally leave the solicitors' office after completing the paperwork, we go our separate ways with a hug, still not knowing quite what to say yet.

About what I said earlier, by the way, about not telling a lie. It's not true. I *can* tell a lie. You know that, you've seen me. But you also know it because you also know that you can too, in case you were tempted into being overly judgemental. Sorry, I don't mean to be spiky. We don't all have to pretend to be heroes you know. Heroes rarely exist, not like our storytellers would have us think anyway. You know, I

197

really don't understand these perfect heroes you see in films or read of in books, with their perfectly simple moral alignments. I can't empathise with them. I'd like to punch most of them in the face, but I won't. Partly because they are fictional, but mainly because they are generally ex-military and armed to the teeth.

Fancy a pint? Don't worry I can afford it. I'm 'celebrating' my windfall. Stick around if you don't mind the sarcasm.

Ted does not mind sarcasm one bit, so he is more than willing to hear all about my meeting, once I send him a text with the 'emergency pint S.O.S.' message. He's rather jolly until I ask him for some advice as to what I should do with the money.
"I want nothing to do with that, Dan. Don't even talk to me about the money. I told you before, it's nothing to do with me," he says insistently, almost angrily. This comes out of nowhere and is somewhat out of character, so it takes me back a bit I must say. It must be contrary to some code or other that he lives by. Or maybe I'm being insensitive in some other way. Hmm, I don't know, probably both. So how do we deal with this conversational bump in the road? Should we talk it through, share our feelings? Like hell we do! Here's what happens.

Ted just takes a few sips in order to avoid eye contact and to give me time to change the subject. And so I do. No need for apologies here, you see. They only prolong the point of conflict. No, just change the subject and move on, that is all that is required. This is an unspoken convention being invoked here, one we are all used to in here, so I oblige immediately, by instinct even. It indeed helps that I previously had not ordered two pints of 'Unexpected Outcomes'. I liked the name, but it came in at a whopping 7.8%, so a glass of that each would have changed our demeanour considerably under such tense circumstances. Instead I opted for two pints of the 'Expected Outcomes', 3.8%. Under this more mellow influence, I swiftly tell Ted about the number of signatures I have for the ACV to keep the pub open, which is the other thing on my mind today, and surely safer territory. Ted stops sipping and congratulates me. Then we try and work out who we can get tonight to fill up the remaining names we need, and in due course get another pint in. Still, it remains a little awkward, in my mind at least. I hastily text Jez and Amy while Ted is next at the Gents to ask them to come along too. I have to be quick, as The Red Lion has excellent hand dryers, as I may well have mentioned before.

Jez and Amy do come in a short time later, in order to rescue me, if only a little. Well, I thought they might rescue me, but I am in slight trouble with them too, I find. I'm spending too much time with my new girlfriend apparently (I'm not sure if they mean the new-new one or the new-old one, take your pick) and have forgotten my friends, they say. Crikey, sometimes it's just not your day, is it? But at least they sign the ACV form, which I shamefully only remember to pass them while looking to change the subject.

And, they are also eventually able to listen to my news about the money I will be getting from Dad. It is Ted who immediately vocalises the idea that has been running around wordless in my head all day.

"Well, you sure can afford that trip around the world with Jen now, can't you?" he says, and sits back, as if his job was done with that contribution. Amy just stares at me over her pint, waiting for a stray facial expression to show her the truth of my feelings, and wondering what else I haven't told her. Fortunately for me I still don't know what that truth is, so I am able to remain a mystery for one more day. In this way we progress to chucking out time, me having successfully avoided any further progress on any subject, and I head home to another inevitably sleepless night.

That previous evening down The Lion was a little more stressful than I would have hoped, so I'm avoiding the place today, which, since it is a Saturday afternoon, is a small yet significant sacrifice. No, instead I am down the park. Not having a run, you understand, but having a sit down on a park bench and listening to the bird song. In happier news, down The Red Lion last night we did indeed get the last signatures for the ACV that we needed, the last one towards the end of the evening. Phase one complete! Debbie will be pleased when I meet her later and let her know. But now what? No idea. I hope she has an idea. She normally does. I'm not sure that I'm going to tell her about the money though. Dad's money. I mean, it's not like it's *that* much. Look, I'm not going to turn into one of these lottery winners whose life is ruined by their windfall, it's not like it's *that* much.

But it will make a big difference to me. It takes away all the major obstacles, so I can do, for once in my life, what the hell I want. I know I don't deserve it, I know that more than anyone, but there it is. Maybe I should just give it all up to charity, but that seems like an easy way out in some way, a few drops in a large ocean that I can just walk away and forget about. A cheap way to buy back my soul. But there is no legacy there, no resolution, and, with that, no forgiveness possible. I mean forgiving myself, of course. No one else is going to even get the chance to forgive me. They are not even going to know that there is anything to forgive. So I plan to bear that burden on my own.

It is while I am in this mind-set that a priest, of all people, sits next to me on the other end of my park bench, to have a sandwich it seems. To my surprise, rather than walk off, pretending to have something else to do, and after the appropriate time to still seem polite of course, I look up and say hello.

Priests talk to people out here in the real world, I guess, in much the same way that I like to talk to people down the pub. The talking is part of their job, if you can describe what they do as a job at all. I have no idea. So, once I have broken the ice, the conversation just flows, since we are both conversational professionals in our own way. As I watch him feed the crusts of his sandwich to the birds, who have already congregated around us (sorry, couldn't resist the pun), I ask him if the birds know him well, or whether it is just the uniform. "The uniform?" he asks, breaking off another piece of bread, splitting it into four pieces, then scattering them to the four pigeons in front of him. I hope he's got some more bread, as there will be more than four pigeons here in a minute, guaranteed.

"Er, is that not what you call it?" I ask, waving my hands generally in the direction of his dog collar and black shirt, and black trousers.

"It's not really how I think of it, no. But I see what you mean."

"At least you don't get people asking you what you do for a living," I observe, hoping this sounds better in real life than it just did from inside my head. "I hate it when people ask me that."

He looks me in the eye and smiles benignly. I must pay attention to how he does that. I can't quite pull off 'benign'. The nearest I get to that is 'happy drunk'. Even when I've not been drinking, apparently. "True," he replies sadly, something obviously already playing on his mind today, "but the garb does get me a lot else besides."

"It does? Er, what do you mean?"

"Well, my friend, it's always an open invitation for people to unload their problems onto me, is it not? Because of this…let's just say attire…people just come up and talk to me, *at* me even, without any introduction, no matter what I may be in the middle of. Or how I'm feeling. I get the saddest stories from people before they even know my name. Or I theirs."

"Tell me about it," I say. He stops breaking off bread for a moment, and looks at me quizzically, wondering if I'm taking the piss or not. I'm not as it goes. "I'm not taking the piss," I say, immediately regretting that particular choice of words. "I'm quite the

202

conversationalist too, at least when I'm in there." I point over to The Red Lion, which stands almost opposite this park. Look, I just said I wasn't going *in* there this afternoon. I didn't say I wasn't going to be *near* there, did I?

The priest looks over to the pub, then at me, and nods his head, as if acknowledging the presence of a kindred spirit of sorts, or so I'm suddenly hoping.

"Sorry about saying 'piss'" I add, "er…again. Sorry." He just laughs and takes a bite of his sandwich.

"I've heard worse," he chuckles through cheese, bread and pickle. "Don't worry. Are you a Catholic?"

"No, I'm not," I reply.

"In which case you can call me Michael."

"Hello Michael. Dan."

"Hello Dan. How's your day going then?"

"Er, fine I suppose. How's yours?"

He looks over to me again. "Funny, no one ever asks me that."

"Tell me about it," I reply. Then "No, I mean it, you can tell me about it. If you want. I'm no expert but you seem like you could do with it."

Turns out my powers of conversation also extend to places near The Red Lion, as well as the pub itself. I have to imagine a pint in my hand though, just to get me in the right place emotionally. Michael, as it turns out, has had a bad week. It's not a crisis of faith, much to my relief. I would have had little to offer him on that subject. His mother is ill though. Back in Ireland. And that I *can* empathise with.

"They've been pretty good with me you know. I've been allowed a bit of time to go back."

"They?" I ask.

203

"The Diocese."

"Right." By 'right' I am letting him know that I understand what he means without needing to offer any opinion on the subject. A common trick we use across the road when the asking of too many questions would just spoil the moment. I actually have no idea what a diocese is. Maybe that's his boss. Not the Big Boss in the sky, just some human one. With a bigger collar maybe. Or a different coloured one. I have absolutely no idea what I am talking about. Which is why I just say 'right' so we can get on with the business of him talking and me listening. This trick gets used all the time. It is the lubricant of the casual chit-chat.

"But we are very busy here. Short-staffed you could say!" he laughs ironically. I'm betting that this is not the style he employs during his Sunday sermon. "And there are people who rely on me here."

"Right." Yes, that's me, at it again. Lubricating.

"I shouldn't complain really, Dan. Actually, I *don't* complain. Not out loud."

I move my hand halfway up to my face, to take a sip from my imaginary pint. Then I decide it probably looks weird, so I pretend to scratch my shoulder and allow him to carry on.

"But these people sometimes come to me with such, I'm sorry, *petty* problems. And I'm just thinking if I could have those problems and swap them for mine, I would be, you know, *happy*. Well, no, not happy. You know what I mean."

"I do know what you mean," I assure him. This time I actually mean it. I could have told him then about the cancer patient I met once, who felt sorry for me, or my Dad at least, while I was visiting Dad in hospital. He had made the calculation that, no matter how bad his cancer was, at least it wasn't Alzheimer's. Maybe this has some relevance, but this moment is for Michael, not for me, so I keep that thought to myself. Silence, from one party, is also another important lubricant sometimes, to get the story told.

"I pray about it. I have confessed. I feel better for a while. Then the feeling comes back again."

"Don't worry, mate. You're only human. Maybe the uniform works to make people forget that. I expect that's the idea, right?"

"Yes, partly…"

"But there's the downside. The, er *Michael* in you doesn't get a fair chance to breathe. *Father Michael* takes all the oxygen, right?"

He then eyes me up with a look of bewilderment. I carry on regardless, on a roll, perhaps buoyed by the proximity of the pub, my hand still holding my imaginary glass. "I don't know, but I'm betting people don't stop to think of you as a real human being at all. I'm guessing they talk to the collar most of the time."

He takes a moment to think about this. I'm betting he doesn't have conversations like this much.

"And what about you?" he asks. Standard stalling technique.

"Me?" I stall in return.

"Do they treat you like a real a human being in *there*?" He nods over to the pub sign, visible through the trees. "When they tell you about all their troubles."

I sit back and chuckle. I wasn't expecting that. I have

205

to have a quick 'think' about that so put on the appropriate 'thinking' facial expression so he knows this too. It doesn't take me long to answer him though.

"They do, actually. Yes. They do."

He stares back at me for a moment, his eye meeting my eye, but not uncomfortably so. Then he says, "Good for you, Dan. Good for you."

I would normally say 'cheers' at this point. But I can't really do that here, so I say nothing at all for a moment. Instead, we just watch as the pigeons land and grow in number from four, to eight, to twenty and beyond.

We might have called it a day there. On another day I might have just shaken his hand and wandered off. But something about the moment made me stay, and it wasn't just that I was scared of wading through quite so many hungry pigeons. I told him about my Mum and Dad, while he was finishing his lunch. How it all gets worse, and how it might get a little better afterwards, in time. How people treat you sometimes. Nice, but different. Like your misfortune is somehow infectious.

"Ha, I feel like I'm in confession or something," I laugh after a while, "talking to you like this."

"You haven't been to confession before then I take it."

"God no. Sorry, don't mean to um…"

"Blaspheme?"

"That's it. Don't mean to…um…anyway…"

"No problem. Really. You don't have to walk on eggshells. I experience the worst, and the best, humanity has to offer every day. You, I think, sit nicely in between." He smiles at me, perhaps playfully, as he says this, waiting for a reaction. "Proud to be average Michael. I am, in fact, an enthusiast for the mediocre. I shall take no offence. But no, I have never been to confession. I take it that it's not much like sitting on a park bench chatting, with a bunch of pigeons listening in."

"Ha, no, not usually. It could be, I imagine, in some churches. But no, it's not normally like this. Maybe I should put that idea to the diocese."

"So long as I get a credit."

"Indeed. So, Dan…"

"Uh huh?"

"Would there be anything you would want to talk about?"

"Sure, loads of things."

"I mean, you know, to return the favour, would there be anything you might feel that you need to open up about?"

"Jesus, no! Sorry…again. I mean, no thank you, but no. Confession is not my thing. Really."

A moment of silence, the gap between our worlds having lost its bridge in that misjudged moment. But it was lost only for a moment, as it goes. Michael composes himself and says "Sorry, I misread that. Believe it or not, people normally want to confess things to me."

"They do?" The surprise in my voice is genuine.

"Yes, it can make you feel better."

"I see. It *does*? Really? I'd never thought of it like that. Anyway, this time let's just say thanks but no thanks."

"I apologise," he tells me.

"No need, really. Actually, you just reminded me of someone I met a while ago. You might know her."

"I might?"

"Yeah, she was, *is* I mean, a Catholic."

"Well there are quite a lot of us, Dan."

"Ha, yes, I know. But she is from round here. I think so anyway. I met her here. By which I mean *there*." I point to The Red Lion again.

"Oh, right?" he says, raising an eyebrow, his curiosity duly piqued. "What is her name?"

"Bernadette…I think."

"Bernadette? Really?" he asks, more surprised than I expected.

"Yes, really. Is there anything unusual with that? I thought it was a Catholic type of name."

"It is, sorry, yes, it is. But you don't really meet that many Bernadettes in real life, round here at least. I don't think I know of a single one in my parish…"

"I don't think she was a regular churchgoer to be honest. She was more of a regular attendee in my, er, parish as it were." I nod over to the pub again.

He nods to let me know he has picked up on my inference. "What did she look like?"

I describe her, as best I can from a hazy memory. He looks at me intently, trying to make the connection from his memory with what I am saying. Presently he gives me that eureka moment face, the one I sometimes get when me and Jez are trying to piece together the events of the night before, after a particularly large bender.

"Yes…" he drawls out, still unsure. "Quite a drinker, yes?"

"Even by my standards, I'm afraid so, yes."

"I think someone like that came to one of our help groups a while back. Last year for a while. Something like that. Don't recall the name I'm sorry to say, or if she even told us her real one."

"Oh, good. Did you manage to help her then?"

That question takes the 'eureka' look off his face. Michael replaces that look with one for which the word 'glum' could have been first coined.

"No, not this one. She stuck it out for a few weeks, but she came back one day in a right state. She was a little abusive, to be honest. Abusive to me would have been fine, I can take that. But she started yelling at some of the other addicts. And she was breathing alcohol breath over the alcoholics. And that was particularly troubling one of the group, Clive, I can tell you. I couldn't risk that. I hated myself, but I had to ask her to leave. What I meant was that she should leave just for now. What I meant to say was that she was welcome back next time. But I never quite got those words out in the moment. Anyway, she did leave, eventually, once she had finished her rant. Trouble is, she never did come back. That's all I know. Can't imagine we had a happy ending there. But I remember her. I pray for her. Do you think that was your Bernadette then?"

"Maybe," I reply. "Sounds like it could be. Hard to know for sure. If so, it seems like she just didn't belong in either of our churches, did she?"

"She would always be welcome back to mine, Dan."

"Well, maybe, maybe not. She'd be best off keeping out of mine that's for sure."

I didn't say it, but I felt that if she was ever to resurface again, it would unfortunately be me who

209

saw her first. Instead, me and Michael chit chat about the strength of communion wine, which I find out has to be pretty potent for some reason. You sure can learn some strange stuff when you strike up a conversation. Then suddenly, as if due to some hidden calling, it was time for him to go.

"Thank you for the chat, Dan. It was nice to meet you. Perhaps we shall meet again." Michael says, as he gets up to leave. We shake hands and I smile.

"I dare say we might," I offer.

"You are always welcome in church."

"And you are always welcome down the pub, even if the wine is not up to your usual standards. That, I guess, is probably the more likely venue of the two, if I'm being honest."

He just smiles as he takes his hand back, turns and walks away with a wave. I wave back.

As I watch the pigeons finally get bored and move away to more promising locations, I try and push away thoughts of Bernadette. I imagine her cleaned up and happy in some other town elsewhere, but the idea doesn't stick somehow. The idea of confession, however, won't go away from my mind, despite being well and truly rejected by my conscious brain. The thought that it somehow might be a healing force is taken by my subconscious, and I know that I won't be able to get rid of it now. What I can do, though, is try and lock it away with all the other crap I don't want in my head, but nevertheless just won't leave.

I used to think that I kept my sanity through a lack of sobriety. Holding back the demons with the beer and all that. Now I'm not so sure that was ever true. Maybe I've been slowly going mad whether I drink or not, and I just notice less when I'm drunk. But where does that leave me now? And how much of my sanity will be left by the time I finally figure that one out? I wish…I just wish this was easier. Is that too much to ask?

Third note inn the mattere of The Red Lion Witch
Matthew Hopkins, Witch finder-General

Your trial begins, witch. If you swim… the mark of Satan is upon you. Then you must hang.

We will know your guilt. You can confess to God and your Devill.

~

I'm at the pond again, and this time I'm not even drunk. It's only lunchtime. Hopkins infects the whole of my days now. The gates are open, so I could walk through if I wanted to, physically. But I stay here on the bench. I can't face him anymore. Dad. So now he has been taken away from me again. But I know that there is no sympathy to be had for me. I will get what I deserve.

I feel a couple of people sit by me on the bench. I don't catch their eye, but I slowly gather that it is a five-year-old child and her father, having some snack or other. I budge up to give them more room, even though they have plenty already. I feel the girl glance over at me briefly before she turns back to her apple, sliced neatly into bite-sized chunks.

I stare at the water, saying nothing, and wonder what the moment will be like when these two come to the end of their own relationship. It's coming. They are not thinking of this today, but it's coming. Time is always running out. We are just so very good at fooling ourselves that it isn't, happy to wallow in the bliss of another obvious lie.

The water stares back at me, inviting me in. Maybe I would sink after all. That would be wonderful. Sink down and down, metre by metre, taking on the same

213

innocence that I myself had as a five-year-old, simply enjoying lunch with my Dad in the park.

But I can't do that now. That moment has to be for no one else but me. I get up, place another stone in my pocket and walk away, head down. Sigh. No matter, I can always come back later.

Chapter 14

Debbie and I have just completed another visit at the care home. I mainly listened to a charming fellow called Duncan, who said that he and his friends came up with the perfect political solution to poverty and world peace. They formulated it in some boozer in London back in the 50's, a place that was then still surrounded by echoes of the Blitz, in all sorts of ways. He was ever so poetic about the scene, which I imagined in black and white at the time for some reason, but I just couldn't do it justice by trying to recreate this for you now. I have no idea whether any of this was true or not, but it was fascinating stuff to listen to nonetheless. I may regale you of the details over a pint later, if you like. Anyway, Duncan seemed very happy when we left, and he shook my hand when I got up to go. I guess he will never see his plans come to fruition now, which is a shame for him, and for us all.

Debbie is in a tremendously good mood with me. Partly due to this successful mission to the care home, but also because I delivered the completed ACV form back to her with all the necessary signatures. We are celebrating by having a pizza and a bottle of Prosecco. In a restaurant, no less, with food. She is holding my hand and looking over the table at me grinning from ear to ear, talking to me about positive things and the future, etc, etc.

This is all, of course, making me feel just awful.

"What's the matter, Dan? Did sitting with Duncan upset you or something?"

"No, no it's nothing. I'm just tired that's all." At least saying I'm tired is actually true. I'm not sleeping at all well these days, even by my standards.

"Oh, I thought Duncan reminded you of your Dad maybe. It's not that long since he's been gone, so I do worry about you doing… this. I know I railroaded you into it a little."

I force a smile, but it is a real one. "Just a little maybe. But it has been good for me, I think. It never upsets me because of Dad anyway. When it does upset me, it's because it is just plain upsetting. Seeing people waste away from the inside. Duncan, though, was a charmer today."

"Good, good. That's a relief. I do worry about you, you know."

She reaches over to hold my hand. Just as that particular hand was considering heading for my glass of Prosecco. Don't tell anyone, but I quite like Prosecco. You can almost drink it like beer. But you shouldn't. Really, take it from me. There are some things that I do so you don't have to, and that is one of them. It's all part of the service!

"So, what are you going to do now with the ACV form?" I ask, to distract me from not getting the imminent sip of fizzy wine.

"Goes into the council, then it's official. Then we can tell Tom."

"Oh, God. I'm not looking forward to that."

"Don't worry. You've done your bit. Furtive persuasion is your thing. Direct conflict is mine."

With that she takes her hand away and takes a sip

216

herself.

"What a team," I say, somewhere between honest and sarcastic. It just came out before I could decide which it was. Luckily, Debbie takes it as being honest.

"I know," she says smiling, and grabs another slice of pizza. "Together we shall save The Lion!"

"Shall we get t-shirts?" I then ask Debbie on a whim. This spoils the moment a little, judging by the look on her face.

Don't worry, we will absolutely not be getting t-shirts. On the plus side, Debbie does not mention Jen again this evening. She probably feels she doesn't have to. Which makes me feel just awful too.

So this is why, on this particular Saturday afternoon, I sent all the necessary texts, messages and calls around, just to make sure I have a full posse together for a Saturday night out down The Lion. This is so Tom the Landlord won't be able to get me on my own, which I don't fancy. My name is on that darn form, I now keenly realise, the significance of which did not occur to me at first, when I was all youthful and enthusiastic about keeping the pub open. Now I'm wondering if it should just close, just to stop me getting into an argument with Tom the Landlord. I don't *really* mean that of course, not quite. I even break my normal habit by not arriving early tonight, just so I'm not exposed and alone for too long. That made for an itchy half an hour in the flat before I left home, let me tell you. I'd have been pacing the halls, if I'd had any. Debbie is working tonight so she will be there, but she will be busy, and won't be able to keep me company. There's a band on tonight, you see, so the Lion will be lively.

By the way, when I say I sent *all* messages etc, I don't mean that I asked Jen to come down too. I may not be the brightest when it comes to relationships, as you may have already gathered, but I'm not *that* stupid. She's got me nailed down tomorrow for a holiday planning session instead. Don't worry, we have arranged to meet in the Lord Palmerston, a pub I never go to normally. They don't have great beer.

Despite all this meticulous planning, I'm still first in though, as I see when I survey the bar area from the doorway. Debbie gives me a wave and a thumbs-up at the same time, from the other side of the bar, while she is getting someone a round of six drinks. She doesn't normally give me a thumbs-up, so I guess that means that she has done the deed with Tom. Not *that* deed, I mean she has told him about the ACV. If she had, in fact, slept with Tom then surely the thumbs up sign would have been distinctly inappropriate in that situation, don't you think? It's also generally inappropriate in Brazil, some bloke told me here one night. I won't say why. Like I say, you can learn all sorts down the pub. No, I'm thinking that she is giving me the thumbs-up to make me feel better, to say that our plans are progressing nicely, and that we will save the pub after all. But all this succeeds in really doing is turning my stomach. Conflict and change always do this to me. I'd better get a beer in to calm my bowels in these turbulent times.

At the bar I avoid being served by Debbie (who wants to be behind a round of six drinks?) and also Tom the Landlord (who wants a blazing row with the landlord before you're drunk?). I furtively check Tom's demeanour, which is hard to read objectively, considering I now know what has just happened. He just looks like what I call 'standard grumpy', which isn't all that unusual. Maybe I can get through tonight after all. I avoid his eye and he avoids mine. What a team! Toby, a new but energetic young member of the bar staff, swiftly serves me a pint of 'High Noon', 4.4%, the top of my ABV comfort zone for a Saturday session. We exchange a few pleasantries, myself and Toby, mainly based around the stain that I have brought with me on my t-shirt. It was the first time I had noticed it to be honest and we try to determine whether it was curry or Italian-based, but are not able to come to a sufficient determination in the allotted two minutes we have to conclude our business. I stop short of sniffing the offending patch for both our sakes, which Toby says he appreciated. He shows much promise does Toby, I think, as I sit down with my pint at a table big enough for four. I would have got four pints in, but that would have guaranteed that the others would be even later than they are already.

As I wait for my tardy friends, now ten minutes late despite my firm instructions as to the importance of punctuality this evening, I check out the band, who are setting up a stage area (of sorts) by the end of the bar. I take a look at one of the flyers that they have left lying around. It seems that this band is formed from the ashes of 'Tantric Love Rabbit', who I have seen here before but do not remember much of, bar the name. Well, you would remember *that* name, wouldn't you? Well, anyway, *I* did. As it goes, I'm guessing that the name had something to do with the band splitting up. Surely there must have been at least some members of the band who found it just too embarrassing to put that particular job title on their CV. However, considering that the new name of the band is 'Hyper-Dimensional Love Heroes', I expect the guy who comes up with the band names is still part of this outfit. Perhaps they are entering their more grown, up artistic phase. Then again, I note that the flyer is promoting their new single 'Blow It', so maybe not.

Amy comes in at exactly the same time as she always does, quarter past. I believe this to be a firm statement of her opinion on today's instructions regarding punctuality, but I'm not going to mention anything. She says hello and heads straight to the bar. Tom serves her, I notice, but nothing untoward occurs between them. She gives Debbie a wave at the bar before she joins me at our table.

"You ok, matey?" she asks, once she sits down.
"Yeah, sure," I say defensively. Do I look 'not ok'? Do I not look 'ok'? Either way, that sort of response is not going to be enough for her.
She eyes me up over her first sip, also a 'High Noon', 4.4%. There's not much else on tonight that isn't going to do us too much damage over a session like this is going to be. She then asks "And what's the Jen situation then. She gone home yet?" You can always rely on Amy for the direct approach.

220

"No, I'm seeing her tomorrow. Just for lunch, you know. Before she goes home."

"And that's it?"

I don't know what to say. I wish I knew myself. I hide behind my glass for a long, but hopefully not suspiciously long, sip. Then the sound of a glass smashing behind the bar sends my heart in a spin. We both turn around to survey the scene. I'm expecting to see Debbie and Tom squaring off behind the bar, with angry stares on both their faces, and a broken bottle in each hand like a weapon. But no, Toby is standing there instead, with both hands in the air, sheepishly grinning, taking the sarcastic applause from the nearby punters and bar staff alike. Then he heads off to get the dustpan and brush. By the way, that's a rite of passage that Toby has just gone through there, one that all bar staff must go though. 'The First Broken Glass'. A full pint as well, more's the pity. It's a relief though, for me anyway, that *this* is all it was. I'm definitely a bit highly strung tonight, I decide.

Shortly, Jez and Ted come in together, laughing away at something or other. It's nice to see them getting along without me, it really is, especially as I wasn't sure that they would get on at all when I first introduced them to each other. But I can't help but wonder when those two becoming particularly pally actually happened. I shall have to try and rise above it all and not be jealous. Everyone had to do without me before, when I lived in London, and may well have to do so again soon. Anyway, my first pint is down to around three sips and Amy is busy making sure hers is too, so Ted heads off to the bar for 'High Noons all round' and Jez takes a seat.

221

"Nice stain," he says, eyeing up my torso. "Hoisin sauce?"

Once again, I don't know what to say. I'm sure a second 'High Noon' will help though.

'Hyper-dimensional Love Heroes' were pretty good, although after four pints of 'High Noon', I expect even Tantric Love Rabbit would have sounded like The Beach Boys. 'Blow It' predictably proved to be catchy but emotionally uninspiring. We all had a laugh though.

A little later, all three of them ambush me on the subject of Jen, and this time I have nowhere to hide. So this time I told them what the situation actually was and waited for the onslaught.

"You said what?" exclaims Jez, with a pained look on his face. "What did you agree to *that* for?" He is referring to me supposedly agreeing to travel around the world with Jen of course.

" I don't know," I say, trying to defend myself. Now looking at the faces of my three best friends, I am gradually feeling more and more like this is all rather indefensible. "It felt like it might be a good idea at the time. And she was very persuasive…"

"Jesus, Dan," Amy says with a tut, shaking her head roundly at me. But all done with love, I'm sure. I carry on.

"…and running away, you know, felt pretty tempting after everything that's happened. You know?" I look to Ted for support, but he chooses that moment to look away, sensibly.

I immediately feel guilty playing the 'Dad card', but Dad being gone *is* a big part of why I let Jen tempt me into leaving, it really is. It just somehow doesn't sound so good if I say it out loud.

"And now you can afford it, right…" Jez tells me, mining another seam in this conversation.

"Yes, he's got the inheritance money now, hasn't he?" Amy sighs, sitting back.

"Yes, right…" Jez nods, then tails off, not knowing what to say next on the subject already.

We all take a sip. If this was pint number one, we may have digressed to chat about our latest favourite box set on tv or something, to save the feelings of the person under interrogation until later. But this *is* now 'later', pint number five, and none of us are going to let this particular conversation just wander off without some attention first, myself included. There is too much conversational inertia now.

"Yes, so I have the money." I admit. "I have the money. Sorry, but it is what it is. I'd give it all back twice to have Dad back though, you know that!"

Nods and a chorus of 'of courses' ensue.

"Thing is though," Jez continues. "This is *Jen*, right?"

"Right…"

"And she, not to put too fine a point on it, messed you right up, right?"

"Right. I believe that this is well documented," I admit.

"You're not wrong there. So, that's a bit of a risk, right? Going around the world with someone who did that to you?" Jez has a point, despite a beer-induced growing lack of eloquence.

"Er, yes, I suppose so. But she has *changed*. She has, er…what's the opposite of 'grown up'?"

" *'Dan'*?" suggests Amy, making quotation marks

223

with her fingers, like rabbit ears, only partly joking. We all laugh way too much anyway. It's that time of the night, and the release was welcome to everyone. "Let's just work with 'grown down'," says Ted, once we have calmed down. "It's still a personal progression when you choose not to be so sensible anymore. I'm not against that."

"'Grown down' is fine. Thanks Ted," I tell him. "Anyway, she's come round to my way of thinking, finally. You know, that life is for living. Not the career ladder and all that. The stuff we used to argue about. It took a decade, but I won the argument!" My triumphalism is left with a modest response around the table and one of those raised eyebrows from Amy. I add a weak "Eventually…" just to temper my statement back down to reasonable levels.

"Yeah, alright," Amy jumps in. "But how do you know she won't change her mind? To me, it sounds like she is just using you. She's having a life-crisis and wants a holiday from herself, so she's sitting there…"

"Where, Amy?" Jez asks looking around. "I may be getting a little lost. Is she *here*…?"

"Anywhere, Jez. A notional place where she's sitting, thinking about her life. Somewhere like this maybe. Or perhaps a wine bar."

"Oh, I see. Hope not a wine bar…"

"Indeed. So she's wondering *'who do I know who would just drop everything and keep me company on a mad trip around the world? I know, Dan would do it. He's up for anything. All I need to do is flash my eyes and apologise then he'll do it'*."

"It's not like that, Amy," I say. "That's a little harsh."

224

But I can't help but think, 'fair enough though'. Like I said, it's that time of the evening, where my mind likes to jump around.

"Are you *sure*, Dan?" Amy replies. "I want to know that you are sure, Dan. As your friend I would want to know that."

Debbie chooses that moment to come along and collect our glasses. To be fair, it was probably not her choice. Our table is now somewhat full of empty pint glasses and rather overdue a clear out. We all stop talking when she arrives, then say hello and so on while she clears the table. She gives me a playful punch on the shoulder and a smile. I give her the standard comment as to not knowing where all these glasses came from. Then she moves on with the tower of glasses balancing against her arm.

"Obvious question, but dare I ask what you are going to do about *her* then?" Ted asks, nodding over to Debbie once she has gone.

"Yeah, good question..." I admit.

"Which needs a good answer, Daniel," Amy states, "So what *are* you going to do then?"

Deep breath.

"I'm going to get another round in."

That causes initial consternation around the table, then a wordless admission from all that it is indeed my round, and that indeed we are all down to our last three sips.

Look here. I know that the answer is never at the bottom of a bottle, or a glass, as the saying goes. This is a true saying. The answer, however, *can* sometimes eventually be found in a good old chin-wag with your mates, especially once they are in a brutally honest mood. So, in that spirit, we do have a go at fixing my life, but the moment in time seems to evade us, and we just end up in the circles I've been going around in myself. It's not their fault. It's all my fault. I'm just not in the mood to find solutions tonight, only punishment. But I'm not going to admit that fact to my friends right at this point. Later, they even start to couch the conversation in terms of which woman is going to 'save' me. I'm thinking who said I needed saving anyway? Or that I even deserved saving? And if anyone said that, is it really that obvious? These are thoughts I keep to myself between sips, while different theories about me bound around the table. They are right though, but what I'm not telling anyone is what I need saving from, or who I need saving from, and why. And what I'm also not saying is this. After all these years of thinking that only Jen could possibly save me, and now realising that life it not that simple anymore, I still can't stop thinking that if she can't, then nothing will. It's a habit I got into. And if she can't save me then maybe I just can't be saved, and the Witchfinder will win after all. And that he *should* win too. I think all this as Amy repeats some point from earlier, but in a slightly different way, and even though I'm trying to listen, the words wash over my head like Toby's spilt pint from before.

The jukebox gets turned up and it starts to form a backing track to our night. I should say something, say something, anything. And I should say it now. I say nothing though, until the subject of best boxed sets comes up again. And I start to hate myself, properly hate myself, for the relief that it brings me.

Chapter 15

Henry, who has a boundless capacity for joy, has decided to keep me company in The Red Lion this evening, before the conference with Jen at the Lord Palmerston. I, apparently, am here to keep him entertained for the duration. If you have not yet noticed the sarcasm, you will shortly. We are both sitting at the bar, and he is currently staring at me, waiting for me to say something else. I am staring instead at my 'Paddington Beer', 4.1%, waiting for me to say something else too.

"Yeah," he says portentously, to nothing in particular that *I* have said.

I'm in a bad mood, for me, and feeling a little naughty today, so I just return the compliment. "Uh huh," I respond, in what I hope is an understanding tone.

"Yeah," he replies, slightly more morosely.

"Mmm," I nod in agreement, to whatever it is. I can't keep this up much longer. I'm just not capable of winning affirmation tennis with the likes of Henry.

"Yeah," he adds, swilling his pint round and around. That's it, I'm done!

"Henry," I say, "what's on your mind, mate?"

He looks away from his pint and up at me. "On my mind? Nothing. I'm fine. What about you?"

Ok then, my turn again. "Well, my old legendary girlfriend came back the other day."

"Legendary? You mean like she wasn't really your girlfriend?"

This causes me to bristle somewhat. Bloody hell, I'm only trying to be nice! I'm not asking to be insulted, as if it is so unlikely I can actually have a girlfriend! But I swallow this brief peevishness with a swig of beer and just say, "No, she is actually real. What I mean is that she was a really big – no, not *big* – I mean *important* girlfriend, from my past, when I was younger."

He nods like he properly understands. God knows if he does or not. I must have been drinking with this guy, on and off, for a couple of years but still know virtually nothing about him. He's slightly older than me but not much, and that I'm only guessing. He always wears the same coat, which either has the same stains on it, or he always spills things in the same place, one or the other. And he tends to drink the house bitter, without risking the guest ales. He didn't go to school in this area, at least not that I remember, and his accent could be from anywhere south of Lincoln. He is a closed book. I can't criticise him for that though, can I?

"But it's weird, you know," I carry on, knowing this conversation is going to be all me now, "her being back and everything. For years and years that I dreamed about this moment. I never got over her, not really, and I guess I would have taken her back despite everything. But we lost touch and I never dared find her again. And now she's back."

"That's great," Henry tells me. Two more syllables to add to the total.

"No, it's not. It's not *great* anyway. That's what I'm trying to tell you. I don't rightly know what it is, what it's supposed to be, what it *should* be. It's not what I imagined."

"Aren't you seeing the barmaid here though? Whatshername?"

What? He knows too? Is it really that obvious? I thought we were being cool. Jesus!

"Debbie," is all I say by way of an answer. Two can play at this game.

"Hmm," he sniffs knowingly, which is just annoying, as he surely does not have the information to know *anything* about my life. I take another swig to calm down. Actually, sometimes I think I don't have enough information to make sense of my life either. I can't help but notice that Henry is now staring at his pint with such an intensity that it's as if he is trying to boil it with his eyes, like some kind of superhero with a beer.

"You alright mate?" I ask.

"Yeah," he says, then downs the rest of his drink in one go. I'm wondering if he is going to have another or not for about a minute I guess, but which felt like five. I would not have left him on his own if he wanted another, but I'm not upset, I admit, when he decides that this is quite enough fun for one evening, then leaves.

Once he is gone I am left to my own devices. Not normally a good idea but after a pint with Henry I will even take a bit of Matthew Hopkins just to change things up a little. A change is as good as a rest is it not? No is the answer. No, it isn't. You see, I have never been one for change, even the good type. But even I have to admit that change can work out well once in a while. Which somewhat reminds me of the day when I was first dropped off at my University

Halls of Residence. There sure was plenty change that day. It was the first time ever that I was to live away from the family home, all the way away in London. But, as things transpired, it was the run up that was worse for me, not the day itself. As the weeks ticked down to days I was getting more and more nervous, thinking about all the stilted conversations I might have, all the jokes that would fall flat. All those new people who would think I was a knob. But as me and Dad drove away, that was gradually replaced by a growing sense of excitement and the joy of possibility. Here's how it went, if you would care to know.

Mum was going to come as well, but I had decided that so much of my stuff was simply just too essential to leave behind that we kind of filled the car up, leaving only seats for me and Dad. So that meant I had to deal with two separate tearful farewell moments that day. Hold it together Daniel, I thought to myself, you're a big boy now, as we drove off. I had one end of a guitar, the small end fortunately, stuck next to my head for the entire journey. I couldn't play, it was Rachel's from when she was at school, but I decided at the last minute that this was the sort of thing that I should be getting into now that I was going to be a student, so I shoved it into the car in the last space available. Don't know why.

Dad asked what I wanted to play on the car stereo. I opted for *The Queen is Dead*, by The Smiths. After that he didn't ask me again what I wanted, but put on *Dark Side of the Moon* by Pink Floyd, once Morrissey and his friends were done. Conversation was a little stilted throughout most of the drive, as I recall. I thought at the time that this was because I was so nervous, but looking back now I guess it was because we were both nervous. Perhaps Dad even more than me. He was definitely more agitated by the time we got into the outskirts of London. He said that he had never really driven here before and it was somewhat of a nightmare compared to the streets around home. I dare say he was right. There was an awful lot more happening on these roads, and a lot more besides going on to the side. I constantly looked left and right, sucking up every scene enthusiastically. Shop after shop after shop, all seemingly selling the same things. Half of them with fruit and veg on the outside, undoubtedly taking on a thick coating of traffic fumes. I didn't even recognise half of what was on those shelves. Then there were the great deals for packs of lager, handwritten in garish fluorescent colours, with spelling mistakes and the numbers written in big stars or explosions. How exciting! Then there were so many people just hanging around, some laughing, some looking forbidding. Thousands of bus stops, it seemed. Dad missed all this, his eyes dead set on the road ahead, and on his mirrors. Conversation dried up as I resisted the urge to point out anything that caught my eye, such as a pink haircut or a turban, in case he felt tempted to look, and then total the car. So even though we were still physically together at that moment, we were also beginning to drift apart already.

Before long, and a few wrong turns later, we ended up in the car park, of sorts, next to the Halls of Residence. I'm not sure if it was really a car park, but it was the only place we could see to stop, and Dad had really had enough of driving in London by then. We were both also keenly aware of the massive amount of stuff that I had packed into the car (all absolutely essential of course) and how much effort it was going to be to shift it into my room, which we shortly found out was on the third floor, much to Dad's dismay. Ok, I was young yes, but not strong, and dad was not a big man either. We were just going to have to struggle through this and try to look as much like 'real men' as we possibly could. As we stood by the car we gave each other a steely nod, as if to confirm to the other that, yes, we can do this, and no, it is not going to hurt. I took the guitar first, mainly because it was in the way of my head getting out of the car, but also because it wasn't that heavy.

Once the car was empty and the room was filled, it was finally time for goodbyes. It was a little rushed in the end, since we found out that we shouldn't have parked where we did about twenty minutes ago, but were not informed of a suitable alternative place, so we just upped the pace as best we could. Those students who saw me on that first day must have thought that I looked like I had a permanent grimace on my face, as if that was the natural state of my visage. Fortunately, I told myself at the time, that would mean that they wouldn't recognise me when I first rocked up to the students' bar, grimace-free. Dad looked at me like he was trying not to be sad. Which meant, of course, that he looked even sadder. Meanwhile, I was trying not to look too excited. God knows what that look actually resembled. Then we had a quick hug, twice as long as our usual hugs I reckon, then a hand on the shoulder for good luck. No tears. He wished me luck and said the date when we would meet again, when I was next back up for Christmas. It's funny how we all do that isn't it? "See you Sunday" or "See you on 28th March 2008 at twenty past twelve". It's not an exercise in fact checking, though, is it? It's just a way we reassure ourselves. Our brains like it, so they make us say it. "Yeah, see you December 16th." I repeated, as Dad got in the car. I waved him off enthusiastically, my guts churning with fear, but also something else. It was like I was ready to burst out, ready to give birth to the new me, the *me* I had always wanted to be. Dad gave me a quick wave, hurriedly scouted the surrounding area then drove off. I watched as the car went around the corner. Then he was gone. I don't like long goodbyes. But rushed goodbyes are even worse, I found out that day. You know, I never talked to him about what he did next, and how he felt on that drive home alone. I wish I had. Too late now. And, as it goes, I did not see him again until December 16th. Actually, it must have been the 18th. I had a couple of parties to go to before we all headed home for Christmas.

From that precise moment, the one when Dad drove off, everything changed. Three hours later, for example, I met Jen. How's that for change then?

I take these thoughts with me as I decamp to the Lord Palmerston, and order something I'd rather not talk about, which was not 'Paddington Beer' 4.1%. And three minutes after musing about this very thing, Jen turns up in my life once again. In order to ensure that

233

I kept our table, I was timing the end of my pint for her being ten minutes late. But she is bang on time today and I still have a third left. That remaining liquid swiftly disappears in one go as she heads to where I'm sitting, so that is one problem solved. That's me, Dan the problem solver! That particular problem, you don't need to tell me, is not my most pressing one, but there you go. I shall take my victories where I can get them. She kisses me on the cheek, all buzzing and full of life, which I can't help but find a little depressing. I do my best to try and drum up some enthusiasm, which is easy enough to approximate after a pint or two.

"So, I hope you have been giving my idea some thought, Daniel," she begins, once she has been provided with her beverage (which will also remain unnamed), and a few minutes of warm-up chit-chat have been adhered to.

"It has been on my mind, yes." I am fond of this kind of lie that is not really a lie. I should go into politics or something. Actually, no, I really shouldn't.

"Good, good," Jen replies immediately. "There are still some really good tickets around, so we haven't missed out yet, don't you worry. I'm checking every day!"

"Good, good," I echo, wishing I had given this conversation a bit more forethought, rather than talking to Henry about her. She senses my tension. Hasn't lost the old skills there then.

"Sorry, Dan," she says, staring back at me with kitten eyes, leaning over to put her hand on my arm, "I know you don't know if you have the money or not for this yet. It's unfair to pressure you in this way,

234

I'm sorry."

"Y…" I reply.

"…it's just that it would be so great, right? Shame if it has to be about money…"

I don't know if it is the eyes, the hand or the earlier pint of 'Paddington Beer' I had, but without my permission I find myself replying by saying.

"Well, it's not the money anymore. I ended up getting a bunch of that after Dad, you know…"

Jen pulls a sympathetic face and nods sympathetically, but I can tell she's really buzzing underneath now. Why is she? I said that it's not the money *anymore*. That could easily mean that there was something *else* stopping me, right? She will surely work that out when she thinks back over what I said. Right?

But as the evening progressed and we carefully slipped into the subject of the perfect travel itinerary, then a very careful foray into 'old times', the subject of the 'me not being able to make the trip' never really came up again. She must have felt that she had got what she wanted for now and did not wish to derail it by pushing further. After a while, she said she had to get back to see her parents for dinner. I, apparently, was not invited. This was some relief in reality, so I didn't press further. And so, in this way Jen left me to this table and my thoughts, promising to give me regular updates for 'the plan'. I thought about all this for a while, wishing for the company of Paddington, but to no particular conclusion. Then it suddenly struck me that she had never once said sorry for what she did to me, nor once explained why she did it. Not back then and not now either. Sigh. Our conversation this evening had achieved precisely nothing.

Even worse, I discovered that the hand dryer at The Palmerston was just rubbish. I swear that it was actually condensing water from the very air directly onto my hands!

"Paddington Beer?" Jez asks a couple of days later, as I fill him and Amy in on what had happened with Jen. "You've been drinking a beer called Paddington?"
"I don't think that's quite the relevant ques..." Amy begins.
"Well, I could have had a 'Rupert Beer', or a 'Grizzly Beer' but, yeah, I chose that one." I chip in quickly, in a rare interruption of Amy's flow. "I did go on about that beer to Jen later on. Oh dear, do you think Jen would have interpreted that as me being all enthusiastic for the spirit of travel and adventure?"
"No. No I do not," replies Jez. "Actually, now I think about it, I think this pint is actually called a 'Teddy Beer'. I just liked the pump clip so went for it without looking. Same brewery surely. Smooth one, as it goes...hey, do they have a 'Pooh Beer', do you think?"
"When you two have quite managed to grow up," Amy counters, "Dan, are you saying that now you are going, or that she thinks you are going? These now do seem to be the only options."
"I never said I was going!" I defend myself robustly. "I only mentioned that I now have the money..."
"What did you do that for?" both Amy and Jez say, seemingly in unison.
"I know, I know...so, yes... it *may* be that she... *may*

think that now, yes."

"Hmm, but is there a chance that you actually *are* going to go?" she asks me.

"Er, well…no. I don't think so. Maybe."

"Nicely decisive," Amy sighs. "So…what *are* you going to do then?"

"Well…I'm kind of doing it now," I tell her, raising my glass in the air.

If I had taken a photo at that point you would see Amy with her head in her hands and Jez with his mouth wide open in laughter, eyes raised to the chandelier above. I didn't actually take that picture, but I still see that image clear as day in my head nonetheless, later on in bed, as I bury my head into my pillow until it hurts.

I recall that Henry normally sits at the bar by that time of an evening, but he was absent tonight. I didn't spend much time thinking about this at the time. He probably found a way to have a better time somewhere else, I thought. It wasn't long before I learn otherwise, however.

Chapter 16

A few days later, Tom the Landlord waves me over from the behind the bar. I think he wants to talk to me. Jesus, I hope it is not about the pub. We've been doing such a good job at avoiding this subject so far, so why spoil it now?

"What's up Tom?" I ask, once I wander over casually.

"You're a mate of Henry, right?"

"Well I wouldn't go that far, but I drink with him sometimes I guess."

"Ok, well I heard this from a mate of mine at the hospital. Henry's only gone and tried to top himself hasn't he. Put himself in the hospital. My mate thought we should try and put word around any friends he's got while he's recovering. He's not had many visitors apparently."

I'm instantly feeling guilty now, as this news sinks in. Guilty for succumbing to that particular temptation myself. Guilty for not helping Henry more before. In my head, Matthew Hopkins tells me that I am guilty too. All the bloody time. In my head, I tell him to bog off.

"Jesus, that's terrible," I reply instinctively. "What did he do? I mean, how did he do it?"

Tom just runs his fingers over one of his wrists. I wince at the thought, as Tom the Landlord picks up a cloth and starts to dry some glasses.

"Will he be ok?" I ask.

"Yeah, he did it all wrong apparently. He'll be out in a few days. Just thought you might want to know, or know who else to tell."

"Yeah, thanks. That's really awful. Poor bloke..."

"You going to go see him then?"

"I don't know. I've had enough of hospitals recently. And it's not like we're mates..."

Tom the Landlord just stares back in my general direction and wordlessly picks up another glass. He may not be sending out disapproval, but that's what I'm receiving.

"Well, I suppose I *could* go..." I say.

As I tentatively walk through the hospital doors, I notice with some relief that Matthew Hopkins decided not to come with me. Good. He's still not there when I walk back out the same doorway again a minute later. Don't worry, I haven't bottled it. I am actually in the wrong building. Henry is half a mile away in some other ward. These places are bloody massive! I literally got off the bus at the opposite end of the hospital complex, which means I now have to walk all the way round. I take a sideways glance at the building where Mum ended up, and then also another building where Dad was when he had his accident. I remember both those doorways like it was yesterday. For the people working here, these doors must mean nothing, but for me they are portals into the past. If I walk through them I will be transported back into much darker times. My stomach churns at the very thought of those moments. I watch people walking through those doors now, as I pass. Some are no doubt having those dark times right now. This makes me sad. Oh well, I guess it's their turn. It's everyone's turn eventually, right?

I make a toilet stop halfway round, which was a bigger diversion than I expected, but a necessary one nonetheless, so there's not a whole lot of visiting time left once I get to the right ward, the one where Henry is. This may well be my bladder and my subconscious working in harmony here, to minimise the duration of the visit. I'm not looking forward to this, I must admit, even after having two pints, which, as everyone knows, is the best number of pints if you need to get something done. At the ward reception, I ask where Henry is. The nurse asks for a surname. "Er, I don't know. I just know him from down the pub, you know? Never asked his surname."
"Right," the nurse says, checking her list.
"Would you like me to describe him?" I flounder. The nurse continues to check the list, and shakes her head. "Lucky for you I only have one Henry today. Third on the left. You're the first visitor, as it goes."
"Really?" I ask, incredulous. What sort of story lies behind no one coming to visit you when you try and top yourself? Not a happy one, that's for sure. Suddenly I can hardly put one foot in front of the other to go into the ward. I feel a mixture of responsibility and stupidity upon me, a heady mix indeed. Deep breath.

The two pints in my belly spur me on. I try not to pry into the situation of the other eight or so people on the ward. Some are sitting up with their family around them. Some of those are smiling. Some are on their own, looking at the doorway, or at the other patients. Some are asleep. One of those ones, I notice, is Henry himself. I sit down carefully. I don't want to wake him. Whether that's more for his sake or mine I'm not

240

sure. He looks pale, but peaceful. I can't see his wrists, thankfully, as they are covered up. I look around nervously for inspiration. But there is none. All I notice is that everyone has brought something. I didn't bring anything. No flowers, no grapes. Not even boiled eggs and nuts. Actually, as I dig in my pockets I just find a half-empty packet of peanuts that I had completely forgotten about, but they don't feel like a suitable gift. I'll give it five minutes. I amuse myself thinking that he is about as chatty now as he normally is down the pub. I note, however, that I am much less so. I stare at Henry like I'm staring into a mirror. After the five minutes, which I count down one by one, I stand up, whisper 'see you mate' under my breath, and then take my leave. With some relief, I'm ashamed to say. That was way too much like staring into a mirror, and I didn't like it one bit.

"Where've you been?" Ted asks, as I sweep through the doors of the pub, half an hour later.
"Now there's a story," I say on my way past. "First of all, though, I need a beer."
"*Another* beer," Tom corrects me, as I get to the bar, loud enough for Ted to hear. Ted follows my progress quizzically, as I shrug in return. "Henry ok?" Tom asks, more quietly, as I peruse the choices in front of me.
"He was sleeping," I inform him. I'm pretty shaken up, so I deliberately adorn myself with my happy-go-lucky persona to get through this exchange. "Never seen him looking happier, Tom, as it goes. Seriously though, the nurse said he is doing well and would be out soon. They need the beds anyway. So that's that really. Er, how strong is the 'Just Desserts'?"

"5.8%, mate. It's a Winter Ale."

"Ooh, no thanks. What about the 'Downward Spiral' then?"

"Er, 4.8% that one."

"Ooh…"

"So, go on then," Ted prompts as I join him at the table, with a safe 'Sesh-On Bitter', 3.8%, "what's the story then? It must be quite something to make *you* late. It's not too often I get here before you. I'm just not used to sitting here on my own anymore!"

We chink glasses in greeting and I fill him in on the situation. As soon as he gets the gist, he steps back to give me the floor, resisting the temptation to chip in. A few subjects are not generally suitable for the to and fro of standard pub banter, and this is one of them. Once I am done though, I take a long gulp and meet his eye, as the cue to finally illicit a reaction.

"Darn it, Dan. He was always an odd one was Henry, you know, but I didn't see *that* coming."

"Me neither," I agree. "I mean, how could we?"

"Did he ever talk to you about, er, you know, how he felt and all that? What was going on in his life, etc etc?"

"God knows. Not to me. He would normally just act generally miserable about something here, like his pint, or his seat or the fruit machine. Mostly he would just rely on me to tell him my stories."

"Yeah, same here. That can happen a lot in this place," Ted nods. "In fact, considering the amount of talk that happens in this place, very little of it amounts to much, when you think about it."

"Oh, I don't know. Just talking about anything is good. Like a distraction."

242

"Yeah, but that only takes you so far, you know?" Ted replies. "If there's actually something going on in your life that's causing you that much grief, you probably should talk to someone about it. Don't you think?"

"I suppose so," I reply warily, unsure of this reasonably new conversational territory.

"And why not? If the people here are the best you've got then definitely, yeah. Better than keeping it all in. Look at what *that* did to Henry." Despite the words, Ted does not seem entirely sure, more like he's trying to convince himself as much as me, making sense of these events on-the-fly.

"Well, we don't know that for sure…"

"Decent guess," Ted offers. "Tries to top himself? No visitors at the hospital? What do you think?"

"Yeah, decent guess," I admit, between sips.

"And this isn't just Henry you know. Not many of us blokes are very good at talking about their feelings. Stiff upper lip and all that."

I'm tempted to bring up that I, eventually, did talk to Ted about Dad, and how ill he was getting, and all sorts of other private stuff. But we are not allowed to talk about that subject anymore. He does have a point though. For all the stuff I do talk about, hardly any of it does amount to much. But, on the other hand, that's partly the point, right? If we were profound all the time we'd just go mad. Or get our heads kicked in or something. Yeah, that is a decent enough point, but there's a balance to be made here and, if I'm being honest, I know that I'm keeping too much to myself once again. I just don't see the alternative. It's difficult. The only person I could in theory talk to

Dad about is sitting here now, but that is now the one thing we *can't* talk about. Ted has made it clear already that this is for the best. And I can't even tell you why we can't talk about it, so just don't ask. See? It *is* difficult. So, I just nod to Ted, to show general agreement, but that I have nothing more to offer at this moment.

"It's a big source of male depression, this is," Ted continues, beginning to get on his soap box, "and then suicide, like Henry. British men just bottle it all up inside, don't they?"

"Can't argue with that," I agree, thinking back to all the overheard conversations I have witnessed while in here. Hardly any of them made me feel like I was prying into where I *really* shouldn't be. Hardly any of these exchanges had any real substance to them. It's true, I start to realise. For all the opportunities we have to bear our souls in here, we hardly ever do.

"One in four of us are going to have mental health problems you know," Ted continues, increasingly fuelled by his beer. "Makes you wonder what that number would be if we could just take that stick out of our arse for once."

"Nice image. Yeah, I do know what you mean, Ted. No one wants to admit they are weak though. Or crazy."

"But we are *all* crazy, right? In our own way. Just because you get depressed or anxious sometimes doesn't mean you are a knife-wielding maniac does it? You'd think that was the case though, the way we are with each other."

I think that there may, in fact, be something behind this tirade that I don't know about yet, considering the passion beginning to build up in Ted. It's what we would think of as a 5-pint passion – minimum - and he is several actual pints short of that state as we speak. But, knowing Ted, I will find out what this story is when he's ready. He is good like that eventually, at least I think so, even if no one else here tends to be, me included. Me especially. His point made, Ted heads off to the Gents. This would normally improve a chap's mood, but he still looks agitated when he returns a couple of minutes later. "What's up now?" I enquire.

"Overly Aggressive Splashback. Him over there." He points to some other bloke I don't know, who is also heading back from the toilets. "Ah…" I say.

In case this requires explanation, 'Overly Aggressive Splashback' occurs when a gentleman, while standing next to or near you at a urinal, engages in the act of disgorging himself of urine with the absolute most effort he possibly can, squeezing like his life depended on it, causing the toxic stream to violently splash back from the urinal itself and onto the trousers, hands, arms and whatever-else, of his unfortunate neighbours. Oddly, the perpetrator himself rarely inflicts a self-splashing. That will be the particular physics of this universe which is to blame for this injustice. There seems to be no possible need for this activity, but it is an unfortunately common occurrence nonetheless. Perhaps it is a very particular kind of alpha-male-type display of muscle strength, or bladder capacity. I have no idea. I do not participate in such activities myself and neither do any of my friends. By the way, Ted is not just guilty of mindless moaning here. He actually is doing me a

245

big favour by warning me, and now we can both avoid this 'alpha-male' for the rest of the session and hopefully, when we leave here, smell a little bit less like piss than we would have had otherwise. An exchange of glances is enough to show my understanding of the subject, and also my gratitude as regards the warning.

"Still, it's not all bad," Ted adds, moving on. There was some interesting graffiti added to the wall above the urinal which amused me."

"Oh yeah? A new one? What's that then?"

"*You should just be yourself. Unless it's* YOU. *Then be someone else.*"

That makes us both laugh heartily.

"I like that. I'm going to use that one." I tell Ted. And so, effortlessly, and instead of where it could have gone, like somewhere interesting in Ted's past or present, or everything that is bothering me, the conversation drifts to the banal once again. Another opportunity gone.

This is no one's fault. This is just how it goes!

And that is what I keep telling myself later when Matthew Hopkins silently walks me home, via the cemetery, as is now my habit. This is just how it goes too. Matthew now knows that he no longer needs to say anything to me. He has already won the argument. He knows that despite pretending everything otherwise, I have in fact concluded this: that I'm worth even less than Henry, and if that is so, then why do I deserve to carry on when he barely did? I mean, I'll probably just make a mess of saving the pub and be an embarrassment to everyone. And

I'm inevitably going to mess up my relationships like I always do. Who am I kidding anyway, to think I can make a difference in anyone's life? They would all be better off without me. They won't even notice I've gone, I say so little that is actually worth listening to. That's right, I can't even talk to my best friends, so what good am I? Well don't worry, everyone, because I won't be dragging you all down any more. I won't be dragging myself down anymore either. There is one way I can stop letting everyone down. I can stop everything. God, what a relief that would be. The pain. Then the pain would stop too.

I look back. Matthew Hopkins says nothing. He just smiles and nods. I've decided. I've had enough. I've really had enough now.

I'm sorry, Dad.

Fourth note inn the mattere of The Red Lion Witch
Matthew Hopkins, Witch finder-General

And so he was tried and hanged by the necke until death.

There is nothing to be done.

~

No one is here, by the pond. It's late. I'm stinkingly drunk. There is nothing to stop me now. I have been secretly collecting rocks for weeks and have filled my *pockets with them. To make sure of my innocence as I step into my trial.*

Matthew tells me to take a step forwards. I take a step forwards. To the edge. Just one more. Please.

Then a stumble. My heart jumps. My adrenal gland pumps out its contents, like my life depended on it. And for just one moment I can see other things. Things beyond me and Matthew Hopkins. I can see Harry, and Henry and Rachel. Ted, Amy and Jez. And I can see Debbie.

Matthew pulls me in. They all pull me back. And we become stuck in a perverse dance, a cruel impasse.

So it is up to me after all then. What's next is up to me alone. Deep breath. Without a word, I take a step.

Chapter 17

Why not get your pint, grab your Financial Times, take a seat over there, lean in and overhear this one? You're slightly late, but I dare say you'll catch up.

"Say that again, Dan."

"Ooh, have I just made some kind of impression for once? Neither you, nor anyone else for that matter, normally ask me to repeat myself!"

"Let's just say I'm curious, and I'm not sure I quite got what you meant the first time."

"Well, I've been thinking, Ted. We want to save the pub, right? And I know we are trying to save it because we love it…"

"Yes, I never thought it was an entirely altruistic campaign for you..."

"I don't think anyone could be accused of being overly cynical, Ted, if they said that you'd be hard pushed to find true altruism anywhere."

"You're digressing already, Dan."

"Hmm, yes, I *do* do that, don't I? Right, so saving the pub, that's all well and good, but we also have to remember what we are saving this place for. To provide a place for the community to meet up and all that."

"Well, yes, plus the drinking…but how does that tie in with your idea?"

"Well, it got me to thinking. What we were talking about the other day, about what we don't say when we are in here. We've been banging on about how great a community pub this is, but look what happened to Henry, right in front of our faces."

"Yeah, that sure was a shame."

"We need to do more than just keep this place open. We need to actually make it the sort of place we have been pretending it is. The place where Henry and the next guy like him, and the next one after that, can actually come in and feel like they are not alone. That they are part of something. Then maybe they wouldn't try to…you know…top themselves."

"I get that, but to change things… it sounds like a tall order. Have you been drinking or something?"

"I have Ted! And, finally, to good effect."

"Yeah, but how is this event going to change anything? Just to play Devil's Advocate here, you understand."

"Nice pint that, the old Devil's Advocate. Anyway, I got the idea from the visits to the care home I've been doing. They really do some good. For me *and* the guys I talk to. As for here, well you have to start somewhere, break the ice, you know? And even if it helped one person it would be worth it, right?"

"…"

"Right?"

"…yes, ok Dan. Yes, it would."

"Plus there's two other benefits too."

"Which are?"

"We can raise some money for charity. Ones that combat loneliness and depression and that."

"Ok. Any in mind?"

"Not really, this is kind of fresh, this idea. The Samaritans! There must be some more. There's a charity for everything these days."

"Don't worry, I know a few. I can help you out there.

251

What's the other thing?"

"Other thing?"

"The other benefit of this night you are proposing?"

"Ah yes, it will also put this pub on the map as being a great community pub. It will enhance our ACV application, and maybe improve our reputation so we can attract another decent landlord in next."

"I must say, Dan, it sounds like you have thought this all through rather nicely. Where did all this come from?"

"You don't want to know."

"Don't I?"

"Uh-uh." Sip.

"Ok, so we host a night where we encourage people to come over and talk to you..."

"Us. Let's ask the others too."

"...us, and that's it?"

"Pretty much. We just make sure everyone knows we are having a sponsored chat marathon. Simple but effective."

"I don't know where you've put the real Dan, Mr. Impostor, but you can stay around for a little while longer."

"Ha ha. Er, hey…if I really *had* been kidnapped by my doppelganger, you wouldn't actually say what you just said, would you?"

"Oh wouldn't I?"

"Git."

"Maybe you'd like to talk about it, Dan?"

"Well, maybe I would."

Sip. Sip.

"Ok then."

"Ok what, Ted?"

252

"Ok then, let's do it. Let's make this night happen."
"Cool! So... now what?"
"Get me another pint, a pen and a beermat. We need to write this down."
"Sounds like a plan!"

I bet you're wondering what that's all about then!

Chapter 18

It's raining. It's raining hard. But only outside. And
I'm looking at all this hard rain from the vantage
point of my living room window. If a view of such a
tiny sliver of sky can be called one. I am reflecting.
But I am merely reflecting this: that timing is
everything. If I had left ten minutes before, I would
be in The Red Lion right now, with an excellent
excuse to stay for the duration of the storm. Ok, so
it's not really a storm. I'm just trying to make all this
sound more dramatic than it is.

I am left, therefore, with a cup of tea and my own
company. Only one of those ever did me any good,
but today I shall manage. Looking away from the
window momentarily, I notice the slight depression in
the part of the sofa where I prefer to sit, for no
particular reason that I can recall. You shall have to
ask my subconscious why the seat nearest to the door
is the one on which I usually place my backside. I
then inevitably turn to look at the armchair. Dad
would sit in this armchair when he came to visit me
here. It must be a generational thing. I don't see the
point of armchairs myself, except perhaps in a pub.
Give me a sofa anytime. Well, you've got to put your
feet up when you can, don't you? I don't know where
I would put my feet if I was sitting in an armchair.
Before you say it, I know the answer is 'on the carpet,
num-nuts', but you do know what I mean. It just
doesn't feel right, sitting in an armchair. Especially
when you could have a sofa. Dad disagreed. He said

he didn't know what to do with his other arm if he tried sitting on my sofa. He always, therefore, went for the chair when he was here. At least that meant we were both happy. I'm now looking for the depression that his posterior made in that very chair, but if there ever was one, it has gone now. One more piece of evidence that he was ever here has now disappeared. Sigh.

We liked to have our usual chats about popular science and stuff like that, while sitting in this room with a cup of tea. Chatting over science was our bonding thing, since as long as I can remember, wherever we were living, back from when he would sit in his own armchair, and I would slouch on the sofa of my childhood home. Looking around my room now, as the rain provides a white noise soundtrack, I am taken back to a conversation we had a few years ago, on the subject of what happened before the Big Bang, a subject neither of us knew much about. That never stopped us though! Between us we had only seen a bit of TV and read a couple of articles on it. That was more than enough for us.

"So for decades, the thing was to work out what the Big Bang actually was…" Dad begins.
"Still is, isn't it?" I ask, not sure if I'd missed that meeting. If there ever actually was such a meeting, I doubt that I would have been invited, so I suggest that this is a fair reaction.
"Well, yes, the details, certainly, but we can be pretty confident about that having happened now, Dan."
"Oh good."
"But now some of the interesting thinking is about

what happened *before*. I mean, the beginning can't just come from nowhere, can it? How can you explain the universe at all when you don't look at why it came into existence in the first place?"

"I must agree," I say, "but I must point out that none of this was in the first astronomy book you gave me, sorry *Santa* gave me, when I was six. That book even gave a paragraph to the steady state theory." That particular theory was that the universe was the same as it ever was and would stay the same forever. Sort of comforting, and popular amongst some scientists for a time, but I can't help thinking that it seems a bit daft now. I mean, *everything* changes, doesn't it? That much is bloody obvious, even from down here, whether you want it to or not.

"Hmm, yes, well sorry about that," Dad apologises. "Um, well, I'm sure that Santa is sorry anyway. It's the best we could do at the time. Got your curiosity going anyway, didn't it? And that was the point."

"Sure did," I agree. "Loved that book. So, what's the situation before the beginning of the universe then? I can't remember much about this one. I've been reading about dark matter lately instead. That blew my brains out quite enough!"

"It would, Dan, it sure would. Well then, how can I summarise this…Hmm. Well, you know that map of the Cosmic Microwave Background?"

"Yeah, of course, Dad. Where the static on the TV comes from. That's a really cool map. I would have liked a poster of that on my bedroom wall, but I thought it might put off any women that I managed to get up there."

Dad shook his head and took a sip of his tea. "I would

rather not know, son. I would merely hope that it would, in the end, attract the right sort of woman."

"I can tell you haven't been dating for a while, Dad. There is currently no evidence for *that* particular theory let me tell you. Anyway, what about the CMB?"

"Well, it shows that the early universe, which was made up of these microwaves…no jokes…"

"I wasn't going to! Honestly…"

"…these microwaves, were not evenly distributed. The universe had hotter bits, and cooler bits. And because of this, gravity was not even. And where it was stronger, matter would start to come together. These random differences caused the formation of all galaxies, suns, planets and everything else."

"Hey, I told you leaving things to random events was a good thing, Dad," I add with a smile.

"For the universe, Dan, yes. For you, not so much."

"Yeah, well anyway, that doesn't tell us about what happened before the Big Bang does it?"

"Not as such, but it tells us something about the way the Big Bang happened. It wasn't tidy and uniform. And that can help clever people think about what that means even further back."

"Like when you look around your room when you wake up on a Sunday morning, and look for clues to work out what happened on Saturday night?" I suggest. This is a rubbish analogy, as presumably, the theoretical me would be present in that scenario to remember what happened. At least some of it anyway. I'm just trying to wind Dad up a little here, that's all. Can't resist. He's about to say something, presumably about my drinking habits, but realises in time what I'm doing here, so carries on instead.

"There are a few theories going at the moment. This is quite new, relatively, so there is no real consensus just yet."

"Ok then, so basically what have we got?"

"Well, I only remember or really understand a few. There's the Cyclic Universe Model…"

"I like the sound of that," I chip in. "Is that like the universe recycling or something?"

"Er, I'm not sure that helps. Look, imagine that our universe has a shadow universe connected to it. Like the two universes exist on different branes that are close to each other, and that collide from time to time…"

"Brains? Ha ha. Sorry, I'll shut up."

"Membranes. I know you know this. They are like other dimensions or something. Well, the idea is that when the branes are colliding, this produces more big bangs and other universes with matter in them, in the dimensions that we experience. When they are moving apart this produces a quieter period where there are no big bangs. Then they collide again and the process repeats."

"It's a beautiful image, I must admit," I say.

"Wouldn't want to be at the point of collision, that's for sure. Or maybe we would? Ha, ok, I sort of get that one. What else have you got?

"Um, then there's Eternal Inflation…"

"Like your beer belly!"

Dad ignores this, expect for perhaps a glimmer of a wry smile, and continues. "This theory, how can I put this, imagines that we are just a bubble popping off from a larger universe. There could be many of these

258

bubbles producing completely different unconnected universes, all with completely different rules, such as our uneven big bang. Therefore, it would suggest that virtually all of them are not producing galaxies, stars and life at all."

I dunk my biscuit absent-mindedly. It must have been absent-mindedly because I'm not usually a dunker. "That sounds sad," I add. "Like we are one lucky lonely universe in a much bigger empty universe. Lucky, but alone." I sip my tea as I think about this and look for another, less soggy, biscuit. The plate is empty. Symbolism, ha!

"I know," Dad agrees, "but this might cheer you up. There's another theory that what is happening is that black holes are bleeding matter out of our universe and creating other universes, But these universes are just like this one, with all the same rules, through this process. We could be giving birth to other similar universes from this universe, right now."

"Wow, gosh, brain overload!" I declare, giving up on the biscuit-hunt. "This is so such a long way from my book with that steady state theory. Man, I wonder what my six-year old self would have made of this conversation. I think it might have made me cry!" Then I take another sip of tea, which is doing a good job as a stand in for a pint. "So, anyway," I continue, "is what you are saying here, is that a Universe, like ours, that is capable of producing black holes, i.e. one that produces uneven big bangs, is going to be better able to reproduce and give birth to more universes like it? So rather than us being one lucky universe amongst a whole load of empty universes, we could be part of one big massive family of similar

259

universes…"

"Yes, I suppose so," Dad muses. "That does seem a bit Darwinian though…"

"… all connected by black holes! Cool! That's the theory I like! I'm going to drop that one in conversation down the pub later. That is a pint-three type of conversation, I reckon. Bleeding into pint four perhaps. Then five…"

"I shall leave that up to you, Dan. So, I'm wondering if behind all of this, all these ideas have some connection. Like, yes, there is just one great expanse of energy. Then, sometimes parts of this energy expanse cool off enough to form mass, and a universe sparks from this mass and we get a Big Bang. Then, that universe, if it is created right, can then spawn other universes off itself that are just like it. And, imagine Dan, we are in the middle of that process right now."

"Awesome, Dad. Just awesome. So rather than everything staying the same, you're saying that good things can be born from other good things! Deep. Can't wait to set that thought-bomb off down The Red Lion later. Meanwhile, shall I put the kettle on?"

I can remember every word of that conversation now. Well anyway, this is what my brain is telling me how the conversation went. It probably wasn't quite like that in reality. I doubt I was quite that prone to analogy. But it was a great conversation nevertheless, and that's how I now choose to remember it. You know what? If there are so many other universes and dimensions around, then I really hope that there's room for Dad out there somewhere, like if death is the way through one of these black holes. The pathway, perhaps, to find him sitting right now somewhere, on the perfect armchair.

I'm just making this up now of course, from nothing but my neurons. I know this, I know this, you don't have to tell me. Sigh. But at least I now find myself looking for some good in the universe. That's an improvement of sorts, right?

Anyway, I hope you don't mind me philosophising about my domestic seating arrangements, especially while we are sober. It's going to be a slow afternoon at this rate, if the rain doesn't budge. Just to conclude though, just so you know, I only have an armchair because I don't have space for two sofas. That's not symbolism or anything, just take a tape measure and check if you like. Jesus, it's *still* raining. When will this ever end? Oh, sod it, I'll just get wet.

On the way, as I trot past Corkscrews, the local wine bar, I see a sign outside which says:
"It's cold and wet and miserable. But not in here! Come on in!" Yes, it *is* cold and wet and miserable, but I'm still not going in there. I pull up my hood and pick up the pace, as the rain begins to harden yet again. This sadly reminds me that I really might have to start going in that bloody place eventually, if all of my favourite pubs keep closing. God, I sure hope this plan of Debbie's works. It's got to.

Jez, who this universe seems to like, and therefore is probably liked in many other universes too, is somehow totally dry and over two thirds of the way down his pint when I arrive through the door of The Red Lion. I am dripping wet. The quantum state of his glass means that I will get him a new pint when I get mine. That's another one of the rules of this universe, and also probably many other universes like it, the good ones anyway.

"You might want to get a strong one, like 'GB Aged'," he calls out, as I wave and head to the bar. "Debs has something planned for you!" He then chuckles and shakes his head, smiling.

Debbie's working today, so she greets me with a stolen kiss, as I get to the bar. Since everyone seems to know we are seeing each other by now that's ok, but we don't go out of our way to display our affection publicly. Especially not while Jen is still in town, from my own particular point of view.

"I'm guessing 'Mild Surprise' for you today," she says by way of an additional hello.

"Er, what is it?" I enquire.

"3.3%. But tastes like 4%, I'm reading here. That might be the surprise, I'm not sure."

"Hmm, what else do we have?"

"Oh, ok then. Just the usual, plus there's 'GB Aged'..."

"'GB Aged!' Sounds like my kind of thing."

"It's not your kind of thing."

"Jez suggested it *may* be my kind of thing..."

"Ah, right..."

"At least just for today, that is."

"I see."

"For some reason."

"Yep."

"That you might know of."

"Ok, ok, well, just don't panic. It's nothing much really," she tells me. Then yells over rather loudly

"Thanks *so* much Jez!", which gives me and my nearby ears more than just a mild surprise, I can tell you. Jez too, judging by the amount of beer now dripping down his shirt.

"Perhaps a 'GB Aged' would prevent any panic?" I ask.

"Look, I've just found out today and I was going to tell you right now."

"Ok, what's up then?"

"I've got the local paper to take an interest in our campaign to keep the pub open."

"Right..."

"I can't front it..."

"No?"

"No."

"Because?"

"Because I work here Dan. It's awkward enough as it is."

"Right, so..." in one part of my brain the penny has already dropped. The other part, the one I normally try and give control to, is still holding onto denial.

"So, I've said that they can interview you about it."

"You actually said that?!"

"Sorry, I couldn't think of anyone else. I mean anyone *better*. You'll be fine Dan. You just need to talk about how you love this pub, and why etc etc."

I'm about to protest, then remember Corkscrews, and the sign outside. Debbie's right. I can do this. More than that, I *should* do this.

"Ok, ok. You're right. I can do this. I'll do some research, prepare a few things to say. It'll be fine. When is it for?"

"Er, in thirty minutes time."

"Thirty minutes? Thirty minutes! How did you know I was going to even be here?"

A moment of silence. We just exchange glances until we both are smiling. I just shrug.

"I thought you might not be here at all with this rain," Debbie tells me. "I was thinking of sending someone out for you in a minute, if you hadn't turned up. I had Jez lined up to drag you down, in fact. He wasn't too keen on getting wet, or my pink umbrella, but he said he'd do it."

"Yes, but he didn't have to in the end," I muse. "That figures. Jez always manages to get away with such things somehow. Ok, you will help me out if I get a bit stuck, right?"

"Of course. Just speak from the heart and you'll be fine," Debbie assures me, then reaches over to fluff my hair up.

"Er, what was that for?"

"Well, there's a photographer coming too."

"What? Oh Jesus. Right, in that case, I *will* have a 'GB Aged' then!"

"Are you sure? It is 7.2%..."

As I return to the table and to Jez, he eyes me up and down to discern my state of mind. But all he actually says is "Ah, I see you have gone for the 'Mild Surprise'."

"You could say that, mate," I reply.

Word about my interview must have got around, as Amy and Ted arrive just before the journalist and photographer do. By the time they join us all at the table, I'm a third of the way into pint number two, which should be perfect for a newspaper interview, now that I think about it. Or any kind of interview, except perhaps the type you go to for a job. I can get quite chatty around pint number two, you see, but can still make some semblance of sense to the sober.

"So," says the chap with the notebook, who we must presume is the journalist, "who's running this campaign then?"
Since all heads but mine turn towards me, that provides the answer for him, in lieu of a verbal one from myself. Pint number two is not quite kicking in yet under this amount of pressure, it seems.
"And what's your name?" he asks tersely. I notice he has failed to introduce himself yet. He looks just as jaded as me when I'm at work. Fair enough I suppose, but that sort of face looks incongruous in a pub. Unless it's on Tom the Landlord these days. Incongruous - ooh, check me using big words already. Pint two must be taking effect at last! So I give him my name and tell him the basics of what we are trying to do to keep the pub open, as I have been rehearsing in my head for the past half an hour. I notice the photographer readying her camera, and my subconscious brain sends my hand up to rummage through my hair as I am speaking, without my say so, as if itself is conscious of the way I can look in a picture without a little rummage.
"So, just so we are clear," my nameless interviewer continues, "are you trying to save *all* the pubs in town, or just this pub?"
"Er, just this pub." I say, suddenly less sure of the validity of our goal.
"*This* pub?" he asks, looking around. His slight, but evident, incredulity causes me to bristle somewhat, and send some adrenaline from my adrenal gland to

265

my bloodstream.

"Yes, *this* pub," I insist. "We love this place. It's the only place round here you can go and get a decent beer, have a good chat, and not risk getting your head kicked in. Don't write that down actually, that might be libellous."

He continues writing anyway, but nods at me in that 'I know my job' sort of way.

"Well, what about that place over the road?" he asks. "'Corkies' or something."

"*'Corkscrews'*. No, that's a totally different sort of place. So totally different! I don't even know where to begin to explain that one..."

"Well don't worry, we haven't got room for that many words for this story anyway. Tell me, what have you done for this campaign so far?"

I notice that Debbie is earwigging the conversation from the bar, and she makes some hand gestures over to me. To try and prompt me I think. I'm busy wondering what any of this has to do with the Village People's song 'YMCA' when the penny finally drops.

"Well, we have put in what is called an 'ACV' to the council. We had to get twenty-one signatures for that."

"What's an ACV exactly?"

"An 'Asset of Community Value'. We had to fill in a form. It means that this place, and other sorts of places, can be designated as important to the community, just as they currently are, and so they should not be changed or similarly mucked about with. You understand? I mean, otherwise everything will be turned into flats and that. Then what will happen? We will be all stuck in those flats on our

266

own with nowhere to go out and meet each other!"
Ted gives me a wink and an approving thumbs-up at
this. This gives me the push to plough on with my
nascent speech.

"Look. So many of our pubs are closing every week
and we have to understand that once they are gone
they are gone forever. They will probably never come
back, but even if, in ten or twenty years' time, we
suddenly realise what idiots we were (don't write that
either) letting all our pubs close down, and open up a
whole bunch of new ones, they just won't be the same
places. Look at all the history and character in this
place. The pictures on the walls, the bizarre collection
of nameless things over the bar. You can't just ship
this into a new place overnight. It takes time to grow.
You can't fake it. And it's important! It changes the
way people feel about the place. Like they belong to
something bigger than themselves, something that has
been here for decade upon decade before, hundreds of
years maybe. And get this. It changes the way people
act. It breeds respect. It breeds *belonging*."

I had no idea that I was going to say any of this
before I started, but it must have been buried in me
somewhere, waiting for an opportunity to get out. I
think I surprised the journalist as well, who is
suddenly writing in his notebook again.

"Ok, that's…great. So, what events are you planning
to do next in your campaign then?"

"Events?"

"Yes, now that the, er, ACV form is in, what are you
going to do next? To promote your cause."

"Well, there's this interview…" I say, understandably
floundering, since I had not given this topic a single

moment's thought until just now.

"Yes, I'm aware of that…"

"And…" I need pint-three for creative thought, so nothing else is coming just yet. Oh dear.

"Well, Dan, there is that charity pub sit-in you're organising," says Ted, "in which we are inviting people to come down to the pub here and talk to people for charity. We are being sponsored for each new friend we make. Well, acquaintance will do, but let's not split hairs."

"So, you are going to sit in the pub all day? For charity?" the journalist asks me. Sounds good to me, so I run with it.

"Absolutely," I say, "but we will not be drinking all day, I assure you. This is a responsible, mature, charity event. We will form teams and pace ourselves and all that." I know it is Ted's spur-of-the-moment idea to mention this, but the cause resonates immediately to me, and suddenly I find myself speaking before I've even thought about what to say. This is only *sometimes* a bad thing, remember. I carry on.

"So, we would like lots of people to come down, who might otherwise have felt uncomfortable coming down on their own, or coming into this pub at all, or whatever, and we will all sit down and have a chat and a beer and say hello. One on one.

About…anything at all. You see, we don't meet enough and talk enough as a community, do we? Well, you can in here. You always could, I guess, but I think people have forgotten how. So we want to highlight that you *can* come down here, and to other places like this, just to sit and watch or talk to people, whatever you feel comfortable with. There's too much loneliness out there now, isn't there? That's what I hear on the radio and TV every day. We've forgotten how to get along with each other. All our towns are going to end up like London at this rate, where you don't even know your neighbours and just go out with your workmates. Don't write that either, I don't want to upset any Londoners. They're not all like that, but you know what I mean. Anyway, so, on the day, of the event I mean, we are going to put a banner up over there in the corner saying 'Charity Chat' or something, and anyone can come up and is welcome to have a chat with us."

"Charity Chat?" he asks, still writing.

"Er, or something like that. We need to, er, finesse the details."

"And what charity will that be for?"

"Um, various local charities, that, er, deal with loneliness in the community. Like visiting care homes and suchlike. Home visits. Trips out. Help with mental health. The Samaritans. That sort of thing." I'm on a roll now. I'll be promising Care-Home-Duncan's perfect society next if I don't rein myself in. I look up and see Debbie is staring at me, grinning from ear to ear, giving me some kind of look I can't quite fathom. It might be admiration, but I'm not used to getting that one, so I shall have to check later. Amy, Jez and Ted just look stunned. I suppose they are scared about what I'm about to rope them into next.

"Well, that's great," says the journalist. "We might do a follow up piece on that. When is that going to be exactly?"

"Just before Christmas," Ted chimes in. "That's the loneliest time of year after all."

Christmas. Oh dear. I might be gone soon after that, if Jen gets her way, leaving the pub and all its patrons to their fate. I take another swig to drown that thought for now.

"Great, really great," concludes the journalist, placing his pen back into his top pocket. "If we can just take a couple of pictures for the piece, that will be fine for now."

The photographer gets up, surveys the light and background, and asks us to shuffle round the table a bit. Once satisfied she asks me, "Can you simulate the delivery of a profound statement?" This causes much hilarity amongst my so-called friends but eventually I provide a look approximating profundity, and she puts her camera away smiling. The journalist shakes our hands quickly and leaves, giving me his card, while the photographer hangs around, sorting her bag out. Once he definitely has gone, she looks up and grins.

"So," she says, "I guess you'll be having another pint then?"

"Nah, we'd better be going," says Jez, checking his watch. One, two, three seconds then we all burst out laughing.

"In which case, do you mind if I join you?"

"The more the merrier," says Jez, and he accompanies her to the bar.

Amy gives me that look of 'what have you done, Dan?' but this time there is admiration in there too. I think that's what it is anyway.

"That went well, Daniel," she tells me. "They *are*

270

going to print that you know."

"I know."

"So we are going to have to do it now, you know."

"I know." I then look over to Ted, who dropped me in it just a little, and raise my glass. "Thanks Ted." I say, meaning it really and meaning it sarcastically in equal measure.

"No problem. That's what I do, facilitate," he replies. The remaining three of us all chink glasses, for the moment revelling in the idea, rather than the details.

"Here's to the magic of pint number two!" laughs Jez, about half an hour later, as we consume the dregs of pint number three. "Works every time. The optimum pint, before it all starts to go awry. You sure did one hell of a job there, matey. What would you have promised if they came in for the interview now, for God's sake!"

"I have no idea," I muse. "That's a scary thought. World peace maybe?"

"I knew you were winging it," says the photographer, who we shall henceforth refer to as Flis. It took a short while for her to explain that this was just short for 'Felicity' and that she always thought that name sounded too posh, so 'Flis' it is. "You did wake up Jon, though, so that's a sign it might be a good story." She then told us that 'Jon' was the journalist's name, which was more than he told us.

"Yes," agrees Amy, fixing me with a stare, "but now you've *really* got to actually do it. Sorry, now *we've* got to actually do it," she adds, once she spots the look of fear leap onto my face.

"Has anyone given any thought as to whether Tom the Landlord will even allow it?" Ted posits. "You, I mean *us*, can't be in his good books at the moment as it is with all this ACV stuff."

"That job I will be delegating," I reply. "Conflict is not my bag. That is *definitely* a job for Debbie."

"To the gorgeous Debbie!" Jez exclaims suddenly, raising his glass.

All five of us simultaneously respond as one. "The gorgeous Debbie!" It's what you do in these situations, right?

Debbie looks over to us from the bar, suspiciously, but with a smile.

"Who's Debbie?" Flis enquires.

"Oh you have so much to learn," Jez leans over, gently delivering that thought into her ear. Well, well, well, he may be in there, you know, the dirty dog.

The night progresses nicely from there, the beer making us immune for a while from the consequences of our decisions. Debbie joins me for her break, and I clue her in on exactly what I have roped her in for, which gets me a punch on the arm. It is firm but playful, I think. She says it sounds fantastic, especially about money for the care home visits, and that she will sort Tom out to host it in good time. She actually reckons he will fancy the extra income before he goes away one way or the other, and that he might be coming around to the idea of selling The Lion on as a pub after all if he can get a decent offer. She also promises to clue me in on all things around ACVs and Tom the Landlord tomorrow. Meanwhile, Jez and Flis start to get a little more snuggly and Amy and Ted embark on some good-natured argument over the meaning of the ending of some film or other.

272

Hold it there. Hold it right there. We are not coupling up here, like some preparation for some sunset-bleached final scene. You don't have to be with someone to get a happy ending. You just don't. I hope I've made myself clear here. Good, thank you.

Sorry, I'm getting a little drunk, and something might be stressing me out. Oh yes, I am now running a campaign to keep a pub open and a charity pub-chat event or something. How did that happen again?

But at least I'm still here. I am still here. And, I notice, Matthew Hopkins isn't.

Chapter 19

So, it appears that we are actually doing this thing. At which point it becomes apparent that deciding to do something is often the hardest part of any venture. Once you've decided to actually do something, the actual doing of it then suddenly seems so much simpler. Just make a checklist, think of one thing at a time, and tick each one off once you've done them:

1. Book a venue
2. Get people to join you to do the show
3. Tell everyone else about the show, and get them to come

That's it! It doesn't mean it's going to work, but it does mean that it's going to happen. The first one was easy. Debbie has been doing an excellent job at making Tom the Landlord feel guilty, plus I think he really is relishing a decent pay day before he leaves, however that will end up turning out. The second wasn't too bad either. Amy, Jez, Ted and Debbie were all with me on this from the start. That in itself felt like a quorum. Safety in numbers. Number three on the list, though. That is a real head-scratcher. How are we going to get to be good listeners if no one wants to talk to us?

Bereft of inspiration, I find my next trip to the care home with Debbie something of a relief. My worries are nothing compared to those I see in here. I make a bee-line for Harry again. Despite the fact that he tends not to remember me at all, we seem to have built up some kind of odd rapport. Maybe it's just all in my head, but it helps nonetheless. Someone is actually with him when we arrive, which is unusual. Turns out it's Harry's daughter. He doesn't seem to know who she is either. I immediately find that this makes me feel a little better about myself, before I remind myself to stop having such selfish thoughts. I say hello. She seems nice, but uncomfortable with the situation. She isn't used to it yet. You never get used to it really, I tell her in a quiet aside while we get Harry a cup of tea, but I add that it does somehow become more of a routine over time. I have no idea how true this will actually be for her, or how true it even was for me, but I hope it helps anyway. 'Hope' in itself helps, when you are lucky enough to have some. There is precious little of that here though. There is just the day today that we have together I tell her, so we learn to be thankful for that, if we can. She just smiles at me weakly, wanting to believe me, no doubt, but not yet sure how she possibly can. Fair enough. I would have been the same.

I was about to find someone else to talk to, but it soon becomes apparent that she has to leave, so I hover around as they say their goodbyes. She hugs him tight. He responds to a lesser degree, not sure who is hugging him or why, but grateful of the human contact nonetheless. I get myself a cup of tea and, by the time I get back, she has gone. Then I sit next to Harry, the seat still warm from his daughter's presence, even if he is not.

"She seems nice," I say, as an opener.

"Yes," he replies simply, unsure of what he is supposed to say, and also wondering whether this new fellow in front of him now is nice too, or not. Harry usually runs with this sort of situation, by instinct, so I will just plough on. He must have been a positive, jolly chap when he was…er, when he was, I don't know, *himself* I guess. So I ask him about his daughter. I very much do not suggest that it was her here just now. That sort of thing just gets people upset. His face quickly beams as he brings up a memory.

"Ever so proud of my little Alice," he begins. "Always such a good girl. Top of her class at school you know. That's including the boys!"

"Brilliant!" I say enthusiastically, between careful sips of still-hot tea.

"She's going to be a doctor when she grows up," he tells me. "Or maybe a vet."

"That's a lovely thing to be," I tell him reassuringly. I wonder what she actually did become. Maybe I'll ask her next time, not that it matters.

"She's a good drawer too. We have a painting she did at school put up on our fridge door. It's a space rocket, with all of us waving out the window! We all laughed when she brought this back home. What a great imagination!"

"That would be a great trip to make," I say but my voice edges to melancholy as the words fall out of my mouth. What a great idea for a picture! I never drew a picture like that for my Dad, but I really wish I had done, so he would have been proud of me too. The nearest we got to space was talking about it. Which is better than nothing I suppose, and certainly more realistic.

"We still keep it on the fridge now," Harry continues. "It still makes us laugh. The picture…"

Ah, these memories locked away in time, stranded from the context of the other memories around them, but still existing in themselves as beautiful islands. Beautiful still, as long as you can accept them for what they now are.

As we continue chit-chatting about his daughter, I can't help thinking more and more of Dad while I stare at Harry. He tells me of her brief, but expensive, flirtation with horse-riding. He tells me of her surprise thirteenth birthday party. So much detail, down to the colour of the bunting and the filling in the vol-au-vents. So much detail buried here still, so much of a real individual human being left in there. But today, the more he speaks, the more I just hear Dad. A wave comes over me, as I momentarily forget myself.

"I'm sorry! I'm so sorry!" I blurt out, taking his hand, then immediately regretting it.

He stops reminiscing and turns to me for a moment, suddenly focussed and in the present. He clutches my hand to stop me from taking it away and looks me right in the eye.

"It's alright, son," he tells me. "Really, it's all alright. It's not your fault." Then he smiles for just a brief moment, lets go of my hand, and continues with his story.

I have no idea what the look on my face reveals when Debbie comes to get me some minutes later, but it must have betrayed something. She looks at me very curiously, you see. She doesn't says anything though. She can be polite like that.

A few days later, my steps feel a little lighter as I head to the local radio station. Debbie, now our 'Head of Promotions', has managed to get us booked into a slot in the weekly listings show, which tells listeners in the area what is happening out and about. Conveniently for Debbie, she is working at the time we have been told to arrive, so she cannot join me. I asked Ted, then Amy, but they were busy too. Since Jez was also there at the time, looking at me expectantly like a puppy, I had to ask him too. I'm not sure how much I can trust Jez to behave himself on the radio, but I really didn't fancy doing this on my own, so he's coming along with me.

"This is weird isn't it," he grins at me. "On the radio, man! After all these years! I've told my folks. They are so excited. Have you told your folk…er sister and that?"

"Yes, yes. I've told everybody I know. That's the point. Look, there's the place already. We've got ages yet. Why did you want to meet so early?"

Jez just nods his head over to the right. I follow his gaze towards the door of The Three Tuns. "Can't do this empty," he beams, dragging me in.

"Ok, but just the one…"

Turns out that 'just the two' is just right for a radio interview too. Nice and relaxed, but not too giddy. I did go to the toilet twice though, as we waited to go into the studio. Jeremy, our host, is even smilier (if that is a word) than Jez, and immediately puts us at our ease once we get seated in front of our brightly coloured microphones, then are told how far to sit away from them, which is not far at all. We are given some water to drink, but I daren't put my bladder under any extra pressure, so just leave it there in front of me.

"So…Dan…and…Jez?"

"Yeah, Jez."

"Dan and Jez are here today to talk about this great new initiative they are running next week, at the… Red Lion?"

"Yes, The Red Lion," I confirm.

"The er... Red Lion Christmas Charity Chat against Loneliness?"

"That's right," chimes in Jez, "or RLCCAL…"

"Rollcall?" Jeremy enquires politely, hurriedly checking his notes again.

"No," I step in, "that's just an acronym. We decided that wasn't quite catchy enough…"

"Really?" asks Jeremy. "Rollcall…I quite like it. Anyway, tell us all about it. What is it and what made you set this up."

"Well," I begin, "we drink a lot in The Red Lion."

"Very much a *lot* sometimes!" Jez interjects. Jeremy chuckles.

"I mean we are *there* quite a lot," I continue, "and we know a lot of people there, you know, just to talk to or say hello. Don't always talk to them about anything in particular, but it's a friendly pub and it's nice just to meet other people…"

"It's good to know such places still exist," Jeremy adds, nodding, encouraging me to carry on. So I do.

"But there was this one bloke in there. I would talk to him sometimes, about trivial stuff mostly, knew him a

279

little bit. He seemed a bit sad sometimes maybe, but you know, he was a normal bloke. A familiar face, you know? Then one day we found out that he was underneath having a really hard time and he, er tried to..um…"

"…top himself", Jez adds helpfully.

"Oh dear," says Jeremy, slipping effortlessly into sympathy mode. "How is he?"

"He's ok. He's ok now. Physically. Was in hospital for a few days but is back home now. The thing is though, even though we talked to him sometimes, we never talked about what was really bothering him, you know? We never really helped him. What he did came as a total surprise to everyone."

"Hmm," encourages Jeremy.

"And it made me, us, think what else was going on here. Right in front of us, you know? Even the people who talk, don't really talk about what is happening in their lives necessarily. We've become used to bottling things up."

"If you pardon the pun," adds Jez, eager to contribute.

"Indeed," chuckles Jeremy. Then adds seriously.

"Male depression in particular is quite a problem. Some of our listeners will remember that we ran a really moving show on the subject a couple of weeks ago. I mean, the biggest cause of death for men under forty-five is suicide, right?"

"Exactly," I agree. "It's like we have been brought up to just put up with things inside and we are er, weak if we ever talk about it, or ask for help. So we don't. Talk about it. Whatever it is…" I tail off, not sure what my point was. Jeremy has seen this sort of thing all before and gets me back on track straight away.

"And so tell us how this ties in with Rollcall?"

Jez nods wisely at me at hearing Jeremy use the name and grins.

"It's not…er yes, well, the 'Red Lion Christmas Charity Chat against Loneliness' is like our response to that," I reply. "So, five of us are setting up in the pub next Wednesday night, The Red Lion, but this time we are taking a table each and just encouraging people to come along and talk to us about whatever they want."

"Lovely idea," Jeremy adds.

Jez takes this opportunity to lean into the microphone and justify his presence. "Yeah, so it could be people who aren't lonely, you know, but don't, like you know, like to talk about serious stuff with their friends. Or it could be people who really are lonely and don't normally get to talk to anyone. We don't care! We welcome everyone and want to talk to all of them! You know, we thought that we already did that, but turns out we didn't really. Not enough. So this time we are explicitly doing that. Yeah?"

Couldn't have put it better myself.

"That's sounds great, guys. So how does this work and when does this start?"

"Just turn up to The Red Lion, any time from 5 o'clock…" I say.

"…we like an early start!" Jez informs the airwaves. Which is fine. That's no secret.

"…and you will see us under our Charity Chat banner. Just pick a table, come join one of us for a drink and talk about whatever you like. We won't judge. We'll just listen. We are not experts or anything like that by the way. Just people who are going to listen. That's it. Anyway, if by chance there isn't a table free maybe you can start talking to each other while you wait. You might not even need us, you never know!"

"That really is great guys. And this is for charity too right?"

"Oh yes, sure," I tell Jeremy. "We are just going to take donations at the bar, no pressure, and these are going to various mental health charities and anti-loneliness charities."

"*For* Lionliness. Against loneliness!" chimes in Jez. I don't know how long he's been sitting on that catchphrase, but he seems mightily relieved to get it out finally.

"That's great, guys," Jeremy says, his tone now effortlessly shifting to conclude the interview. "I wish you good luck with all that, I really do, and I hope you can come back and tell us all about it. And may I just add that it's great that there are still some pubs around where the community can get together and do this sort of thing. Great stuff."

"Yes, indeed," I add. "Use them while you can. Anyway, um, thanks for having us."

"Thank you. So please do join Dan and Jez down The Red Lion, next Wednesday from 5pm if you can. Now, it's time for the travel and weather. What's happening out there Julie?"

I meant every word in there, including those that came out of Jez's mouth, but I suddenly remember Jen and her plans for me and can't help but feel a fraud as Jez heartily slaps me on the back, tells me what a great job I did, and herds me back into the Three Tuns again. A well-intentioned fraud, but a

282

fraud nonetheless. Pint three helps with that a little but I know I can't put this off forever. I'm sick of being between everything to tell the truth. I need to belong. I need to belong somewhere.

Anyway, regardless of all that, with that interview we are double-officially up and running. So we really, really have to do it now! We all meet up in The Lion the next day to sort out logistics, which takes all of a pint and a half, then settle down to fantasise and worry, in turn, about how it will all go. Jez is getting all the plaudits from the gang for his performance, but that's ok, he deserves them. Ted takes notes and makes a list. It's a long list, but it's all achievable.

I know I don't talk enough, and this isn't much, but I think you should know this next thing, at the very least. I walk home later again, again a little drunk, but this time alone. Completely alone. Matthew never said goodbye, but I think he's gone for good now. A bit rude, but I'm not complaining. I take the stones out of my pockets, dropping them on the street one by one as I take each step home.

Chapter 20

"Hold it. No, left a bit."
"Are you sure?"
"Right a tiny bit."
"For God's sake, Dan."
"It's got to be right, Ted."
"Whatever for?"
"I'm a perfectionist."
"Really? It doesn't show."
"I'm hurt. Ok, that'll do."
"Still looks wonky maybe…"
"Sod it. Get the next one."

The 'Red Lion Christmas Charity Chat against Loneliness' sign is now up and in place in our corner of the pub. I know, it's a bit of a mouthful. I see that more clearly now than when I last looked at this sign. Jez has added 'Rollcall' underneath in marker pen. It's pretty cool, I have to admit. Now the sign is actually up though, all this is starting to seem more real, and I'm beginning to wonder what the hell we are trying to do here. Ted being Ted, he immediately clocks the worry on my face.
"What's up chum? Does it need to go right a bit?"
"Jesus, Ted. What are we doing? What are we doing here? I'm not qualified for this. I shouldn't be doing any of this. I'm not a psychologist or a psychiatrist. I don't even know what the difference is! What if we do more harm than good here, for God's sake?"
"Hmm," says Ted, looking me up and down, "I thought you might have a crisis of confidence at some

point."

"Thanks for the vote of," I mildly retort.

"Well, I do know you pretty well, right Dan? It sure took a while, but I think I'm getting there."

"Ok, ok. Yes, I *am* having a crisis of confidence," I admit. "Why aren't you?"

"How do you know I'm not?" Ted replies.

"Well, are you?"

"No."

"Arrghh," is all I manage as a response. "Why is *everyone* always calmer than me?"

"They're not really," Ted replies calmly. "It's just that you can see too much of you, and not enough of everyone else. That's all. And that includes me too. Yes, even me. But do you know why I'm not having a crisis of confidence just now?"

"Illuminate me," I ask, immediately regretting the sarcastic tone. I blame the stress. Christmas can be a stressful time, can it not?

"I've been thinking about all this since you came up with the idea, and it boils down to just one thing that you have to realise. Then you'll be fine."

"Further illuminate me," I request, less sarcastically this time I hope.

Ted tells me, "We are not providing the end of the road for any of these people here, Dan. Just the beginning of it. This is not the destination. But the starting line is important too."

"Oh, right." I say.

"Any of us are qualified to start to help people, Dan. Any of us are qualified to listen and be there when people want to talk."

A short pause, as I fiddle with the second poster.

"Ted?"

"Yeah?"

"Two things."

"Uh huh?"

"One, thanks."

"You're welcome. The other?"

"Shut up and help me put up this sign."

Doesn't that show what a bit of clear thinking can do for the soul, as opposed to over-thinking? Wish I had the knack. But I've got Ted instead, and that's a decent alternative.

Once the second poster is up, a couple of the tables are adding to the background noise at the other end of the bar, with a bit of singing.

"*It's Christmas Time!*" a group shouts, and *almost* sings, from around the corner. Ted and myself pause to look up at the table it is emanating from. This looks like a crowd from one of the nearby offices, having a long lunch or a half day today, for Christmas. Probably the former, and they are no doubt all praying it will magically somehow turn into the latter.

"*And there's no need to be afraid!*" they continue. Ah, now I get it. They are going to attempt to recite 'Do they know it's Christmas?', a classic Christmas hit. There are various versions, but there's only one really. You know the one. Hey, did you know this song can be a really good sobriety barometer? What I mean is, and you may know this already if you think about it, that we will soon be able to tell how drunk they all are over there by how far they go into the song before they just give up and jump to the rousing climax. You have to be very drunk indeed to get to "Feed the World" without skipping a bit. This lot joyously carry on for a few lines until one of them stands up and hushes them.

"*And tonight thank God it's them instead of you!*" he shouts tunelessly, but with great enthusiasm.

Everyone cheers. The alpha male will always want to sing the Bono bit, so he must be the alpha male of the group. That's ok though, because this particular alpha male makes everybody cheer and laugh, then raise their glasses. Once that is done two of the others start the singing up again.

"*Feed the World!*" they sing, way too soon, and then the rest of them join in and repeat until they end in a big cheer.

That's a big skip. This lot must have missed out over half the song. So they can't be that drunk yet then. As yet they are too sober and excited, too scatter-brained, with too many other things to say. No, they are not yet all-consumed by the moment, and instead are still partly consumed by themselves. That will change later, when they get plastered enough to open up and perhaps give this tune another go. Ted catches my eye, and we smile knowingly at each other, having had a conversation on this topic before.

"Amateurs," he laughs, looking at his watch. "But even if they go back to work now, there's a whole lot of things will need undoing tomorrow."

He's not wrong. That's why I took the day off.

We take a break and grab some food in a nearby café, a radical departure from our normal modus operandi, but not a bad idea in the circumstances. I get a message from Rachel, apologising for not being able to make it, but also wishing me luck. That's ok, I didn't really expect her to, with the boys and

287

everything, but it's nice to know that she cares.

"Are you going to eat that sandwich, or stare it to death?" Ted asks me, through a mouthful of carbohydrate, fat and protein.

"This feels weird, doesn't it?" I say, by way of reply.

"What, tonight you mean?"

"No, you and me, eating food and having a soft drink."

He laughs heartily at this and holds his sandwich up. I soundlessly 'chink' it with mine.

"Cheers!" we both say in unison, then proceed to line our stomachs. Not long now.

Once we return to The Red Lion and get in position, I notice that the same work crowd we heard earlier are still here, having somehow managed to avoid going back to the office at all that afternoon. Good for them. They have not yet burst into song again, but that could happen any time now. Bono, or at least the guy who sang the Bono line, is staggering back from the Gents when he notices our signs and tables. All his inhibitions, if he had any to lose in the first place, are now entirely lost. So, of course he comes over and politely asks us what we are up to.

"What the living chuff is all this about then?" he enquires.

"It's a charity thing," I offer tentatively. "We are setting up a few tables in the corner here where anyone can come and have a chat. About anything they like."

"Bit lame. Doesn't everyone just do that in here anyway?"

"Yes," I admit, "it's not much of a stretch for me. But it's about the other people who come here who don't tend to talk to anyone, or people who are too scared to come into a pub on their own. That sort of thing. We've put it about in the papers and stuff that anyone can come down here and just talk to us."

"Who's us?" he asks, looking around.

"Currently me and Ted." I point over to Ted who is laughing away happily with some old bloke.

Bono (he hasn't given me his name, so Bono it is) scrunches his nose up a little at this prospect. I would like to think that, if he was sober, his inhibitions would have allowed him to hide his disappointment.

"No women?"

"Well, yes there will be some later. But it's not that sort of night, Bon – er, my friend. It's not speed dating or something. It's just having a chat."

"For charity?"

"Yes," I confirm, "and after that chat you can donate how much you thought it was worth to you. Or just walk away a bit happier I hope."

"Hmm. Where's the money going to then?" asks Bono.

I hand him our flier. "There's a couple of places it's going to. Anti-loneliness initiatives and work against male suicide, mental health support, that sort of thing."

"Jesus. And here was me having a good time here…"

"Yeah, sorry! I don't mean to bring you down. It's just that some people, you know, men in particular, can find it hard to talk about how they feel and it's a… it's a problem right? Also, there's a lot of lonely people out there who have just lost the knack of meeting people."

"Yeah, I guess. Too busy on their phones!"

"Not you. You have the knack I see," I tell him.

"You've got a load of mates here…"

"Who? That lot. Oh, they're just work mates. Don't see them otherwise, really."

"Oh, ok then. Er…anyway, Christmas can be the worst time of year to be lonely. Sitting on your own imagining all the fun everyone else is having. So…"

"So?" he asks, turning his body away from the bar and towards me for the first time.

"So…we are going to sit here and talk to whoever comes in. About anything they want. For the rest of the day."

"Good for you then," he says, not sure what to do next.

"I expect you have a lady over there to chat up though," I offer, to break the silence in advance of its anticipated arrival, "rather than talking to silly old us."

He looks over and pulls another face. "Nah, not really. That's not going so well actually."

"Oh sorry? How so?" I ask.

Bono raises a finger in the air, to pause the conversation like you might a CD, then leans over to grab his pint from the bar and proceeds to sit down next to me.

"See that redhead over there with the cocktail umbrella in her hair?" he says.

"Uh huh. And the…er…is that a beermat in there too?"

"It rightly is. Yeah, that's her."

"Right. What about her?"

"Well, it's like this…" he begins.

290

Bono's life changed the day the beermat girl (who also remains nameless, so we shall call her Siobhan) walked into the office. 'Life changed'. These are the exact words he chooses to use. However, he is a bit drunk, so he might be overestimating a tad, I can't say. Do I do that too, I begin to wonder? Am I also prone to the over-dramatic? I would not bet against it, but it's so hard to tell from here. Anyway, to get back to Bono's story, Siobhan swept into the office all nervous and excited on her first day, dressed in her best suit, and was quite the attention grabber. In one fell swoop, for Bono at least, she breathed life back into a dull office and gave him reason to get up in the morning and come into work again. He helped with her initial training and they got on well, very well, having a laugh while only being slightly flirty. He then let the other office Romeos try their luck in more obvious ways, hopeful that they would be dispatched with proficient ease, thus leaving the way clear for them to get together. And thus it began to pan out, to a degree. They even exchanged knowing smiles as Bob from Accounts found excuse after excuse to stop by her desk and initiate a discussion about something or other, before he finally gave up and turned his attentions to the new temp, poor soul. Bono also started spending more time in the pub with the office crowd, as Siobhan was there. Well, as much as you can call Corkscrews a pub. He became less interested in dating other women, in favour of the mere friendship that he was developing with Siobhan. He felt sure, you see, that this should grow naturally into something very special. It was just so obvious.

291

Bono reaches the end of his pint, then gets that look on his face which normally accompanies that feeling of nakedness in public places, in dreams at least, but can also mean that you are in a pub with nothing left to drink. Normally this might be a cue for us to part company, but I can tell that he wants to finish his story, so he goes off to quickly get a pint, telling me to 'Hold that thought'.

You know, I have always liked the idea of being able to physically hold a thought, to either hold it close or throw it away. As I wait for him to return, I start to imagine which of my own thoughts could go into which list. I conjure up a past moment with me and Dad on the bridge, a mere few years ago, with the future seemingly endless in front of us, playing poohsticks when we thought that no one was looking. All in the name of science of course. I would hug that memory now if I could, as tight as I could, until it felt real again. Then there are the other more recent memories of him, too many of them, that I would throw into that river if I could, and watch them drift away from me forever. I wish either scenario was that easy, but our brains just refuse to work in that way, no matter how nicely we ask.

Bono then speedily returns with his new beer, eager to continue his tale, casting a nervous glance over to his table, where Siobhan is chatting happily with a couple of her colleagues. By the way, in case you are worried, I'm not even half way down my glass, and we are not in a round, so Bono knows he doesn't have to get me a drink. That's ok with everyone. And so he

292

carries on, as if the intervening two minutes at the bar never happened.

The trouble was, he tells me, as the friendship progressed, the relationship never seemed to. Where Bono saw a clear blue-sky future, Siobhan only seemed to see a ceiling. Me and Bono at that point both look up at the old battered ceiling above us now, a little worse for wear, but clearly one that has witnessed so much human experience. That seems to sum it all up in one image, as he looks back at me and carries on. Siobhan, it transpires, earlier confided in Bono, after a goodly amount of white wine, that she might be a little bit interested in Andrew, who unfortunately happened to be Bono's boss. This somewhat broke Bono's heart in that moment and left him with confusion, frustration, disappointment and a host of other of our 'favourite' feelings. Feelings that he still is carrying around with him right now, he tells me. He describes each and every one to me as the level on his glass gradually descends. He then asks, to the ceiling, how could she not see that this would hurt him? Does she really think that little of him? What does Andrew have that he doesn't? I ponder on these unanswerable questions. At least unanswerable by me, at any rate. On another day, with a closer friend, I might have pointed out that Andrew has 'the promotion' and Bono doesn't, just as a joke you understand. But today is not about me, and we are not friends, at least not yet, so I resist. In my world, you have to be friends with someone before you insult them. The better the friend, the worse things you can say. There's a logic in there if you look for it, help yourself. I just can't explain right now, as I'm a bit busy!

To fill a pause in the proceedings, brought on by a particularly hefty swig from Bono's glass, I ask if that is Andrew with her over at their table. He looks over and says that it is. Oh dear, that scene suddenly looks a bit cruel, now I have Bono's side of the story. Siobhan and Andrew, who looked like two normal people just having a laugh in a pub, now look spoiled and corrupt as they stand there chatting. I mean, don't they know it's Christmas time?

So…

So never judge a book by its cover, as they say. Bono is not, in fact, an arrogant, or even confident, alpha male, but rather a delicious mess of self-doubt, bravado and unused affection. Yes, it turns out that this girl over there, wearing the beermat with more grace than you would ever imagine, is the one he has been building up the courage all day to ask out, to stop the 'Andrew thing' developing before it is too late. Yes, today was supposed to be the day. Now it looks like it might not be the day. I don't know what to say, I really don't. I'm particularly unqualified in this field, after all. Bono's day is absolutely not going to plan. I know that, and so does he too, painfully so. Therefore there is really no point in saying it out loud. Instead I just muster up a look of sympathy, and tell him that I'm sorry, and that I've been there too.

That seems to break him out of his cycle of misery, and he looks up at me and smiles.
"Cheers," he says. "You know, I thought you lot were

weirdos when I came in..."

"We might actually *be* weirdos," I interrupt, as we are now back in a phase of conversation where interruptions are allowed again.

"Yeah, maybe," he laughs, "and I was thinking that all this pub chat stuff was a load of old crap..."

"Bit harsh..."

"No, no I don't mean that *now*, really. I mean that it's not. Crap I mean. It's like...er...well, it didn't take much to hook me in, did it?"

I laugh. "I guess not. But you have had a few. Look, I'm happy to listen and all that, and I hope it helped, but I'm sorry I can't offer any solutions or anything. It's a tough one."

"Yeah, yeah, no worries, bruv, don't expect you to," he says shaking my hand, and I feel his nerves jangling through his own fingers to mine as we touch. "Well look, I'm ready to go back into the fray now at least, now I've got all that off my chest. And we'll just have to see what happens, right?"

"Good luck mate," I tell him, as we chink glasses, "Happy Christmas!". He takes a deep breath and gets up. He winks as he turns from me, by way of thanks, then changes his face from the vulnerable, self-doubting chap that I now suddenly find I quite like, to the wide-boy, good time, laugh-a-minute geezer that replaces him. He walks back over to his table, giving a hearty cheer to his colleagues on his return. He gets a big cheer back. Siobhan, I notice, smiles at him and steps back to include him in her circle. But God knows what *that* actually means.

So, I am up and running! And as I briefly sit alone, waiting for my next victim to pluck up the courage to

join me, I sit back and see what else is going on. Amy
and Jez have since arrived and have a guest each.
Debbie is here too, which means the whole team is
here. For a moment I stop to watch Debbie, who had
earlier arrived with a wave during my time with Bono
and has now started a charity-chat over at her table. I
cannot hear her, so instead I watch the way her hands
move in glorious enthusiasm. Glorious enthusiasm for
the act of sharing a story with another human being. I
watch the way her mouth forms the words, words that
will fall upon the ears of her grateful companion. (All
tumbling out at 767 miles per hour, don't you know,
the speed of sound.) I watch her ears, ears that bend
towards the person who is speaking to her now,
welcoming into her their ideas, their thoughts and
their dreams. I watch the head that contains the brain
that makes all of these beautiful things happen. Then I
watch the smiles that result on the faces of these two
people, just a few feet away from me now, but
wrapped up in their own safe, secure and private
space, for as long as the moment allows.

Love can be a complicated thing. But when it turns
out that it isn't, you have to be sure that you
understand just how lucky you are. This thought hits
me like a ton of bricks. Gorgeous, beautiful bricks. Is
it just me, or my analogies getting worse?

I recognise my next victim, as it goes, and I can't help
but grin widely and laugh audibly as he sheepishly
sits down, along with his dog collar. But this is not a
collar for a dog, but rather the one worn by Father
Michael, or just Michael as I shall call him. He smiles
back at me and just shrugs, pint in hand.

"Glad you have a pint," I begin.

"You are? Why's that?"

"Well, a half just tells me that you aren't really planning on staying. I believe that you need a pint to allow yourself time for a proper chat."

"Ha, well I'm glad not to let you down, Dan!" Then a pause and we check each other out again, the first time since our meeting in the park. "Anyway, just say it…" he adds, then pauses. I chuckle, immediately knowing just what he means.

"Welcome to my church, Michael," I say, just to get it over with. We both laugh. "Hey, thanks for coming though. Really. It is good to see you!" I add, with definite sincerity. Then I chink his glass. "It's part of the ceremony," I then inform him.

"I know your ceremonies better then you know mine, I suspect," he replies, still smiling. "Good to be here. I heard about your event from one of my parishioners. I thought I would come down and show my support."

"Well, it's a pleasure to have you here. Well, er, I must admit that I don't quite know what to say now. You are not typical of who I was expecting today. So… hmm, at the risk of being unimaginative, how is your day going today then?"

"Just fine so far thank you, but this makes a welcome change of scene."

"And your mother? Is she ok?"

"Um, no, not as such. On the way downhill, as they say. Thank you for asking though."

"Sorry to hear that, Michael. Are you going to be going back home again to see her?"

"Yes, I am being allowed away again, probably for the last visit. She wants me to give her the last rites."

I take a swift swig, to swiftly dismiss thoughts of potential parallels with recent events. "Oh," I say, "is that er…good? I mean is that er…normal? Sounds tough. To be asked to do that yourself, I mean."

"Yes, it's not uncommon. Mum has always been very proud of me, becoming a priest. That has always helped keep me going in darker times. And she wants me to be there to see her on her way when her time comes."

"That sounds nice. I hope it helps."

"I think it will help her, yes. Maybe me too, I don't know."

"Seeing her off though? Does that really help?" I ask him.

"Sorry, Dan, I said 'seeing her on her way'."

"Sorry. I mean that you think she is 'on her way'. Somewhere. Rather than just stopping existing. Does that help?"

"Yes, it helps. It is a big part of our faith. But, look you previously made your beliefs clear. I don't want to make you feel like it's going to be better for me and worse for you. That's not what…"

"No, no, sorry," I interrupt, eager to turn us away from a conversational wrong turn, "I was just curious. I don't mean to compare. If it helps, I can think of the afterlife in terms of quantum physics, if thoughts of mortality all become too much for me."

"Really? How does that work?" Michael asks, genuinely curious, and equally eager to steer us back to safer territory.

"Well, no one knows how it works, not even quantum physicists…"

Michael chuckles. "That sounds familiar," he says,

298

then his smile drops a little, perhaps through a guilt reflex. I distract him from it.

"But I try to imagine the consciousness as like an electrical field, a very specific pattern of electrons…"

"Yes, I see…"

"And these electrons exist in the normal world like this table and this pint…"

"Uh huh."

"But they are made of sub-atomic particles, like gluons and quarks, or even just strings of energy. And these things don't behave like objects in our world. They operate on probabilities, not certainties, they can be in two places at once, and they may even exist in many other dimensions."

"Interesting."

"And maybe one of those dimensions is where that pattern of electrons can continue to exist after they cease to exist here. Which is, I guess, a kind of afterlife."

"But no one knows this for sure…"

"No," I admit. "I guess you could call it my belief system too, if you were wanting to challenge me."

"I came here to congratulate you, Dan, not challenge you! But it does sound like we have more in common than you might think."

I ponder this for a sip or two, while he waits for a sip or two. "Think of it this way," I eventually reply. "As history has progressed, more and more of our understanding of the world around us has fallen out of the realm of magic and into the realm of science. Like us not blaming witches for crop failures and all sorts of other things anymore. I see that continuing to the point where science will eventually explain everything."

"Yes, I know what you mean, but I think some things will just never be known or understood by man."

A wave of alcohol washes over me as I take a bigger swig than I consciously intended. I can maybe sympathise with that statement, but just in one specific way, specific to me and my actions and the secrets we keep. I could tell him that too. I could tell him right now how there are things about me that will never be known, and because of that I myself will never be understood. My heart skips as I imagine just coming out with the words. Part of me wants to say them. Right now. But that part is just not big enough, so instead I keep to topic, and will the surge of adrenaline away. And, oh yes, I can do this again and again if I want to. Watch me. Sip. And, yes, I do know that this makes me a hypocrite.

"And I can admit that what I was talking about is one of the things we as yet, in science, do not know," I continue. "In the end though, we are both just trying to understand how the universe works in our own ways. Can we drink to that?"

"We can. Cheers, Dan." We chink glasses. "I'm happy to agree with that." He sighs. "I'd be happy just to understand how my parish works."

I don't quite know what to do with that more immediate topic, and struggle for an answer until he smiles playfully at me. I then relax, look around, and say "Me too. Me too."

And so, in such inconsequential exchanges as these, even with so much left unsaid, the most unlikely of friendships can arise, and bridges can be built. It's not all I can be, I know, but it's better than nothing.

300

After his pint though, Michael tells me that he has to go to a meeting, and that he did not want to take up any more of my time. He thanks me for what we are doing, wishes me luck then disappears, scanning the room quickly before he goes. No sooner than he leaves, I scan the room too, and see Henry perched at his normal place at the bar. But this time he is facing towards me rather than the optics, as if waiting for me to become available. I raise my eyebrows as the universal sign of query, then beckon him over. It's that kind of day. And over he does indeed come.

"Alright, Henry?" I begin, using the typical question that demands no honesty, or even any answer at all.
"Dan," he replies. "This is a change for you."
I think this is humour but he's not smiling with his eyes so I'm not entirely sure. I shall give him the benefit of the doubt, all things considered. "Yeah, it's going well. Better than I hoped really. But expectations have been kept deliberately low. Care to join me?"
"Sure," he says, as if the thought had just occurred to him. He's got a lot of barriers up, this one, but he finally takes a seat anyway. This chat, I find myself thinking, may well be the most challenging one of the night.
"Um," he begins, in between sips. "Um." He is struggling for the words again, but this time is determined to find them.
"Yeah?"
"Just wanted to say thanks."
"What for, mate?"
"You visited me, right? At the, er…hospital?"
"Er, yeah. But…you were asleep, right? I didn't want

301

to wake you, so…"

"That's ok. The nurses told me I had a visitor. They didn't get a name so tried their best to describe you. I recognised the description of the t-shirt. So I knew it must be you."

"Ha. These things I wear betray my anonymity," I joke. "Must take a note of that next time I want to rob a bank!"

Henry looks at me a little blankly. I remind myself to avoid random conversational tangents like this when I'm with him. "Anyway," he says. "I just wanted to let you know I appreciated it. That you came, I mean. That meant a lot."

"No worries, buddy," I say, meaning it but not sure how to add to it further. Henry actually helps though, by changing the subject.

"So how are things with you?"

"Me?"

"Yeah, you. I mean, what made you do all this? You can't need company *that* badly can you? You seem to do alright for that as it is, as far as I can see."

"Er, that's not really why…"

"I mean there was that lovely lady you were with not so long ago…"

"You mean Debbie?" I ask, pointing over to where she is sitting, chatting merrily away to some bloke or other.

Henry looks over and shakes his head. "Nope. The other one."

"Ah, you mean Jen," I reply. Then these next words just spill out of my mouth, as if under their own volition. "She isn't anything…I mean she *was*. She used to be *everything*. But times have changed, and

we've moved on. That's not going to go anywhere."
I'm still looking over at Debbie, as I hear myself say those words, and they suddenly seem so true and obvious, like I always should have known this was so. "I'm with Debbie over there, where I should be."
Henry nods, perhaps a little sadly. "Oh right. Good, good. I did wonder about that. Good. Hey, you know what?"
"What's that?" I prompt him, in a definitely friendly way.
"You should be running this pub, once Tom's gone. You and Debbie." I just stare at him blankly, so he carries on. "I'd still come if you did," he adds, as if that would end any argument.
"Really? I just know spreadsheets," I protest. "Wouldn't know the first…"
"You know people, Dan. People come here for booze, right? Debbie knows all about that. But they come here for the people too. That's the heart of this place, I can tell you. A smile and a few words from a stranger has often made a massive difference to my day." I can't help thinking that it doesn't really come across that way when you are with him, but I keep that to myself and let him carry on. "Many times. And you'd be really good at all that, I reckon, if you were running this place. I mean, what do you think this place is going to be like if someone else takes it over?"
I continue to stare blankly, afraid of the consequences of saying anything. Afraid that there might *be* consequences of saying anything. But it's too late. The idea has seeped from my ears to my cerebrum, which is used for hearing, and then to my Superior

temporal gyrus, where ideas occur. And I can't figure out which part of my brain to use to stop any of this happening. So I use my mouth instead.

"That sounds great and all, but it's not that simple…" I begin.

"*Everything* is that simple when you've been through what I've been through," Henry tells me, in the full knowledge that he is right. He has now seen life from a different angle, the very bottom, so no doubt has gained some kind of new perspective from there. I have too, almost, which is why I understand. He doesn't know that, but I do so I can secretly share his viewpoint. He takes a sip and looks me in the eye until satisfied that he knows that I know that he is right too.

It's then that I realise that this statement is his 'thank you', his gift to me.

Anyway, this evening is not supposed to be about me, so I steer the conversation away from my suitability as a pub landlord, and back to how Henry is feeling after his 'thing', as I regretfully describe it, for lack of another way to talk about attempted suicide, without actually talking about it. If you can think of a better word, please let me know. And once this is mentioned, it doesn't take a long time, or much beer, to get down to the topic of his relationship with his father. Like I said, it is that kind of night.

"It was my Dad who taught me to keep my feelings to myself," Henry recalls, staring at his pint rather than me by now. "'Pull yourself together' and all that, whenever I looked like I was going to cry or get upset about anything. So I would just go up to my room and

304

cry on my own when something got to me. Been like that ever since." Blimey, he's drinking something strong or there's just something about this night that is opening people right up. As if all they needed was just to be genuinely asked how they are, then the floodgates open up.

"I hope I don't teach my son that," he continues, "if I ever get to have one. I don't think what Dad taught me did me any good at all. What about your Dad?"

"Well, he died recently…"

"Oh I'm so sorry! No, didn't mean to…"

"Hey, look, it's no problem. It's ok to talk about him…"

"Ok, well only if you want to, sorry."

"It's cool really. Well…what to say…I mean he wasn't like your Dad. We tried not to get emotional either, the both of us, but if we had to, you know, it was allowed. But we never really talked about deep things either. Actually, that's not entirely true. We talked about lots of really deep things. But none of those things had anything to do with us, now that I think about it. We would talk about the universe but never the bit of it that was me, or him. We only skirted around the edges when talking about things that affected us personally, even after Mum died. So I've also never really learned myself either how to be…what's the word...emotional, if you see what I mean."

"Hmm," Henry says, over a sip. I know what he wants to say. He wants to say that his upbringing was worse than mine. He'd probably be right, but one-upmanship such as this surely is pointless and would really kill the conversation, so is best left unsaid. Like so many other things. Either way, with more damage or less, neither of us has been taught how to open up properly, and so we agree on that. Then we sit there for a long moment, wondering where to go from here. This ale will give me something to say in a moment. Any time now. Surprisingly, Henry starts up again before it does.

"This *is* a good pub, you know," he states.

"Yes, it is. It's my favourite!"

"It's a safe spot. For me. Do you feel that?"

"Well, mostly. Saturday nights can get a bit shady sometimes…"

"Hmm. I don't mean that. I mean that a good pub should feel like a safe spot. Where you can be safe from yourself."

"Oh," I say, and take a long sip. I wasn't quite expecting that. He's quite right of course. "Yes, I do know that, Henry. Couldn't have put it better myself."

Once Henry has gone back to the bar, Amy gives me a happy wave then Jez pops over to say that he has started his session and has already managed to talk to a guy about his recent prostate examination. He left it late apparently but hopes not too late.

"He specifically came down here to tell me to let everyone else know that you shouldn't leave it too late," Jez explains. "So maybe mention that to folks if it feels right."

"Sure, I will, thanks," I reply.

Jez puts a thumb up, in the normal way I mean, and turns to go back to his table. Then he stops, turns back and says this.

"Your Dad would be proud of you, you know. Doing all this. He really would. See you later."

Then he leaves me to let that thought sink in. As it does, I feel it finally begin to warm me up, deep from the inside. It's only then that I realise just how long I have been feeling so cold.

Chapter 21

We're still here. Same time, same place. I just needed a toilet break, that's all. In fact, I'm in the Gents right now. Wondering what you are doing here, to be honest. Apart from the obvious. Tell you what, I'll just be using this excellent hand dryer and see you outside.

When I emerge, I see that Debbie is just coming back in the door. I had not realised that she had gone. I then gather that she has brought Harry in from the care home, along with his daughter, who, I had previously gathered, normally lives miles away up North somewhere. Debbie and the daughter both wave at me, so I now finish drying the last of the water off my hands on my trousers, in anticipation of imminent hand-shakes. No hand dryer is *that* good after all, when you're in a hurry. Harry, though, does not wave at me at all. He is just looking around, trying to take in his new surroundings. Since I have now met him half a dozen times and his daughter only once, this should feel a bit topsy turvy. But this sort of thing isn't weird to me now, not at all. That's just the nature of his disease. It makes the victim retreat into themselves, and the family come out of themselves, in equal measure I often find.

Debbie gives me a quick kiss on the cheek and asks me how it's all going, quietly into my ear. I give her a cheery thumbs-up. The daughter (Alice I seem to remember her name is but am not sure enough to use it) is already holding out her hand to me to shake it.

She oozes gratitude and guilt, bless her. I remember that feeling. We shake hands and she thanks me for looking after my Dad. I don't really feel that I've been looking after him, I've just been listening to his stories occasionally. But I suppose that is part of looking after someone too, isn't it? The less messy part, but still important. She introduces herself again thankfully, indeed as Alice, and I can immediately tell that she certainly seems to think I've been helping. "So nice to meet you again, Dan," she tells me. "Dad has spoken so much about you. I think it's you anyway. We're all really grateful, you know, that you keep him company." Debbie smiles at this and pats me on the shoulder before heading back to her own Charity Chat designated table.

"I had no idea that he remembers who I am," I reply. "I normally have to introduce myself again each time." I then turn to Harry, who is arm in arm with Alice and is gazing around the pub with a look of something akin to awe. I get like that sometimes too. "Hello Harry, nice of you to join me here at last." "Hello there," he replies, shaking my hand, squinting slightly at me. "Nice to meet you." Ah well, so it goes. No problem.

"Why not take a seat here," I say pointing to my table, "and I'll get you a drink." As they sit down I ask Alice, "Can he, er, have a drink? Is that ok?" She shrugs "What harm is it going to do now? Just a little one though. Maybe, I don't know, something old fashioned and not too strong?"

"Ah yes, no worries, leave it with me. And for you?" "Oh, for me? Um, no thanks, I'm driving. Do they do coffee?"

"Not as such no, unless I ask nicely."

"No, no need for that. Orange juice is fine. Thank you."

The staff are on alert to serve us Charity-Chatters as priority today, so I manage to get the drinks straight away. I could get used to this! I place a half of 'Dark Delight', 3.2%, in front of Harry. Alice looks at this quizzically, obviously having no idea what I've just presented him. Probably because it actually looks a bit like the unlikely coffee that she had asked for herself.

"Half a mild, Harry?" I ask him.

"For me?" he asks in return.

"For you. Happy Christmas."

He smiles. Which, in itself, is enough right there.

"I used to drink here," Harry tells me and Alice, after a few sips.

"Did you now?" I reply. "I did not know that. I don't think that could have been when I was coming here. I'd have remembered you."

"No," he shakes his head. "Don't know you. I used to come here when Alice was little. Alice is my daughter you know." He smiles at us both, looking for some sort of confirmation. Alice just gently squeezes his arm. I'm not the only one here who has got used to being forgotten it seems.

"I used to bring her here on Sunday afternoons with her mum," he continues. "We would sit at the table over there and have Sunday dinner sometimes."

"I don't remember that, Dad," Alice says.

"I don't remember them ever doing Sunday dinner," I can't help but add, a little sceptical.

"Yes, I loved those afternoons," Harry continues,

taking another small, but appreciative, sip of his mild. "Sunday afternoons was for family down here then. Ah, you know, my Alice, she would just never sit still. She had to keep running round and around. And, cheeky monkey, she would always ask people what they were drinking. And she would occasionally get a sneaky taste! People didn't seem to mind then, you know. My girl was just another part of the big Red Lion family. She was as welcome as anyone. In the afternoons. That chandelier. That was there then too. Blimey, it's exactly the same. See that bit that's missing there, on the right? That was when Alfie Jackson threw a bottle at Kevin Borthwick and missed. It all kicked off that night, let me tell you. Something to do with Alfie's missus, I never did find out…"

Ah, so he does know where he is then. He even remembers the name of the pub. I guess he could have noticed it on the way in, but for Harry it is more likely he would remember something from thirty years ago than thirty minutes ago. That's just how his disease works, sadly.

You know, I wish I could remember a time when The Red Lion was the way he describes. The Sunday family thing I mean, not the Alife and Kevin thing. I love this place now, as you know, but it obviously isn't the community hub that it once was back then. But hey anyway, for one day at least, me and my friends are doing our best to bring a little bit of that old spirit back. Moreover, looking at this father and daughter sitting here with me now, and imagining those same two people in this same space all those years ago, I feel a strange rush of comfort. Their roles

311

have reversed since then, but they are still the same people, and they are enjoying this same space in the universe once again. And sharing this space with them too helps me realise that perhaps what we are trying to do today really is worth a little something.

I pause to look around this place that we have created today. As I watch Ted laughing along with some fella, and watch Debbie nodding animatedly at another old boy at her table, as I hear Amy's and Jez's laughter waft over from the corner, and as I watch Harry continue to tell a beaming Alice all about his little girl, I can't help but smile. And I can't help but begin to wonder what else we should be doing here, once this one night is over.

And it is just as I'm thinking this, and realising that I am sitting back, probably looking a little bit too satisfied and happy, that I also realise that Jen is watching me, from across the pub. More than that, I get the impression that she has been watching me for some time. I blush, suddenly feeling like I've been caught out. I guess I have been. I would certainly not have been looking like I'm the sort of chap who is about to leave and go off around the world. I would have instead looked like I was right at home, just where I was. And now she knows it, without me having to say a word. I should have told her using words, though, I do know that. Even she deserves that.

But even knowing this, in lieu of going over to her immediately, I give her a friendly wave and motion some kind of sign language, which may or may not have suggested that I just have to go to the bar first. I do this mainly just to gauge her reaction and thereby her mood. I want some clue on which to base my first response. She waves back, which is something. But the way she does it looks a little sad, which is something else. For a further few moments neither of us takes a physical step towards each other, each of us hesitant. Oh God, another metaphor. Hey, sorry, sometimes they just happen. Deep breath. It's me who is on home territory here, so I had best go over. So I do. We lightly hug and perform a vague peck on the cheek.

"I thought we weren't meeting up until the weekend?" I begin tentatively, realising too late that this doesn't sound entirely welcoming. I try and recover with, "Nice of you to come down though! Cheers."
"Yeah," she replies, "I just thought I would take a look, see what this was all about…"
"Cool..."
"Yeah…"
"Well…"
"So…is it going well then? Do things like this even go well…or not?"
Nervous chuckle from her. Without that chuckle I may have been a little miffed at that last comment, but with it I can let it slide. "Yes, it is going well Jen, so I guess they *can* do, judging by events so far. I've had a few good chats. Maybe some have made the universe a tiny bit better, I don't know…"
"Good, good…" she says, continuing to look around, perhaps for some kind of understanding, which up to this point is eluding her. Which only serves to clarify

an understanding of my own. At which thought I realise that she is going to see Debbie in a moment. I know that this should not be a problem at all, on the outside, but now I realise just how much my feelings have suddenly distilled between Jen and Debbie, even tonight. Although this too is another secret locked inside of me, my body again reacts as if everyone knows. My adrenal gland kicks in, preparing me for trouble, or so it is thinking. But it is a blunt instrument, the poor thing, designed for the fight or flight reactions of a lifestyle from thousands of years ago. Here and now it is only more likely to get me into trouble. Evolution is just too slow to help us out sometimes.

So…my eyes start to move around nervously, I begin to sweat, and I shuffle my feet. All these being attempts to quietly dissipate the extra energy my glandular friend has just mistakenly given me, attempts to hide my internal thoughts that only serve to accentuate them. Jen, of course, notices all this right away, just at the moment when she scans the Charity Chat tables and my compatriots there. This could now go one of several ways, none of which I am in control of. But as our eyes meet, she opts for resignation, a scenario that she has no doubt already played through in her head. That's the option I would have picked too. In fact, if I care to remember, it's the option I very much did pick, when she dumped me all those years ago. 'This is not revenge' I tell myself again and again in this moment. And I am right. It isn't. It's not that at all. It is just what is *right*. So why I felt the need to mention it to myself, I have no idea.

314

I should say…something. She should say something. Someone should say something! Oh well, I guess that someone really should be me.

"It's really made me think about how important home is to me now really," I finally force out. "So…I guess this means I am going to stay. Here I mean. Not…er, go away…" Not the most impressive speech, I know, but in this context, it is life-changing nonetheless. She is more than ready for this now, so slips into a dignified stance, and we continue to chat about how *her* trip is going to go, without needing to mention that this will now be without me. We talk just for long enough to prove to each other, and also to ourselves, that we are all ok. Whether we actually are or not, the pretence is required. A slight pause, then the vague cheek kiss again, then she is gone. Just like that. Sorry for the anti-climax.

How long will she be gone for this time? Who knows. Once she is gone I feel…actually, I don't know how to describe what I feel. There's relief, yes, but there's other things as well. Regret too, and also flipping between the fear that I've done the wrong thing, then firmly flipping back to being convinced that I was right after all. Overall, it's mainly relief though. Anyway, I shall have to park all of this for now. Time speeds up again, just at the moment that I realised it had slowed down. I look away from the door and back around the pub and gather myself. I have things to do after all, people to see!

Actually, as it turns out, I don't. Debbie, Amy and Jez are mopping up the last few stragglers and, barring any late surge, that will probably be that. But that is fine, as things have already gone better than I dared hope, and I don't want to spoil anything now. I'm getting pretty drunk to be honest, even though I've been on the session ales and trying to remember just to sip occasionally. Ted is free now too and he comes on over to my table.

"Good to have a rest now, buddy," I say to him as he approaches, wiping imaginary sweat off my brow and finding that there is, in fact, something on my brow after all, a substance yet to be determined. I find that I don't really care, regardless of what it is. It hasn't killed me yet, so not likely to now. Ted, surprisingly, shakes his head at me.

"Not quite a break for you yet," he tells me, somewhat seriously.

"You what?" I enquire eruditely, or at least with as much erudition as I can currently muster.

"I think *I* still need a chat, Dan."

"Eh?" I add, in much the same vein as before, not being sure what he's aiming at.

"I need a chat."

"Of course. When don't we chat?"

"But not like our normal chats…" Ted adds, perhaps a little awkwardly.

"Oh, ok…sure. Like…er… no civil war or witchfinder or stuff like that?"

"No witchfinder. You know, one of *these* chats, like we've been doing today. It feels like the right time, it's been that sort of night, to be a little different to how we normally are. So tonight, for once, we can actually talk about ourselves, rather than anything but." He points at the banner we put up earlier, which now feels like days ago, as I feel his words echo those

I said to Henry only moments ago when thinking how me and Dad were.

Depending where you come from, a moment like this should not be awkward between friends. At all. Not between friends who spend so much time together and talk so much about so many things. But that is just the theory, isn't it? *This is different.* As much as we pretend that we can talk about anything, me and Ted, that is actually not necessarily true. We can talk about anything that's safe, is what we really mean, perhaps unless we are too drunk to remember, which doesn't count for either party. Just like me and Dad, we can talk about anything in the universe that isn't us. There's always a line, you see, a safe line that you draw with everyone, a line that is not to be crossed. The line is in a different place for everyone you know, and can move as your friendship progresses, but there are two things that I understand about the line. One is that it should always move of its own accord without intervention by a single party. And two, it can never be even mentioned by either said party. Observation of the line would automatically alter its position if that happens, just like what goes on in the inside of an atom, or if you do something shameful. Despite this, we still know that line is there and roughly where it is in any given relationship. But I realise at this moment that Ted is overtly moving the line himself right now, all by himself. Hence the awkwardness. Hmm, I'm glad I'm drunk. Oh well, since he's gone and done it now, we had better just push past it and see what happens. Rules can be bent or broken I guess, especially the stupid ones.

"Next customer!" I say to him with a smile, and

317

beckon him down to sit next to me, regardless of how nervous I suddenly feel.

"I just wanted to say this now, Dan, so it's done. Then we can go back to normal."
"Ok, matey, no worries."
"This feels stupid."
"Can't be as stupid as I've been lately, Ted, so you're in good company."
That seems to help him a little, as he chuckles, just for a brief moment, and sits back into his seat. Then a pause as we wait for the real conversation to begin.
"I've…I've not been well recently, Dan," Ted tells me. Blimey, it's all coming out tonight, I think. I try to stifle the familiar dread in the pit of my stomach, suddenly remembering the moment when I worked out how ill Dad was, or when Mum made her own announcement all those years ago. Ted sees this in my eyes and hurriedly adds, "No, I'm not dying! Well, no more than we all are."
"Oh phew!" I say in palpable relief, not even sure if that's how I should be feeling yet. I compose myself, not easy after this many pints, and put on my serious face. "So… what…er is it then?" I ask him, with as much bedside manner as you'd expect, presuming you'd been expecting very little.
"It's er…it's hard to say it out loud really. So I'll just say it straight. It's er…it's depression I guess. I have depression. There. I said it."
This hits me like a kick in the guts. I'm not sure how much is in sympathy for him, and how much is in embarrassment over the situation we now find ourselves in, but both are in my stomach somewhere, fighting for dominance, and confusing my reactions. I

318

opt for the pop-science response out of habit and start gabbling until something else happens.

"Oh. You mean, like medical depression, Ted?" I ask. "I read ages ago that there are two types of depression, well at least two anyway, these being the two I understand. One being depressed about things happening, or not happening, to you in your life. The presumption, lazy or not, about this one is that you can at least do something about that in theory. Then there's the second, that being medical depression, where your brain has trained itself to be your worst enemy and give itself the worst chemicals from your cornucopia of glands without you having any say in the matter at all. And there's no telling yourself to cheer up with that one – it's chemical. Just like any physical illness. You might as well try and turn water into wine, or lager into ale…"

Ted looks at me spouting all this with a look of what I can only describe as knowing affection, as if this response, as unemotional and over-factual as it was, is just what he expected of me, and perhaps just what he needed. But as I watch Ted search for the next words to rescue me from my impromptu lecture, I listen to myself as if I was bystander at the next table. This bystander starts to wonder which one of these forms of the illness has dogged me all this time. And whether it would even help if I knew.

"Yeah, that one, the chemical one," he admits, jumping into a gap I have just left for inhalation. "I've had it for years. Since I was a kid really."

"You hide it well, mate."

"Long time practiced, that particular skill," he muses, "long time." I let that sit there for a moment. This conversation is about to take on a life of its own, now that it's premise has been laid out, and will take us gratefully both along with it, as long as I don't mess up the next few words.

"Well, I for one would not have guessed, if that is any help at all."

"I don't know, maybe there's hiding it *too* well."

"Yeah, I can concur with that."

"You do like a nice concur, don't you Dan?"

"Well this time, my friend, I mean it."

A pause for a much-needed swig from both of us, then we reach the point where we are both ready to let the conversation take control. Ted then looks me in the eye, in some ways a diminished character, in others much stronger. Honesty can do that to a person.

"I lie a lot, you know," he tells me. "About things I have done and that. Well, some of it's true, it just depends on whether I need to pretend or not, in the moment. When I need not to be me for a bit."

I don't know about you, but I did have my doubts over a few things he may have mentioned. The conversation tells me, firstly to find this amusing, then to quiz him on a few of these before I can even think about whether or not it's the right thing to do. But it's what I would have done if we were talking about anything else, so I don't expect that Ted would want to be treated any differently now. In fact, I know that's the last thing that he would want. He joins me in a chuckle, and thus we begin.

"So…you being up in court, was that true?"

"Nah, I did hit him, but he didn't press charges or nothing…"

"Paratrooper?"

"Applied. Didn't get in…"

"Turd in the word search?"

"Oh, no that was true, that one. Have to hold my hands up to that one!"

"Of all the things that could have been true, it had to be that one!" I cry.

That broke the remaining ice. The chuckles turn into laughter at this and the last of the barriers are down. Maybe I have half-decent people instincts after all.

"I always knew you were a bullshitter, Ted," I say, buoyed by this, "just not a depressed one." Maybe I'm being a little over-exuberant now, as Ted then looks at me quizzically. The resulting panic though, and the beer, finally brings out the thing I should have said all along.

"Well, look, that's a surprise, I can't tell you any different. But look, I have to say this. Thanks, mate. Look, I'm glad you told me. Thanks for telling me. It means a lot that you felt you could share that with me, you know? And you know that I still love you the same, mate!"

"Yeah, cheers. Me too, but, just so you know, not like *that*!"

"Oh, no not like *that*! How drunk are we?" and we laugh again, definitely more than a little this time.

"Just about the right kind of drunk," he replies.

"Seriously though. Thanks too. Thanks for not being weird about it. It took a lot just to say that out loud. And you don't have to do anything, you don't have to say anything in particular. I just wanted you to know so it's out there. Well between us I mean. I'm still me. I just wanted you to know that sometimes there's another me, one that's not so much fun to be around, in case you happen to meet him."

"But it *is* still you though mate, it's all still you. That's how you are. I get it! And hey, that's a brave thing to do, to say it out loud, believe me I know. I'm darn impressed, let me tell you!"

And as we talk about it a little more, tipping gracefully over the line from drunk to rather drunk, I wonder if I will ever be that brave myself. And what might happen if I am. And what might happen if I'm not. But as we carry on talking, the magic of a pub conversation proves itself again to be a great healer. Ted loses all his initial nerves, even starts to look mightily relieved, and all is soon back to normal. A new normal anyway, which will work just fine for us. This is what Ted wanted after all. For me to know the truth, but for everything else to remain the same.

That all sounds marvellous of course but, just so you know, I'm still going to stay in my particular shell. For now, at least. Don't judge me, but I think we've had enough honesty for one day.

When Ted and me finally find a suitable point where we can break off, we see that the place is really starting to thin out. Amy and Jez are starting to tidy up a bit so Ted joins them and helps. Debbie is at the bar talking to Henry and Tom the Landlord. They are somewhat animated, which for once I find a little disheartening, as I am myself feeling pretty tired by now. As they realise that I'm coming over to them, they all suddenly stop and look at me. I'm not normally paranoid (am I?) but they do seem to be staring at me rather intensely. And they have all stopped talking at the same time. Oh dear, what have I done now? That's the best thought I can come up with, such is my state of mind. Then Debbie hugs me and brings me into the group.

"Henry's had an idea," she says.

"It's a good one," Tom the Landlord adds.

"It's a very good one," Debbie further adds, "as long as you agree…"

Chapter 22

So.

I am going to make amends. I am. Not just for the things I have done. I always had reasons for the things I have done. Whether those reasons were good enough or not I am happy to leave that to you. You don't have to like them. I have never asked you to, though, have I?

No.

No, I need to make amends for the things I *didn't* do. I never had any good reasons for those. All those wasted years. All that time wallowing in my own disappointments. Ok, I know that I did come back here determined to have an easy life. Despite that, I was handed things to do. A lot of them were bad, but I did them anyway. And now I have been handed something good to do. And this time I am going to do that.

And I *am*, you know. I *really* am.

Right after this pint.

The End

Postscript From the Author

Thank you for reading my book. Really. I hope you found something in it that spoke to you.

I would love to carry on writing more books and what really helps new authors more than anything can be summed up in one word.

Reviews.

The more reviews we get online the more those algorithms notice us and promote us to other readers. So if you could please take the time to write a review, such as on Amazon, that would be really helpful. Even just a few words is fine.

Reviews also let me know what is working for readers and what is not, and that is also a very good thing, as I sit here in the pub with Dan, deciding what he is going to do next.

We both hope you meet you down The Red Lion again soon.

Cheers.

Mark Fryday

July 2018

Printed in Great Britain
by Amazon

18269867R00190